I0777476

The Ghost of Mackey House

R.A. Johnson

CROW Books

Cover art by Lance Buckley

First Edition
October 2021

ISBN 9798740777535

To Cathy and her wonderful statue.

1

Saturday, Late September

The tapping of steel on stone, followed by running footsteps, drew Jan to the porch railing as a spotlight shone on the strange statue on the lawn. After scanning the darkness for a moment, the light switched off, leaving only the full moon to illuminate the scene below. When the moon-cast shadow detached itself from the statue and slid across the lawn, Jan's rational mind dismissed what he saw as a trick of the light, but a seed of fear was planted deep in his subconscious.

He heard a muffled curse from the ancient Crown Vic cop car that was the source of the dazzling light. More indistinct mutterings cut off as the driver's window rolled up. Exhaust fumes blurred the taillights of the cruiser as it pulled away, descended the hill, and disappeared around a bend. Jan's eyes followed it, then tracked further down the hill to where the moon reflected off the waters of Lake Wallenpaupack.

Wind-blown leaves, their fall colors turned to shades of grey by the moonlight, danced around the enigmatic statue standing proudly on the lawn. Like a magnet, it drew his eye. As he had many times before, Jan wondered about its origins and why it seemed more alive than simply a chunk of granite.

Damn, it's getting cold.

He rubbed the gooseflesh on his arms and suppressed a shiver.

I hope that Tomlin couple is done, well, "coupling," so I can get some sleep.

Turning to his laptop, which had long since gone to sleep itself, he sighed and closed it. The new novel it contained just needed a final polish before going back to his publisher.

I'll wrap that up tomorrow after I head home.

Scooping it up, he re-entered his suite and stopped to listen. The century-old floorboards in the Mackey House bed-and-breakfast announced hurrying footsteps in the hall outside, which were followed by the squeal of the Tomlins' door closing, then some rustling and murmuring, the squeak of bedsprings, and ultimately silence.

If they start up again, I'm going to bang on their door. Maybe they'll let me join them.

He chuckled to himself. It had been two long, lonely years since he returned home from a writing retreat at this very bed-and-breakfast to find an empty house and divorce papers on the kitchen table.

I should write more, now that I'm up, he thought.

But he had nothing to write. He should be drafting his third novel, now that the second was nearly finished. His agent talked about his growing readership, and her expectation that "the next one" would be a bestseller. Her encouragement was a much-needed boost to his chronically deflated ego, though he knew the reality of his "success" was but a shadow of the publisher's expectations.

I can't. I just can't. I've got nothing to say anymore.

Each time Jan sat down to write, his mind wandered. When he forced himself to reread what he had written so far, he ripped it apart and littered it with comments and corrections. As edits piled on top of edits, he realized the story was tedious and worse, boring. His agent insisted his growing fan base would eat up whatever he wrote. The book contract that launched his second career, and had probably saved his life, led to a second one and a third. Even though this third novel was barely begun, his publisher was already pestering him for progress reports.

It's crap. Everything I write now is crap. It was all luck before, not talent.

What he couldn't explain to his agent or publisher, though, was that his previous stories had evolved in his head for years before he put fingers to keyboard. They'd still be floating in there if he hadn't lost his wife, his house, and his job in the space of a month. He couldn't just spit out another one. So, he fled to here, where this new career that he had sacrificed everything for had begun, looking for inspiration.

At least here, in the mountains of eastern Pennsylvania, he felt a semblance of peace. In the past, in this place that was the antithesis of his "real" life, he had the solitude he needed to capture his dream life in words. Not this trip, though.

Perhaps it was the company of his fellow guests, the strange Tomlin couple whose noisy sexual antics in the suite next door had driven him out onto the chilly porch an hour ago. Jeff's loud crassness and Naomi's tittering, faux-girlish laughter set Jan's nerves on edge.

He looked to the bottle of bourbon on the sitting-room table, then tilted his head to listen.

Silence. *I guess they're done.*

With a goodnight wave to the bottle, he turned into his bedroom.

I'm leaving tomorrow. Maybe when I get home, I'll be able to write something, or at least get a decent night's sleep.

Sheriff's Deputy Kathy Jensen cruised the dark, lonely roads of Wayne County. These midnight shifts suited her disposition best. Alone, drifting through her duties as she drifted through life, she had always found it easiest to fulfill others' low expectations of her, rather than try to prove the worth of the intellect and ambitions she kept locked away out of the world's view.

With one eye on the dashboard clock and the other scanning the countryside, she turned onto the Mackey-to-Dundee road for the first time that shift. The Mackey House, its Mission style architecture and vibrant gardens, now withered and brown awaiting the onset of Winter, glowered down at the Deputy as her ancient cruiser labored up the hill. Its normally welcoming countenance, which had greeted Kathy on the many occasions when she visited its proprietors, Dan and Sandy Adams, loomed sinister in the darkness above. Its upper and lower porches protruded like a pair of pouting lips, while its roofline formed a scowling brow ridge.

Her instincts alerted by some unconscious difference, Kathy focused her attention on the most famous feature of the Mackey House: the granite statue incongruously overlooking the front lawn. In contrast to the subtle, almost demure architecture of the house, the statue that had come to identify the place, was almost obscene.

Dressed in a flowing, diaphanous gown, the voluptuous Roman goddess stood proud. An ever-present wind, captured by the sculptor and as frozen in time as the statue herself, pressed her thin shift tight against the sensuous curves of her legs, hips, belly, and her breasts, whose nipples rose to meet the sculptor's chilly wind. Rendered as it was from native granite, her body nevertheless appeared as soft as any woman of flesh and blood. With her back arched, her head tilted skyward, and her lips parted, the young goddess stood, frozen forever in a moment of pure ecstasy.

Kathy knew this form almost as well as she knew her own body, although the difference between them could not have been more pronounced. What drew her attention this night, however, was not the erotic nature of the statue, but the movement she saw behind it. Something rhythmically rose and fell as if a hammer tapped a chisel.

Bastards.

Flicking on her door-mounted spotlight, Kathy expected to see local kids bolt for the woods bordering the property. Instead, to her surprise, a single large male figure ran around the side of the house and disappeared into the shadows. Panning the spotlight across the lawn, Kathy drifted her car forward until she could illuminate the side yard. There was no trace of the vandal, though.

She looked at the thick line of brush that separated the well-tended expanse of grass from the thick woods.

Whoever it was is long gone, and I ain't traipsin' through the woods in the middle of the night chasin' them.

She glanced at the dashboard clock again. It read 2:40 AM.

I'll stop by to talk with Dan and Sandy tomorrow.

Turning off the spotlight, Kathy stepped on the pedal and the wheezing cruiser rumbled toward Dundee.

3

Sunday, Late September

When Jan came down to breakfast the next morning, Jeff and Naomi Tomlin were already eating. He poured a cup of coffee from the pot warming on the sideboard and took a seat at the dining table, as far from the Tomlins as possible. This put him to the left of Dan Adams and across the table from Sandy Adams, co-owners of Mackey House.

Sandy stood as he sat and asked, "The usual this morning?"

Jan nodded, "Please," and she headed for the kitchen, rolling her eyes as she passed behind the Tomlins. Jan hoped to avoid Jeff's attention, but the eight or ten feet of separation was not nearly far enough.

"I was just telling Dan, here, but I don't know if I've told you," Jeff said around a mouthful of scrambled eggs, "that I have a special connection to this place." He had, in fact, told Jan this, and anyone who would listen, multiple times in the past two days. "We came up here this weekend to check the place out and kinda connect with my family history, you know?"

Naomi gave one of her fingernails-on-a-blackboard laughs for encouragement.

"I had always heard growing up that my great-something grandparents were filthy rich, but lost it all in the stock market crash and Great Depression. I always figured the family legends were just stories you tell the kids to impress them, so we wouldn't think we had always lived in a shithole." Naomi tittered. "Oh, sorry. Not proper breakfast language, is it?"

Dan frowned and Jan almost did a spit take. Undeterred, Jeff continued, "Anyway, I always thought it was a load of bullsh—crap until my Mom died this past summer. She had been living alone in the family rowhouse since my Dad drank himself to death when I was in college. Since my good-for-nothing brother had moved south, I was stuck with cleaning the place out and putting it up for sale. The little shit didn't want to do any of the work, but he sure as hell wanted his cut of the profits. Since I was the executor, though, I fixed his wagon. I got my drinkin' buddy, Joey, who's a contractor, to write up a bunch of receipts for work he never did—a new roof, plumbing, electrical, all kinds of stuff. Joey made some nice cash for doin' nothin' and most of the sale price just, ya know, evaporated."

Jeff smiled proudly and Naomi let loose with her loudest "hee, hee, hee" yet. Jeff took a break to shovel more eggs into his mouth, as Sandy backed through the swinging door from the kitchen holding a plate of eggs-over-easy, rye toast, bacon, and hash browns. As she set the plate in front of Jan, his mouth watered in response to the delicious aromas wafting up from the plate.

"Mmm, this smells delicious," Jan smiled up at Sandy, who beamed in response.

Jeff continued around a mouthful of eggs, "Anyway, I was cleaning out the attic when I found this," he leaned down to the satchel alongside his chair and pulled out a small leather-bound book. "This," he waved it back and forth, "is my great-something grandmother's diary."

He looked expectantly at each of the others, but got nothing back, only blank stares. "My great-something grandmother Jennifer Smythe Mulberry." Apparently, Sandy's gasp was the reaction Jeff was fishing for.

Dan stood, alarmed by his wife's reaction. Sandy retreated a step and covered her mouth with one hand while the other flew to her heart.

"Honey, are you OK?" Dan took a step toward her.

Sandy took a deep breath and said, "Yeah, that name—I haven't heard that name since I was a kid."

Jan had turned around in his chair, his breakfast momentarily forgotten. "Who's Jennifer… whatever?"

Jeff started to respond, but Sandy spoke first. "She was here when the original Mackey Hotel burned down."

"Exactly!" Jeff seemed desperate to regain everyone's attention. "And this," he waved the diary above his head like a semaphore, "is her account of that fateful night." Without waiting for encouragement, he began to read.

December 26, 1920

Dear Diary,

This is the hardest entry I have ever had to write to you. My dearest friend, my lifelong companion and playmate, dearest

Flora, has been taken from this life in the most horrible way. And I fear I am at least partially to blame.

Mother and Father, as was their custom, planned to spend the Christmas holiday at the wonderful Mackey Hotel. Before this year, they left Charles and me to celebrate Christmas morning with our nanny Beatrice. Mother always says that Christmas can be any day of the year we wish it to be, so we would celebrate a family Christmas when they returned. Though this may be nontraditional, the absence of my parents meant I could spend the day with Flora. And since Flora's mother, being Mother's handmaid, was attending Mother and therefore also absent, we spent Christmas Eve and Christmas Day engrossed in our playtime fantasies.

This year was different, however, as I had made my Debut in the Spring making me a member of Society, which meant that I would spend the Christmas Holiday with Mother and Father. And, since I was now an eligible debutante, I required a personal maid of my own. The natural choice, of course, was my playmate and my dearest friend, Flora.

Our roles necessarily became very different, though. I was beyond needing a playmate, instead I now needed to find a husband and a maid to take care of all the details of a woman of Society. My wardrobe, hairstyle, makeup, everything was new. How fortunate I was to have Flora, whose mother had attended my own Mother for so many years and who quickly taught her daughter how best to meet my needs.

So it was that Flora and I set out with three of our four parents and Father's valet, Simon, by train from Philadelphia two days before Christmas 1920. I barely slept the night before, so high was my anticipation of the trek along the rattle-trap railroads that took us into the wilderness.

The morning of our departure, Flora dressed me, and I took a light breakfast in my room. Mother scowled when I informed her I was too excited to eat with the family.

Simon, Flora, and her mother saw to our luggage at the train station, and we departed around noon for the Mackey Hotel—a place I had heard about for years. As we wended our way north, the landscape grew more and more rural and the mantle of snow deeper and brighter. The cold of the northern clime and higher elevation seemed to produce a powdery snow that glistened in the low afternoon sunlight like tiny diamonds.

Mother had prepared my wardrobe well for the cold, though. It was almost dark when the train pulled into the station below the edifice that was the Mackey Hotel. We disembarked, comfy in our furs even though our breath formed great clouds of steam as we climbed the stone steps to the hotel's entrance. We were met there by a jolly man, Mr. Ephraim Mackey himself, owner and proprietor of that magnificent spot of luxury and sophistication in what seemed to my eyes to be the middle of the wilderness. Little did I know how much my life would change in that mountain hideaway.

The first change came when I met Mr. Jonathan Mulberry, of the banking Mulberries, whose parents had travelled with us from Philadelphia. Jonathan had made his way from Boston after the close of classes at Harvard, where he was pursuing a degree. We were introduced and my heart went into palpitations. I feared I would faint away when he bent and kissed my hand. My blush must have been visible to all. Turning away to hide my embarrassment, I noticed Mother and Mrs. Mulberry exchange a knowing look.

Mr. Mackey escorted us to our suite of rooms at the top of the hotel's grand staircase. They comprised a small sitting room flanked by two bedrooms, one of which Mother and Father occupied, while the other I had to myself. After a brief inspection, which met with Father's hearty approval, Mother, Father, and I descended to join the other guests in the formal dining room where Mr. Mackey's staff had laid out a "wintry supper" and glasses of what I took to be simply orange juice.

Father laughed at me when I sputtered over a thirsty gulp of the orange elixir which Mother, scowling as she often did, informed me is called a Mimosa—orange juice spiked with illicit champagne—and I should drink it like a lady, not a sailor. This admonition drew more laughter from Father and chuckles from the other guests present.

The evening passed quickly, sitting with the ladies in the parlor, gossiping about the new Paris fashions, while the men smoked cigars and played billiards, thankfully in another room.

Christmas Eve morning, we enjoyed a hearty breakfast, followed by a sleigh ride through the forest to the tiny town of Dundee, where we stopped for mugs of hot chocolate. The rest of the afternoon was spent in preparation for the Christmas Eve Gala that evening.

That evening, Christmas Eve, was the most momentous evening of my life, beginning with such joy but ending in such tragedy. It began when I entered the sitting room of our suite after Flora had dressed me and done my hair up into the most fantastic *coiffure*. Father beamed at my appearance while Mother inspected me like a military commander reviewing her troops. With a reluctant nod to Flora, who stood in the doorway to my room, she twirled her finger, telling me to turn around. Assuming that she simply wished to continue her inspection of the lay of my frock, she startled me when she lowered a necklace over my head and fastened the clasp about my neck.

I recognized it immediately, though I had only seen it on very special occasions. It had been Mother's mother's. The weight of it surprised me, and lamplight danced among the diamonds, rubies, and emeralds when I spun to face the mirror on the wall. Mother whispered, "Welcome to Society," as she turned me back to face her and Father. But that was only the beginning of that wonderful and ultimately horrible night.

Jonathan and I—yes, we progressed from Mr. Mulberry and Miss Smythe to Jonathan and Jennifer straight away—were seated next to each other at dinner, and I became instantly infatuated with him, as any eighteen-year-old debutante would. His handsome face and well-muscled arms, which brushed against

my own bare ones several times
throughout dinner, seemed taken straight
out of my deepest fantasies. His shy smile
yet manly scent made my body tingle all
over, and I feared my arousal would be
evident through my silk slip and beaded
satin gown.

After dinner, we danced and
chatted together throughout the evening.
The music, the champagne, several cups of
punch, and being on the arm of the
handsome Jonathan, transported me and
freed any inhibitions which may have been
loosely held, anyway.

The evening seemed to last but a
moment, and we found ourselves alone
after the older generation had said their
"Good nights" and their "Merry
Christmases." That is when Jonathan and I
gave in to the desire that had been building
all night and demonstrated our newfound
love for each other in the most intimate
way. I fear our recklessness and
abandonment of all social conventions that
night had immediate, tragic consequences.

When my parents retired to our
suite, Jonathan gallantly promised them he
would escort me up to our rooms in short
order. Instead, I practically dragged him
through the doorway under the grand
staircase to the back stairs. From there, we

descended to a cold, dark hallway lined with servants' quarters.

Trying first one door, we found an empty room that looked so bleak, I refused to enter. But the second door opened to a room with a neatly made bed and signs of recent occupancy. With the gas lamp turned down low, we threw ourselves at each other.

We tore at each other's clothes until I beheld Jonathan in all his glory. The sight melted me inside. Before joining him on the narrow, sagging bed, I unclasped my necklace and laid it on the bedside table.

After Jonathan was sated, we shared a cigarette, huddled together for warmth. As I lay half on top of him, I felt his chest rise and fall rhythmically and a quiet snore escaped his lips. Content in the knowledge that my sole ambition—to land a quality husband—was coming to fruition, I too felt my eyes grow heavy.

I awoke to Jonathan scrambling out of bed, slapping at his thigh. The smell of smoke was heavy in the air from the bedding, which was smoldering where our cigarette had fallen. Jonathan bravely tried to smother the fire, but his flapping of the blanket only fanned the flames. As the fire climbed the wall toward the old gas jet, Jonathan pushed me out the door into the

hallway. I barely had time to grab my slip
and frock.

It is still amazing to me how one
drunken escapade can change so many
lives. I had just made it to my room when
the terrible cries of "Fire!" rang through
the hotel. It was with only the clothes we
wore, I, half-dressed, and Mother and
Father in their night-clothes, bundled in
our heavy coats, that we fled down the
back stairs into the frosty night.

I shall never forget the heart-
wrenching cries of Stephanie, Flora's
mother, when Ephraim took a count and
Flora was not among us.

Jeff closed the book and sat back with a self-
satisfied grin.

"That's it?" Sandy asked.

Jeff shrugged. "That's the last entry in the diary.
She wrote nothing after that."

"But what happened afterwards? Was Jennifer, or
at least this Jonathan Mulberry prosecuted?" The pitch of
Sandy's voice rose in exasperation. Again, Jeff just
shrugged.

"I want to know how the love story ends," Naomi
chimed in, accenting her comment with her distinctively
obnoxious giggle.

Jeff snorted. "Well, considering she and Jonathan
got married six months later and my grandmother was born
shortly thereafter, I'd say it was 'happily ever after.'"

"Wait." Sandy slapped the table. "A young woman died in that fire. Her life was snuffed out before she had a chance to live any of it, and all this rich whore, who started the fire, can talk about is clothes and jewels and getting knocked up on a blind date?"

Red anger rose up Jeff's neck. "Hey! That's my great-grandmother you're talking about. Show some respect!"

Sandy slowly rose from her chair, her napkin clutched tightly in her fist. Despite her five-foot-four-inch height, she seemed to tower over Jeff as she leaned across the table.

"And Flora was *my* great-great-aunt, you pompous jackass. Your family never showed her or my family any respect. I can see nothing has changed." She threw her napkin onto the table and stalked through the swinging door into the kitchen.

Jan, Dan, and the Tomlins sat in stunned silence for a moment. Dan had been curiously silent during this exchange. Jan figured he knew from first-hand experience that Sandy could handle herself in an argument, and he appeared to be correct.

Finally, Dan spoke. "She has a point," he said, deliberately keeping his voice low and even. "Jennifer did seem a bit self-centered."

Jeff seethed. "She was only eighteen, for Christ's sake. She lived a sheltered, privileged life up to then."

Dan just spread his hands in an "I rest my case" gesture.

Jeff took a deep breath before saying, "Come on, Naomi." He pushed back from the table and stood, but Naomi just looked up at him.

"I thought you were going to ask them about—"

"Shut up!" Jeff barked. He took a deep breath before continuing. "Come on, I need to take a drive to cool off."

"I think that would be best," Dan said as Jeff stalked off.

Naomi threw an apologetic half-smile to Dan, then hurried after her husband.

Jan, who had been holding his breath, let it out and said, "Well, that was exciting."

The old Crown Victoria coughed once, then dieseled for a few seconds before finally going silent. Kathy Jensen opened the squad car's door, which complained with a rusty squeal, and climbed out. She was bone tired. The kind of tired that comes from too many lonely nights and too many restless, sleepless days. The duty schedule had her locked into the midnight-to-eight shift, and sleeping during the day didn't suit her.

It's probably not worth complaining—again.

Maybe it was her tiredness, or being distracted, but her push on the car door left it half-latched and the yellowed dome light still glowed.

Crap. The damn battery will be dead tomorrow.

With practiced ease born of long experience, she stood with her back to the stubborn door and slammed her butt against it. The latch made a satisfying click, and she bent over to make sure the dome light had gone out.

"Hip check and a beauty!" said Deputy Jonah Spatz, known to everyone as "Spaz." He and Deputy Tom Gheringer walked from the police station to their new Ford Escape squad SUVs.

"That was more of an 'ass check and a beauty,'" Deputy Gheringer sneered.

"So, which was it?" the first deputy asked.

"I told you. It was an ass check."

"No, I mean, which was a beauty? The check or the ass?"

Both men guffawed.

"Good check, great ass."

"Nah, it's too small for me," Spaz said as he made a fondling motion with his hands and broke into a song about big butts.

"Very funny, assholes," Kathy said as they passed each other. She was used to their high school harassment, which never seemed to let up.

From behind, she heard Spaz say, "Hey, Jensen, you got dirt on the back of your pants. Let me wipe it off for you."

Kathy yanked open the station door and, without turning, she said, "Touch my ass, Spaz, and I'll break your arm."

Gheringer laughed at Spaz's comeuppance, because both men knew Kathy would do just that.

Spaz didn't laugh, though. He just muttered, "Fuckin' squaw."

Holding the door open, Kathy called back, "I ain't that kind of Indian, Dickhead."

Kathy handed her car keys to Cindy, the morning shift dispatcher, and signed her Ford back in.

"I don't know why you put up with all that," Cindy said sympathetically.

Kathy looked up from the clipboard. "Well, you do, too."

"Not like that," Cindy said, shaking her head. "My dad would kick their asses good." Cindy's dad was a former Marine and head of the County Tactical Squad. Cindy, whose full name was Cynthia Blackfox Cattaraugus, leaned across her counter and whispered, "He shouldn't call you that. Do you know what 'squaw' means?" Her voice was barely audible when she said the word.

Kathy, whose actual name was Kaveetha Shwethaparma Jensen, and whose East Indian heritage linked her to her mother's family ten thousand miles away on a different continent, scowled. "Yeah, I know. It means 'cunt.'" When she saw Cindy blush, her voice softened. "What it really means is 'men are disgusting pigs.'"

Cindy, a year out of high school and still dreaming of the Big Romance, nodded. "Not all of them, I hope."

Kathy shook her head and chuckled as she walked back into the station to do her after-shift paperwork.

"Good luck with that."

5

The two men refilled their coffee mugs and sneaked out to the front porch, hoping to escape the clatter and muffled curses emanating from the kitchen.

"Best we let her cool down," Dan said as they settled into rocking chairs on the wide wrap-around veranda.

Birds chirped in the overhanging trees, and robins hopped across the lawn looking for sluggish worms flushed to the surface by the previous night's rain. The absence of the Tomlins was marked by the sun breaking through the clouds on an otherwise gloomy morning.

"How's the writing going?" Dan asked as they sipped their coffee.

"Not very well, actually. I'm really stuck on this third book."

Dan crossed one of his work-boot-clad feet over the other and ran a calloused hand through his jet black hair. "Didn't you just finish a book?"

"Pretty close. I'll turn in the final edits tomorrow."

"Congrats. What's this one about?"

Jan gave a little laugh. "Same as the last one, basically." Dan raised a questioning eyebrow. Jan continued, "Suburban angst. Failed marriages, neighborhood affairs, that sort of thing."

"Ah, 'chick lit.'"

Jan winced at the pejorative, but then reluctantly nodded. "I guess so. I'd never buy the stuff." He laughed.

"At least it pays the bills," Dan said as he turned to look out over the lake.

His comment produced a derisive snort from Jan. "Not by a long shot. And my contract is very light on the advances."

Dan's can-do attitude shone through when he said, "So, what's the next one about?"

Jan sighed. "Good question. That's what I came up here this time to figure out."

"Any luck?"

Jan just shook his head, and the two fell silent as they drank their rapidly cooling coffee.

After a minute, Jan spoke. "The first two books just, I don't know how to describe it. They seemed to flow straight from my brain to my fingers. They had been kicking around up here," he tapped the side of his head, "for so long that I didn't have to do much more than write the draft, then edit it. This next one isn't so easy."

"Maybe you're overthinking it. Too anxious about it."

Jan shook his head. "It's kind of the opposite. I rewrote my first book in a fit of anger after Lorraine filed for divorce. The court took my house, and I got fired from my job. I was a total basket case, drinking too much and nearly suicidal. But I put all of my feelings of betrayal toward Lorraine and the company I worked for, along with my growing hatred of her shark of a lawyer into the antagonist. Then I turned the protagonist from a wimpy victim into a strong, kick-ass heroine who fought back. That inspired me to climb out of the deep hole I had fallen into."

"Your marriage, your house, and your job? That's the Bummer Trifecta."

"No shit. I was in a bad place, man. But the writing was, cathartic, I guess. All that anger's, if not gone, at least tamped down now. But it's been replaced by money worries." He looked over at Dan. "This may be my last trip up here … at least for a while."

This got Dan's attention. He turned to face Jan. "But you're our most-frequent guest. Sandy wants to give you a plaque or something."

Jan chuckled, but then got serious. "We split the sale of the house in the divorce, and I've been living off that for the last two years. That pile is dwindling, though, and the advances on the books are a pittance, given the effort I put into them. I'm goin' to have to find a real job soon."

"Well, maybe this last book will take off. I know Sandy really liked your first one."

"Yeah, maybe."

The two fell silent again. Dan finished his coffee and stood. "If this is your last visit for a while, you need to have some fun before you go home," he said with a smile.

"What did you have in mind?"

"I was going to take the dirt bike up in the mountains, but Sandy has stuff to do today, and I don't like to go alone. Ever ridden a four-wheeler?"

Jan nodded enthusiastically. "Oh, yeah. Love 'em."

"Excellent. Meet me at the garage," he nodded toward the property's outbuilding, "in ten minutes?" Jan practically jumped from his chair. Eyeing Jan's Dockers and Top Siders, Dan said, "Dress for mud."

***

Three hours later, Jan helped Dan roll the mud-spattered motorcycle and ATV down the ramp at the back of Dan's pickup. Between the two of them, they hosed the mud off both bikes, the bed of the truck, and the ramp which they hung on wall hooks in the garage.

"Thanks, man, that was a blast." Jan couldn't have wiped the grin off his face if he'd wanted to.

"Hey, thank you," Dan replied. "If it wasn't for you, I'd be painting or fixing something around here."

"Those trails are really extensive."

Dan nodded as he pointed toward two folding chairs leaning against the wall of the garage. "They run all through the state lands, which make up a good part of the county. It's like another set of roads between towns up here."

Jan unfolded the chairs while Dan opened the old refrigerator rumbling in the corner and pulled out two beers. They clinked their bottles as they sat down.

"You heading home today?" Dan asked.

Jan nodded. "And I don't know when I'll be back. I wish I could stay longer, but…"

Dan looked thoughtful for a moment, then, without looking at Dan, he said, "If you need a discount, I'm sure we can arrange something."

"I appreciate the offer, but I have to get my shit together up here." He tapped his temple. "This place is a great escape, but escape isn't what I need right now. I've got to face up to some stuff."

"It's that bad?"

"I'm not livin' on the street—yet—but if I don't do something now, it could come to that soon."

Dan used the condensation from his beer bottle to slick back his black hair. "How'd it get so bad, if you don't mind me asking?"

"Oh, it's been a rough couple of years."

***

Two years earlier, Jan lay on the recliner that passed for a bed in his studio apartment. Boxes of his stuff occupied the couch and coffee table—the only other pieces of furniture in the small room. Attached to a low-end cable box, an old computer monitor sitting on a TV tray next to his chair served as his entertainment center. A nearly empty Jim Beam bottle stood on the floor within arm's reach. As the last two months had progressed, his taste for bourbon had followed the decline of his financial assets. Seventy-dollar bottles of Blanton's had given way to thirty-dollar Maker's and finally to twenty-dollar Beam. He supposed he would be trolling the bottom shelf in the local State Store later today.

How did this happen? He asked himself that question hourly, never with a better answer than *life sucks, Loraine is a fuckin' bitch,* or *I brought this on myself.* None of them reflected reality exactly, although all of them were true.

Back in October, when he returned from his first solo writing retreat at Mackey House, he found his house empty and divorce papers lying on the kitchen table. There was no great surprise there. His relationship with Loraine had been strained for most of a year. Apparently, his solo foray into the Poconos had been the last straw.

It wasn't like I didn't invite her to come along.

He had told her many times that she was welcome to join him, but after their first visit, meant to be a rekindling of the embers of their nearly extinguished romance, she announced she wouldn't be going back. Each time he asked, her refusals had gotten more and more accusatory, and the threat of consequences seemed to hover just below the surface, like a shark cruising just off the beach.

While he was gone, Loraine cast her bait into the water and a divorce shark gladly broke the surface. Things moved quickly after that. A series of court orders followed, forcing him out of his house—though he was still responsible for the mortgage, of course—and garnering fifty percent of his salary as "separate maintenance." His own divorce shark, a toothless bottom-feeder, had simply shrugged.

The next blow came when his badge refused to open the door at work. When he asked the security guard to buzz him in, Sam just held up a hand and dialed his phone. A minute later an anorectically thin young woman with stringy brown hair and glasses much too large for her angular face opened the door to the office suite from the inside and waved Jan in.

"Mr. Sorrensen, I'm Tammy Newgarden, your Human Resources Liaison." She didn't offer her hand or meet his eye. "Please join me in my office, please." Her voice trembled a little on the repeated "please."

"Tammy, what's going on? Why didn't my card work?" Jan had a sneaking suspicion he knew exactly what was happening but wasn't ready to admit it to himself.

Tammy remained silent until they sat in her closet-sized office. She motioned for Jan to close the door.

"I'm afraid I, ah, I have some bad news, Mr. Sorrensen," she glanced down at an open file folder on her desk, "ah, Jan."

When she finally looked up and made eye contact, realization hit him.

"Wait, let me guess. You're laying me off." His voice was a mixture of resignation and the faintest hope that she would tell him, "No, no, of course not." She didn't.

Instead, she shook her head and said, "No, not exactly." Hope raised its head a bit, but then Tammy swatted it like a whack-a-mole.

"Actually," her eyes dove back down to what was obviously his personnel file. "Actually, you're being fired, for cause."

"Excuse me? Wh-why?"

Tammy still wouldn't make eye contact, and her voice trembled more than ever. "Your supervisor, Mr. Thomas, feels you have been too … distracted … by your outside activities to devote sufficient attention to your duties as a Senior Software Engineer." She finished reading from the folder and finally looked up. Jan sat, open-mouthed. "Sam will escort you to your desk." She pointed to an empty box next to Jan's chair. "You can take your personal items in that."

Jan found his voice, which rose in pitch and volume. "Wait a minute. I've never missed a deadline, and my performance reviews have always been good. What the hell is going on!"

"Mr. Sorrensen, please! Mr. Thomas, ah, feels," she looked back down to the file, "you have been too distracted by your outside activities to devote sufficient attention to your duties as a Senior Software Engineer." She finished her second reading with a distinctive note of finality.

Someone knocked on the door, and Tammy practically jumped out of her chair to answer it. Sam the security guard stood in the hallway. Tammy stood back from the door, clearly indicating the exit interview was over. In a daze, Jan stood and followed Sam.

"Don't forget your box!" Relief was obvious in Tammy's voice.

That box was just one of several that sat unopened around the studio apartment. Jan knew on some visceral level that if he started unpacking, he would have to admit the last two months had really happened. Despite the best efforts of his subconscious, the evidence was all around him, both physically and electronically. His inbox was empty of any responses from all the resumes he had posted to every job search site he could find. Nobody wanted a fifty-something programmer when they could hire a fresher right out of college.

Loraine's shark had frozen their joint accounts, his two weeks of severance was long since spent, and already the mortgage payment was late.

The house has to go. Loraine won't like it, but... He smiled despite himself. Anything that pisses her off, I'm all for.

That decision made, he reached for his laptop. The first two weeks after his world fell apart, when he still had hope that Loraine would come to her senses and he would find an even better programming job, he had written every day, working on the novel that, in his mind, had caused all of his current problems.

That novel, an angst-filled contemporary lit piece, was the "distraction" that cost him his job and the obsession that led to "lack of marital attention", according to Loraine's shark. As his depression deepened, however, each time he reread his edits the story soured, the plot tarnished, and his opinion of his authorial skills dipped.

It had been a month since he last saved the file in a huff, then almost deleted it permanently. The spark of spite he was feeling from his decision to sell the house, though, prompted him to reopen the novel for a final look. Eight hours later, he sat back and stretched his neck.

It's not great. But it's not terrible, either. And best of all, now I know how to fix it.

The months of heartache had taught him how to add dimension and depth to his characters and how to traumatize them, making the story much more interesting and realistic. Jim Beam ignored, he leaned back in over his laptop and set to work.

The recent crises in his life taught him to punish his protagonist with emotional and physical trials, which made him less a stoic hero and more a living, breathing, flesh and blood person with wants and needs that conflicted with each other. He also learned how to make his damsel-in-distress less of a victim and a more strong-willed, speak-her-mind woman whose "f-you" attitude drove her to make one mistake after another until she faced her ultimate existential crisis.

But most of all, he learned how to make his villain truly evil. Every drop of hatred he felt towards his wife, her shark lawyer, his own do-nothing lawyer, his former boss, and the legal system that stripped him of the life he worked so hard to build, all of it he poured into his villain. He wove the smarmy side comments, the public emasculation, the destruction of his old life and the assassination of the person he had been, into the fabric of his female antagonist.

For a month he did little but write and revise and edit, then start the cycle over again until he was just changing it but not improving it. Then, with the Literary Agent Directory open in one window of his laptop, he sent his first batch of ten queries. Then his second ten, then his third and fourth batches. The bottle of Jim Beam that he had ceremoniously tucked away in a kitchen cabinet sang its siren song every time a "We're not interested in your novel at this time" response came back, and it sang even louder when weeks went by and no responses, even rejections, came back.

The ice cubes rattled when he dropped them into the glass, and the cabinet door banged when he pushed it closed. His hand shook a bit and his mouth went dry when he twisted off the black cap. He held the bottle horizontal, its open muzzle poised to shoot the brown liquor over the welcoming ice when his laptop dinged with incoming mail. The spell of anticipation broken, he set the open bottle upright and resignedly read what he expected to be yet another rejection.

Dear Mr. Sorrensen,

I found your query and the chapters you included quite interesting. If the rest of your manuscript, which I am formally requesting, is as intriguing and well-written, I would be interested in representing you.

Regards,

Lisa Lagrange (she, her, hers)
The Abernathy Agency

The next two years flew by in a whirlwind. The sale of the house went through, which floated his financial boat significantly, and the small advance he received when the book sold was icing on the cake.

***

A cycle of writing, revising, editing, and promoting left him mentally exhausted yet exhilarated. Now, with one so-so seller that had yet to earn out its advance, and another poised to be published, the reality of this new life did not yet match his dreams, but at least the vibrant Fall colors reflected his hopes for a new life.

"Wow, that was quite a journey. You're OK now, though, you know, mentally?"

"Oh, yeah. Financial worries aside, I'm the happiest I've been in years. Plus, Lorraine married the Mercedes dealer she had been banging behind my back, so no more alimony." They both chuckled, then Jan continued, "I think that's my problem. My writing before was fueled by anger and hate. I don't have that in me anymore."

As they walked to the back door of the house, Sandy stepped out and held up both hands. "Stop right there. There's no way you're coming in my kitchen covered in mud." She pointed at Dan. "You, sir, need to fix the fence post that heaved last winter, and you—" She held a bathrobe out to Jan. "Leave your clothes in the laundry room," she said, then turned back into the house.

Exasperated, Jan turned to Dan, who gave him a knowing smile and shrugged. As Dan turned to gather his tools, he said, "I guess you'll be getting home later than expected."

6

"Like I said, it was the discovery of my great-grandmother's diary that brought us to Mackey House," Jeff Tomlin explained to Dan and Sandy while they sat in the formal parlor. A roaring fire in the fireplace popped and crackled and gave off the sweet scent of burning oak. The firelight cast flickering shadows that danced across the bookshelves lining the walls, and with the wind whistling outside the windows, it was the perfect setting for a ghost story.

Jeff, it turned out, knew a lot more about the history of Mackey House than Sandy and Dan did. Dan quietly sat back in his chair, sipping his mug of mulled wine, a skeptical smirk on his face when Jeff enthused about the site's rich, yet gruesome history. Sandy, on the other hand, leaned forward, hanging on Jeff's every word.

"The current building," Jeff explained, "was built between 1921 and 1922 on the site of the Mackey Hotel, which was a late-Victorian structure. This house sits on most of the Hotel's original foundation. The Hotel provided lodging, dining, and entertainment for its upscale guests far away from their daily lives in New York and Philadelphia society."

Jeff paused to sip from his mug of Irish coffee before continuing. "The railroad serviced the hotel—you can still see the short line tracks down by the road—with a station conveniently located just across there." He pointed to the dark front bay window, though they offered only a view of blackness beyond. Jeff was catching his stride and Sandy could see in her mind's eye men in top hats and tails, carrying walking sticks and escorting corseted ladies in high-necked bustle dresses, their hair piled high upon their heads.

Naomi sat to Jeff's side, a far-away look in her eyes, probably because she had heard this story many times before. She sat passively in the firelight, perhaps picturing a scene similar to what Sandy imagined, or just fantasizing about the hero of the romance novel on her e-reader. Dan, too, was quiet, but not passive. He wore an expression of wry amusement, as if he only half-believed what Jeff was relating.

"The hotel thrived for over two decades, having attracted a following of repeat customers among the high-society families of New York and Philadelphia's Main Line. They could board a train in the morning and be at the hotel by dinner time. Both the Reading and Penn Central railroads ran weekly excursions on trains complete with French chefs for their dining cars, salon cars with crystal chandeliers, and luxurious Pullman sleeper cars. The maids and valets had their own, much more utilitarian accommodations, of course.

"So it was that Ephraim Singletary Mackey, the owner and proprietor of the hotel, hosted a Christmas Gala for his most loyal—and richest—guests on the twenty-third through the twenty-sixth of December, every year. The final one was one hundred years ago, in 1921."

Dan broke his silence. "That's when the place burned down?"

"Exactly. There was a huge scandal following the fire. A Board of Inquiry investigated the death of your great-great-aunt Flora and other aspects of the fire."

Sandy interrupted. "What were the findings of the investigation?"

"A tragic accident, I'm afraid. They blamed the fire on a poorly maintained gas jet in the basement. At that time, they were converting the hotel to electricity, but the basement was still lit by gas wall fixtures. Flora, I'm afraid, was trapped in her room by the flames."

Sandy shuddered. "What a horrible way to die." Jeff nodded.

"I take it neither Jennifer nor Jonathan came forward and admitted it was their carelessness with the cigarette that started it?" Sandy asked.

After a moment to gather his thoughts, Jeff said, "No. They both held their silence. Anyone else who knew the truth did, as well."

"What 'other aspects of the fire' did they investigate?" Dan asked.

Jeff caught his breath, and Naomi's attention snapped back to the conversation with a scowl.

"Well, since everyone had to rush out of the hotel in the middle of the night, the guests left a lot of expensive items behind."

"You mean like that necklace Jennifer referred to in her diary?" Dan was leaning forward now, as well.

"Yes, exactly. That and other pieces of jewelry that the other guests had brought."

Jeff hesitated and glanced quickly at Naomi, whose features practically shouted for silence.

"Did they find any of it?" Dan asked.

"Ah, some of it."

"But not all?"

"No. The pieces were all insured, though, so the insurance companies pored over the wreckage of the hotel for months before finally giving up and paying the claims." Jeff swallowed. "They figured everything melted in the intense heat."

Dan raised an eyebrow. "Diamonds don't melt."

Jeff hurried on with his recitation. "The next morning, after the fire was extinguished and a headcount of the guests and staff revealed that Flora was missing, a search of the ruins began. They found her body later that afternoon. Why she was in the empty room at the end of the hall was never revealed—until now." Jeff Tomlin sat back in his chair.

Sandy sat in a horrified silence, but Dan remained aloof. He said, "So, this is, what, family lore? Pretty strange for your great-grandparents to pass down such a sordid 'first date.'"

Sandy gave Dan a disapproving sideways glance, but Jeff chuckled, not taking offense. "No, of course not. Their liaison was a secret they took to their graves, although the speed of their subsequent engagement, and the speed with which my grandmother arrived, raised some eyebrows." He chuckled again. "No, it was a family secret known only to the two of them, until I found this." He pulled the tattered old diary from the satchel he always carried.

***

Sandy washed the wine glasses while Dan dried and placed them in the cupboard.

"I still don't know why you wouldn't let me throw them out after they were such douchebags."

Sandy shrugged. "Jeff's note was very apologetic, and we don't have anybody else coming in for a couple days. Besides, rent is rent."

Dan paused hanging up the dish towel and turned to look at Sandy. "Well, at least they're leaving tomorrow."

Sandy rinsed the suds out of the sink and took the towel from Dan and gave him a sly smile. "Then it'll be just the two of us—for now."

Recognition dawned on Dan's face. "Wait, are you—"

"No," she dropped the dishtowel on the counter and put her arms around his neck. "At least not yet."

As Dan looked down at the fire in her eyes, the grandfather clock in the hall began striking midnight. "Happy Anniversary, my love," he said before kissing her deeply.

The dish towel never got hung up that night—or the next day.

7

Monday, Late September

"Did you call the Tomlins, Babe?" Sandy asked as she put the finishing touches on breakfast.

"I knocked on their door and called to them twenty minutes ago. They wanted breakfast at eight, right?" Dan headed out the backdoor for firewood.

"All this food'll get cold," she muttered as she grabbed the master key ring and headed up the back stairs.

Her first knock drew no response, so she rapped her knuckles hard on the thick wood paneled door. Still no response.

They were probably up all night doin' it, she thought, and smiled at the memory of her own previous evening.

Turning the key in the lock and pushing open the door to the suite's sitting room, she called, "Hello. Good morning!"

Still getting no response, Sandy stepped into the sitting room and was met by a dry, stuffy heat that felt nothing like the house's century-old hot water radiators. A strong coppery smell overwhelmed her senses and Sandy trembled with a fight-or-flight anxiety originating deep in the primitive parts of her brain.

She tried calling out again, but only a croak emerged. Drawn inexorably toward the open bedroom door, her rational mind refused to believe what she knew instinctively. But when she stepped into the doorway and saw the bodies on the bed, all conscious thought evaporated and the breath she hadn't known she was holding erupted in a full-throated scream.

8

Deputy Kathy Jensen stood in the Mackey House hallway just inside the front door. She clutched a clipboard in one hand and a pen in the other with which she wrote "Det. Lewis" on the empty line below the coroner's name and checked her watch. "9:28 AM" went in the column marked "Arrival."

"Jensen," Detective David Lewis puffed, out of breath after the climb up the outside steps from the street below. "That statue has always given me the creeps," he said while he gulped air.

"Wait 'til you see upstairs," Kathy mumbled shakily.

He studied her ashen face. "You look like Hell."

"Tired. I was coming off shift when I got the call."

"You were first on scene?"

Kathy nodded, then steadied her voice into an official monotone. "I was doing my after-patrol paperwork when the call came in at 8:05 AM of two deceased individuals at the Mackey House. Deputies Spatz and Gheringer were on other calls, so I responded." Detective Lewis raised an eyebrow. He knew they were probably having coffee and donuts somewhere. "I arrived on scene at 8:12. When I arrived, I found Mr. and Mrs. Adams in the parlor. They're still there. Mrs. Adams was … overwrought, but Mr. Adams, who appeared to be in shock, directed me to the Veranda Suite upstairs."

"The 'Veranda Suite?'" the detective asked.

"All the rooms and suites have names." Kathy made a what-does-that-have-to-do-with-anything face. "Anyway, I drew my weapon in case there was an intruder and proceeded upstairs to the scene." Kathy paused and swallowed.

Detective Lewis spread his hands expectantly. "Well? What did you find?"

Kathy gathered herself. "Upon entering the suite, I observed copious amounts of blood splattered on the walls and ceiling, soaking the bedclothes and pooled on the floor."

"How did you know it was blood?" Lewis asked.

Kathy's initial irritation at such a stupid question turned to appreciation as she thought for a second. "The smell. It was the smell, Detective. That copper smell of freshly spilled blood."

Lewis raised an eyebrow. "You a hunter?"

Kathy nodded. "Crossbow. Sometimes bow and arrow."

He looked at her face and the wisps of black hair that had escaped her hat. "That figures," he grunted.

I'm not that kind of Indian, you idiot.

"What else?" His impatience was obvious in his tone.

Kathy was impatient, too, but for a different reason. "I observed the two decedents—"

"Never mind. I'll see for myself. Make sure you submit your full report by the end of the day." Kathy nodded. "Good."

He turned to the stairs and started to haul up his immense bulk. Kathy had the distinct impression that her "report" had simply been a chance for the fat old detective to catch his breath.

I didn't even tell him the weird parts.

"Holy shit!" The detective's shout echoed through the house.

There ya' go.

9

Friday, Late Spring

Jan stood watching the early morning rain fall. The launch of his second novel with the attendant interviews, conference panels, and readings pushed his springtime retreat later than usual.

His change in career had transformed his life, at least on the surface. But really, he had exchanged programming deadlines for submission deadlines and "What have you done for me lately" bosses for "Your next one needs to be even bigger" publishers. But all-in-all, he felt proud of his success, modest though it was, if not entirely satisfied.

The one thing he had truly lost, and which disturbed him on a visceral level, was love. He had honestly loved his wife, even after she left him and, on some subconscious layer of his psyche at least, still did. It wasn't hearts-and-flowers love that he missed, although he considered himself quite the romantic. It was more the general intimacy of sharing a home and a life with someone.

He had, of course, channeled the pain of loss into his characters, which both his agent and publisher correctly predicted would make for great book club sales. The first novel had been cathartic. It had washed his soul of much of the heartache and downright hate that he had harbored. He

51

rode that wave of emotion for another novel, but then that fount of creativity ran dry. But contracts are contracts and deadlines are deadlines, and daily email requests for progress reports on his next novel did nothing to make that creative fountain flow.

As he had each Spring for three years, he returned to Mackey House overlooking Lake Wallenpaupack, hoping to find the spark of an idea that would become a story that he could nurture into a bestseller.

The rain continued to fall as it had for three days. And for those three days, all Jan had done was stare at the patterns of rainwater that poured from the overflowing gutters. The floor of the porch creaked as he shifted his weight. Something in those little nuances of reality brought him back from wherever his mind had gone. He noticed, for the first time since his most recent arrival, little things about the old house that seemed different somehow.

In the many weeks he had spent at Mackey House, he'd seen his fair share of thunderstorms march down the thirteen-mile length of the lake. Never before had he noticed the rain gutters overflowing. They collected the fallen leaves from the overhanging maples and oaks every Fall, but now the trees were in full foliage, their newborn leaves that vibrant shade of green that proclaims their health to the world. Clogged gutters in the Spring meant the detritus from last year hadn't been dredged from the roofline channels.

The steady overflow drew his eyes to where it splashed off the porch railing. Dark green paint, which from a distance lent the trim an appealing contrast to the reddish-brown stucco, was peeling. Now that he thought about it, there were a lot of differences this trip. His air conditioner, stuck in the suite's bedroom window, seemed to groan and clatter a lot more than he remembered. And a plumber, not Dan, had been working in the bathroom next door yesterday afternoon.

It occurred to him he had subconsciously noticed a few other things, as well. The B&B was abnormally empty. In fact, he was pretty sure he was the only guest, which was very unusual for this time of year. Even the strange statue of a woman seemingly in the throes of either religious or sexual ecstasy that dominated the front lawn looked a little dingy.

Dan and Sandy Adams, the thirty-something couple who owned Mackey House normally kept the place in tip-top shape, which was something they needed to do to attract guests, since the B&B was so far off the beaten path of Pocono ski slopes and gambling resorts.

Come to think of it, I haven't seen Dan yet this visit. Why wasn't he working on the plumbing?

Normally both Dan and Sandy met him when he arrived, helping him with his bags and welcoming their "best guest." This time, though, it was only Sandy, looking more harried and frankly older, who gushed over his arrival. He made a mental note to ask her about it at breakfast. Resignedly, Jan turned from the falling water to his laptop sitting inert on the small glass-top table. With a sigh, he closed the screen and carried it into his room.

"Getting much work done?" Sandy asked as she slid the plate of eggs, bacon, multigrain toast and a homemade blueberry muffin onto the table in front of him.

"I wish," Jan said. "My well seems to have run dry." Sandy gave him a wan smile. "Thanks, by the way. This breakfast looks amazing."

Her smile brightened a bit. "You're welcome. I hope you enjoy it."

She turned to return to the kitchen, but Jan spoke up before she could leave. "I'm surprised I'm the only one here. It's usually jumping this time of year." Actually, he was glad of the quiet, but he felt the need to chat. And Sandy wasn't her bright-eyed self this morning.

"Yeah, I guess there's a lot of competition and, you know, the economy hasn't been that great."

"Sure," he responded, but he also knew that the country's economy was in fact booming. "I haven't seen Dan around—" His words died mid-sentence when he saw the tears welling in Sandy's eyes. "Oh, my God. I'm so sorry. Did something happen?"

Sandy collapsed into one of the many empty chairs surrounding the dining table. She sniffed back the tears and met his eyes. "He's gone."

Is he dead? he thought, and his face reflected his shock.

She continued, "He took off last winter, right after the…incident."

"Took off? You mean he left you?" Jan felt a surge of anger at Dan, and a stronger affinity for Sandy. How could somebody cheat on a sweet, pretty woman like Sandy?

"He didn't so much leave me. More he left this place."

That made more sense. The upkeep of a big old house like this one was certainly an uphill battle and a full-time job.

"So, he got tired of the constant maintenance?" He saw her hesitate, so he quickly added, "Look, if I'm out of line asking about this, just tell me. Believe me, I know how hard talking about a spouse leaving you can be."

Sandy shook her head hard, her blonde ponytail flapping back and forth. "No, he loved fixing this place up. This house was his baby." She stifled another sob and sniffed back more tears. "He got scared off, like all of our guests…except you."

"Scared off? Why would anybody be scared off?"

This conversation is baffling. I'm clearly missing something.

She gave him a surprised look and wiped her hands unnecessarily on her apron.

"I guess you don't follow us on social media, huh?" Her tone was borderline sarcastic.

"Actually, I don't really 'follow' anyone. I barely have the time or energy to do what the publisher demands by posting a few blogs and tweeting occasionally. That's plenty."

Sandy looked genuinely surprised, but then her face fell back into a look of resignation.

"Oh, that explains why you weren't scared off, too. You don't know what happened." Jan just shook his head in bewilderment, so she continued. "You know the Veranda Suite upstairs? The one that faces the front of the house?"

Jan nodded. He had walked past its hall door at the top of the main staircase and shared the upstairs porch with its occupants many times.

Sandy hung her head, and whispered, "Back in the Fall, a man killed his wife and then himself in that room."

Holy shit.

A million questions came to mind, but Jan's sense of decency kicked in before he could voice any of them. He reached out and took Sandy's hand.

"I'm so sorry. That must have been a terrible shock."

She looked up at him from under her bangs. "It was, especially since I'm the one who found them the next morning." Sandy looked startled for a moment. "In fact, it was right after you left."

"You mean the Tomlins?" Jan sat stunned when Sandy nodded.

"After you left, Jeff and Naomi came back from wherever they had spent the day. He had left a note apologizing for the argument we had over breakfast, so the four of us hung out by the fireplace in the parlor. Everything seemed normal, if not a little awkward—I never did like them very much." Jan nodded his assent.

"They went to bed before midnight, then Dan and I cleaned up and went to bed ourselves."

Despite the deeply disturbing narrative, or maybe because of it, Jan's authorial story sense started itching. Jeff's recitation of the socialite's diary came back to him, as well.

There's a lot of strange history in this house, he thought.

Hesitantly, and as gently as he could, he asked, "And you found them?"

Sandy nodded, and a sob escaped her lips. "It was horrible."

11

Jan sat quietly as Sandy's voice trailed off into silence and her eyes stared into the past. They left the breakfast dishes on the table and sat side-by-side on the couch in the parlor.

"You don't have to tell me the details, if you don't want to." Jan's tone was reassuring, although he desperately wanted to know more.

She shook her head, coming back to the here and now. "There's nothing else to tell about that night. Shortly after Jeff told his story, he and Naomi went to bed. Dan and I cleaned up a bit and went to bed ourselves."

Sandy stopped again, and Jan covered her hand with his. She looked up at him and smiled, squeezing his fingers as she did so. When he relaxed his own responding squeeze, she turned her hand palm-up and interlaced his fingers. Jan felt a spark of something pass between them where they touched, and he knew Sandy felt the spark, too, as her eyes met his and a smile curled her lips.

"Like I said, you don't have to continue." His voice sounded deeper, even to his own ears.

"No, I want to. I had to tell the police what I saw over and over, but I've never told anyone what I *felt* about the next morning. I feel...safe enough with you." She dropped her eyes, but he caught a glimpse of tears appearing in them first. Then, barely above a whisper, "Even more than I did with Dan."

Jan leaned forward and kissed the top of her head. "You are safe with me," he whispered in return. Sandy nodded, and the words poured out.

"It was awful. I mean, there are no words I know to describe it. We had agreed to have an early breakfast so they could get on the road. Dan and I got up about six-thirty to get everything ready. Frankly, I was glad to see them go. They weren't my favorite guests by a long shot, plus I wanted some quiet time with Dan. The stresses of running a business in a big house almost a hundred years old were wearing on our marriage. I was looking forward to some downtime when we could reconnect, you know?

"But eight o'clock came and went with no sign of Jeff and Naomi. I didn't want the food to get cold, and I was getting pissed, so while Dan was fetching wood for the fireplace, I went up to find out how long they would be. I knocked on the sitting-room door but got no answer—" Sandy swallowed hard.

"Anyway, I didn't get an answer when I knocked, so I used the master key."

She paused to take a breath, and Jan figured she was stalling, not wanting to relive what had happened next. She still gripped his right hand, but he replaced it with his left and gently placed his right hand on her back, just below her neck. To his surprise, she leaned into him and lay her head on his shoulder. He dropped his hand to her waist, completing the embrace.

Sandy took another deep breath and spoke into his chest. "I opened the sitting-room door and called out to them, since I didn't want to barge right into the bedroom. Then I stuck my head in and called their names. When I got no response, I got worried, so I crept into the sitting room and knocked on the open door of the bedroom, without looking inside. They still didn't answer when I called to them, and I knew in my gut something terrible had happened, although I couldn't have imagined what I saw when I stepped into the doorway. My first thought was, 'Why did they splash red paint on the walls?'"

Jan felt her body shiver and heard the sob she tried to stifle, so he pulled her even more tightly against his shoulder and laid his own head on top of hers, telling her through his touch that it was alright to let it all out, which she did. Sobs wracked her body, and tears dampened his shirt as she buried her face in his chest and expelled months of pent-up emotion.

When the sobs and hiccups finally stopped, she lifted her face to his and lightly kissed his lips.

"Thank you," she said. "Thank you for letting me get all of that out." She glanced down at his shirt. "And for letting me get mascara all over you."

They both laughed. Again, she took a deep breath, held it for a second, then let it out.

"Forgive me if I don't go into the details. Suffice it to say, the scene was a bloody mess. Jeff and Naomi were naked. She was face down on top of him. If it weren't for the blood everywhere, I would have thought they were still—you know."

Oh, I know, he thought. *I heard them going at it enough when I was here.*

Sandy's voice faltered, and Jan jumped in. "That's enough. I get the picture." Then he winced at how trite and dismissive his words were. "You don't have to tell me anymore."

Sandy nodded and mouthed "thank you" before extricating herself from his embrace.

"I need to go to my room."

Her abrupt tone clearly meant it was not an invitation, despite the intimacy they had shared just a moment before.

"Sorry, I'm just wiped out. I'm going to take a nap. I hope you make progress on your book."

With that, she stood and left him sitting on the couch, confused by her sudden departure.

12

Saturday, Late Spring

Ideas flew through Jan's head, but not ideas for the book he had come to Mackey House to work on. The story of the fire nagged at him. His stories always had some historical aspect, which meant Jan had learned that what people remembered, and what actually happened, were often far apart. The natural inclination of a storyteller is to embellish the facts, making them more interesting and sometimes making up new ones to fit their own narrative. Jan had certainly done that in his own writing.

He had also developed a keen sense for when the supposed facts seemed a little too pat, a little too convenient for the story. That's why the story of Flora and the Fire—he had already titled it in his thoughts—tickled the back of his mind for the rest of the morning. His laptop sat unattended while he tried to remember exactly what Jeff had said the previous fall and reconcile that with Sandy's account of the following evening. The story didn't quite hang together, and he knew he was missing pieces of the puzzle. Finally, he slapped his laptop closed, collected his car keys, and headed downstairs.

Facts. I need facts. I need to know what really happened here a century ago.

He felt the first whispers of his interest growing into an obsession, but he also felt the seed of a novel growing, crowding out the sappy love story he had gone there to write. He could tell the tragic story, shaping it into a real page-turner with Lost Generation characters, a high-society love story, and a tragic death, all set in an eerie, isolated hotel.

Halfway to the nearby town of Dundee, driving along a winding country road lined with little blue periwinkle flowers, he thought about heading to the library. The library in Dundee was small, but he had used it for research before. Plus, it had good Wi-Fi—much better than Sandy's—and it was next door to a cute little coffee shop. Still undecided, he pulled up to one of the few stop signs in town at the intersection with Dundee's Main Street.

The library, he knew, was two blocks to his left, but another destination popped into his head and he smiled. The local Historical Society occupied an old storefront a couple of blocks to his right. Inspired by the prospect of local color, he turned right. He hadn't gone a block, though, when red and blue lights flashed in his rearview mirror.

Crap. Damn small-town cops.

Pulling into the parking lot of the town's combination gas station and convenience store, he hoped the county sheriff's patrol car would pass him by, but he cursed again when it pulled in behind him. The wait while the deputy ran his plate seemed to take forever.

Damn small-town cops with small-town network service.

Finally, a uniformed officer stepped out of the county vehicle. Jan was surprised to see a distinctly non-masculine form approach his open window from behind.

"License, registration, and insurance, please." Her voice was a contralto but carried a clear note of well-earned authority.

Jan had learned from his neighbor, who was also a local cop, to get his wallet out of his pocket and cards out of the glove box *before* the officer was standing at his window. Reaching into your back pocket or opening your glove box was the quickest way to get a cop to draw a weapon.

"Certainly, Officer," he said as he handed his identification cards through the open window.

The standard-issue aviator style sunglasses obscured the deputy's eyes. "Do you know why I stopped you, Mr. Sorrensen?"

"No, sorry. What did I do?"

"It's what you didn't do, sir. You failed to come to a complete stop at the intersection."

Jan thought back, and was pretty sure he remembered feeling the car recoil, but it wouldn't do to argue.

"Sorry about that."

"Distracted thinking about your next novel, Mr. Sorrensen?"

The *non sequitur* took Jan by surprise.

"Excuse me? You know who I am?"

The deputy just held up his ID in response. Her patronizing expression spoke volumes, but she otherwise remained silent.

"No, I mean, you know what I do?" Jan sputtered.

A smile tugged at a corner of the deputy's mouth. "Dan and Sandy never made a secret of their famous house guest." The smile broadened. "Plus, the library carries several copies of your books—all of which you donated, I understand."

Jan smiled back. Maybe he could get out of this ticket after all.

"Never hurts to spread a little 'bread on the waters,'" he said. "I'm actually a little blocked on this next one, which is why I came up here—to clear my head, you know?"

He wasn't sure why he shared that particular detail, but he figured the longer they chatted, the less likely he was to get a ticket.

"Well, I hope Cara and Nick finally get together," the deputy said, referring to the main characters of Jan's first novel. She pulled off her sunglasses and Jan saw the twinkle in her eye.

"Why…" he read her nametag, "… Deputy Jensen, you've read my stuff."

She patted the phone clearly outlined in the pocket of her tight uniform pants. "I have a lot of time on my hands in this job."

An idea struck him. "I just heard about the murder/suicide at the Mackey House last fall. Anything you can tell me about that?"

The smile vanished from Kathy's face and she shook her head. "I can't discuss that," she said. Her tone shut down any further questions he had.

"I was headed to the library, but changed my mind. I think I'll check out the Historical Society instead. Maybe that's why I rolled through the stop sign."

Kathy's lip curled and her voice dripped sarcasm. "Yeah, maybe that was it."

"So, are you giving me a ticket?" Jan tried to keep his tone light.

"Why? Do you want one?" Her tone was still sarcastic, but with a hint of playfulness, too.

He shook his head quickly and smiled. Her returning smile sent a thrill down his spine. Deputy Jensen put her sunglasses back on, flipped closed her ticket book, and handed his license and registration back to him. Jan suddenly realized he didn't want this traffic stop to end, even if it cost him a ticket.

"Did I really roll through that stop sign?"

She slid the sunglasses down on the end of her nose and looked at him over their rims.

"Nah. I was just bored."

She turned on her heel and strode back to her patrol car while Jan watched her go in his mirror.

13

The Dundee and Northern Pocono Lake District Historical Society occupied an old storefront building right on Main Street. Its double bay windows held a collection of Native American artifacts, a chronological display of photos depicting the development of Main Street, and a montage of pictures showing aerial views of the area's many lakes and ponds, which formed a patchwork landscape.

Jim and Barb Donnelly ran the Historical Society with the fervor of retired empty-nesters still used to going to work every day. When Jan entered the building, Barb was busy laying out another photo spread, while Jim sorted through a box of recently donated papers. They both stood from their seats at the room's large worktable when he entered. Jan introduced himself and got a reaction he wasn't expecting.

"It's about time you paid us a visit," Barb said over her half-sized reading glasses.

"Are you researching your next page-turner?" Jim gushed. "Your last one was a real bodice-ripper, it was."

Jan wasn't sure he liked his book being called that, but he smiled anyway. "So, you've read it?"

"Oh sure. Read them both," Jim said.

"We have a very active book club here in Dundee," Barb continued.

Jim completed the thought. "Sandy insisted we all read them. Any hints about your next one?" Barb scowled at him, but he just shrugged. "It doesn't hurt to ask."

"Well, I'm not sure. I'm staying at the Mackey House—"

"Of course you are," Jim interrupted. Barb slapped his arm. "Oh, sorry."

Jan opened his mouth to speak, but Barb jumped in. "You're looking into that horrible murder they had up there last fall, aren't you?"

Jim nodded enthusiastically, but frowned. "Can't really call that 'history' yet though."

Barb slapped his arm again. "It happened in the *past*. That makes it history."

Jim fell silent, and Barb turned back to Jan with an expectant expression.

Jan, who had watched this exchange with a bemused look, took a breath.

"Well, yes, I'm interested in the details of the murder/suicide, but I also want to know the entire *history* of Mackey House and its predecessor, the Mackey Hotel."

It was his turn to return an expectant look.

"Of course, of course. Where should we start?" Barb asked.

"Best to start at the beginning, I always say," Jim chimed in.

Another slap on the arm. "I didn't ask you, you old fool!"

She turned back to Jan as if neither had just spoken. Same expectant look.

Jan couldn't help chuckling at these two.

"How long have you two been married?" he asked, smiling.

"Too long!" they both said simultaneously, eliciting laughter from all three.

"Actually," Jan started, looking at Jim, "I'd prefer to work backwards, starting with Dan Adams' sudden departure."

Barb's hand flew to her mouth and Jim shook his head. "Cryin' shame that. Him takin' off and leavin' her to her own devices like that."

"Well, maybe he had reason to," Barb shot back. "There were strange goings-ons after the killings."

"You don't believe that nonsense, do you? That's just her story."

Barb wagged her finger in front of her husband. "No, no. That couple who came a week after the killings only stayed one night. They probably saw *her*, too."

"Would you stay someplace where a guy killed his wife, then himself? Of course, they left. Probably as soon as they heard the story."

Barb and Jim were on a roll, completely ignoring Jan, who, despite his amusement, had become totally lost.

"Wait, wait, WAIT!" Both husband and wife turned back to Jan with sheepish grins. "Thank you. Tell you what. Whoever I point to gets to answer my question, OK?"

Jim and Barb looked at each other, shrugged, and nodded.

"Good," Jan continued. He put a finger to his chin as if contemplating a major life decision, then pointed at Barb. She grinned and delivered yet another slap to Jim's arm. He rubbed it absent mindedly as Jan asked, "Why did Dan leave Sandy?"

"This is just hearsay, you understand. The 'official' reason, as told by Sandy at least, is that Dan was tired of all the upkeep the B&B demanded, so he just up and left. She claims they were arguing all the time about money and what repairs were needed next."

"But—?" Jim tried to jump in, but Jan held up his hand.

"You'll get the next one. Be patient." Jim sulked, but remained silent. "Anyway," he turned back to Barb, "that sounds reasonable enough. Maintaining that old place must be nonstop, and expensive."

"Oh, I'm sure it is, but that's the point. Dan loved doing it." Jan looked skeptical, hoping Barb would elaborate, which she did. "There's only one hardware store in town, and the closest Home Depot is, what? Almost an hour away."

This is exhausting, Jan thought.

"Stanley at the hardware store—yeah, his name is Stanley, ironic, isn't it—says that he was always enthusiastic when he came in to buy materials."

It's a clever coincidence, Jan thought, *but not ironic*.

Again, he kept his comment to himself just to keep the train on its track.

"And," Barb held up her index finger for emphasis, "whenever he needed a new tool, he didn't go the cheap route. Oh, no. It was top shelf tools for Dan."

"So you don't think there were money problems, either?"

"No way. That B&B was full all Spring, Summer, and Fall."

Jan nodded knowingly. That had been his observation, as well. "So, you think they had other marital problems. One of them was cheating, maybe?"

Barb looked confused, but shook her head. "No, that's not—"

"Hey!" Jim interrupted. "It's my turn." Jan shrugged and nodded, then pointed to Jim, who grinned and continued. "By all accounts, they were devoted to each other. No rumors of cheating that I—we've—heard of. No, some say," he nodded toward Barb, "it was the ghost that drove him away."

"Wait, a ghost? What ghost?"

This is getting better and better.

Jim and Barb gave each other the "typical tourist" look.

"Flora's ghost, of course. After the killings last fall, Flora came back full force."

Jan just stared, mouth hanging open, but he recovered quickly.

"OK, clearly I don't have enough background here. So, we had better start at the beginning."

Jim gave him an I-told-you-so nod. "To do that, we need to go up to the Archives."

Barb motioned for Jan to follow as she led the way past an old rowboat and various glass cases on their right, and neat rows of bookshelves on their left, to the back of the first floor. At a door set into the back wall, Jim unclipped a carabiner from his belt, which held a set of keys.

"The Hotel file is on the second floor," he said over his shoulder as he turned the key and swung the door outwards.

Behind it, a stairway climbed steeply to the left. "We lived upstairs when we first bought the place," Jim said as he started up the stairs. "But once we filled up the third floor with archives, then the spare bedroom on the second floor," he had reached the first landing and used the keys again to open another door to what was once their apartment, "we decided we needed more space."

"And an escape from your obsession," Barb chimed in.

"It's not an obsession. I just love the history of this place."

Barb made a face but stayed quiet for once.

At some point, the rooms of the apartment—parlor, two small bedrooms, kitchen, and bath—were transformed into a storehouse with racks of boxes and mismatched filing cabinets protruding from the walls. Jim led them through the parlor to one of the bedrooms in the back. The sun shone through the window and Jan noted how well-organized the space was. To prove the observation, Jim went straight to a particular rack and pulled a box off the second shelf.

"Turn around. We'll use the table in the kitchen."

Retracing their steps out of the bedroom, Barb, who was now in the lead, crossed the hallway into a small kitchen. A coffee maker stood on the counter, a drop-leaf table set against a wall, and a relatively new mini-refrigerator hummed in the corner.

"Jim practically lives up here with his treasure trove of ephemera."

What a turn of phrase, Jan thought, and he tucked it away in the part of his memory he had trained to remember overheard snatches of conversation.

Jim set the file box on the kitchen table and pushed it back against the wall. He offered Jan the one 1950s kitchen chair, with its cracked yellow plastic upholstery, while Barb fetched two folding chairs from a closet. When they were all seated, Jim started pulling pictures, newspaper articles, and other bits of paper from the box.

He laid an old, faded photograph on the table and spun it around so Jan could see it. "This is the Mackey Hotel back in—" he lifted the edge of the photo and looked at the back. "—1906. That would be fifteen years before the fire."

"When was it built?"

"The Hotel opened in 1896. This area was the real boondocks back then."

Barb jumped in, "Before the dam was built and they flooded the valley, and inundated the town of Wilsonville, to make the lake."

"After that, the place *filled up* with outsiders."

Jan had done his homework before his first visit, so he knew Jim was exaggerating.

The lake has over fifty miles of shoreline, only about ten miles of which is developed. This place is still the boonies.

He studied the photo for a moment. "It looks a lot bigger than the house that's there now."

"Right. Jamison Mackey was the original owner. Ephraim Mackey, his grandson, inherited it when his grandfather died in 1910. Word is that Ephraim never really liked being a hotelier. Once he was free of it—

because of the 1921 fire—he built that house on most of the same foundation, but smaller at the front. Once the house was built and the statue was up—"

"He became a recluse." Barb had been silent longer than any time since Jan had met her. "Not only did he stop having hotel guests, he stopped having any guests. Lived in that big place mostly by himself, just a live-in maid for a while. Had his groceries delivered and everything."

Jim was nodding along and trying to break in. "Yeah, they say he was living in just one two-room suite on the second floor."

"The one named after a bird—"

It was Jan's turn to interrupt. "The Raven's Nest?"

"Yes, yes, that's it. Apparently, The Raven was Ephraim's nickname on account of his jet black hair and beard," Jim said.

Barb interjected in a whisper, "They say his hair was still black as coal the day he died."

"At one hundred and four years old."

Jan was becoming overwhelmed with these trivial pieces of information. He held up a hand and Barb and Jim fell silent.

"So, the original hotel opened in 1896." He paused for nods of assent, then continued. "Old Man Mackey died in 1910. Did he build the original hotel?" More nods.

Odd that they've stopped speaking, he thought, but then he realized he was still holding his hand up. *Well, whatever works.*

"His grandson Ephraim ran the hotel for ten years until it burned down in 1921 when someone died—Flora, the maid. I heard about her last fall. She was trapped in the basement when the fire started, right?" Neither Barb nor

Jim spoke. They simply nodded. "He then built the current house, lived in it, apparently in my suite, until he died at age one hundred and four. Did I miss anything?" He finally dropped his hand.

Both of his hosts shook their heads. Jim let Barb answer. "Nope. That's the timeline."

"OK. So when did Ephraim die, and who owned the house until Dan and Sandy bought it?"

Barb and Jim were silent for a few seconds, then Jim rifled through his papers, pulling out a yellowed newspaper obituary. "Ephraim Mackey died in 1992."

Jan waited during a silence that was quickly becoming awkward. What happened to his chatty hosts to turn them into sphinxes? Finally, a note of exasperation in his voice, he said, "So, who owned it until the Adams bought it?"

"Ah, nobody," Barb said.

"Excuse me?"

Jim took a deep breath. "That's right. The house stood empty for over twenty years."

"Wow. Dan and Sandy must have had a lot of work to do to fix it up after it sat empty that long."

Jim nodded. "It was a mess. It took them the better part of two years before they could take in guests."

"I can see how Dan would get tired of all of that work."

"Oh, no," Barb said. She looked at Jan intensely. "He loved the work. He had a contracting business before moving here, so it was right in his wheelhouse. It doesn't make sense that he would leave it all behind after putting his heart and soul into it."

This line of thought confused Jan, but he sensed a deeper implication. "What's your point? Why do you think he left?"

Barb and Jim looked at each other, obviously reluctant to answer. Finally, by some form of marital telepathy, they decided Barb would respond. "Well, some folks say ... they say maybe he *never* left."

"At least not alive," Jim finished in a whisper.

14

It was late afternoon by the time Jan left the Historical Society. He had to assure Barb and Jim that he wouldn't repeat their suspicions before they let him take photos of their records and press clippings about the Mackeys, their hotel, and the House. Once they had his assurances, the gossip floodgates opened, and it seemed he heard about everything and everyone in Wayne County. With their stories, from the absurd to the sublime, running through his head, he sat at the mahogany bar in the Towne Tavern.

So absorbed was he that he didn't even notice when a striking young woman, dressed in jeans and a button-down chambray shirt, walked into the bar. He couldn't help but notice, though, when she sat down next to him. At first, he didn't recognize the straight black hair framing high cheekbones and an angular jawline as it fell past her shoulders and gathered at the open collar of her shirt. Backlit by the front windows and the dim bar lights, her dusky skin stood in stark contrast to her piercing blue eyes. Jan stared appreciatively, yet uncomfortably, at this person with no sign of recognition until she took a pair of mirrored sunglasses out of her shirt pocket and put them on the end of her nose.

Oh, wow.

"Deputy Jensen. Are you following me?"

The bartender placed a glass of draft lager, unordered, in front of her.

"Thanks, Lloyd," she said as she smiled at Jan.

"I guess you're known here," Jan said, and they both laughed.

She raised her glass and said over its rim, "Learn much from the local gossips?"

Jan's eyes shot up. "So, you have been following me."

"Jan, your vanity plate says 'JAN WRTR'."

Jan lifted his bourbon and took a sip. "So, I'm 'Jan' now? You have me at a disadvantage."

She held out her hand. "Jan Sorrensen, I'm Kathy Jensen, nice to meet you."

He took her hand and got a firm handshake in return.

"Nice to meet you too, Kathy, unprofessionally that is."

They both took another sip.

"So, what stories did Barb and Jim tell you?"

Jan's suspicion antennae started buzzing, but he kept a smile on his face and tried to keep his voice normal.

"Just a lot of boring Dundee history."

"Grist for your fiction mill?" she asked.

Perhaps he was just being paranoid and Kathy just wanted the inside scoop on his next book, but he felt a bit like he was being interrogated.

"Maybe. I'm kind of stuck right now and I'm looking for new ideas."

Kathy emitted a half-laugh. "Well, if you're looking for fictional stories, you went to the right place today."

He looked sideways at her. "You don't think much of the Donnellys, do you?"

Kathy sighed. "Oh, they're basically harmless, I guess. I just have an innate dislike of gossip."

"Well, you can relax. All we talked about were the facts around the Mackey Hotel property."

He had struck out asking about the killings when she pulled him over, when she was still Deputy Jensen. He didn't want this conversation to end, so he didn't mention the 'incident' this time.

That's why he almost choked on his bourbon when Kathy said, "You mean they didn't tell you how they think Sandy killed Dan?" She smiled at his reaction, but also gave a rueful shake of her head. "I thought so. Let me tell you, it's a pile of crap. Sandy and Dan were like two lovebirds. At least they were before ..."

"Before the killings, you mean."

"Until afterwards, actually. They pulled together, clung to each other really, after the investigation was over and they cleaned the place up." She shook her head and finished her beer. Lloyd brought fresh drinks for them both. Jan caught his eye to make sure the drinks went on his tab.

"So, what happened? To their marriage, I mean."

"Fucking social media." Kathy's voice was venomous. "Once word got out about the killings, then the incident a couple weeks later, the trolls set upon Sandy and Dan. You couldn't search for Mackey House without getting these horrible posts full of stupid, totally unfounded allegations." Kathy took a big gulp of her beer and practically slammed the glass down on the bar. "All of their reservations got cancelled. Reservations for the entire year, except yours apparently. Didn't you get the memo?"

"I don't do social—wait. The entire year's reservations were cancelled? And what other 'incident' are you referring to?"

Kathy nodded, but ignored his second question. "Everything got cancelled almost overnight. By mid-January Dan was talking about selling the place."

Something clicked in Jan's brain. "You must know them pretty well."

The dim bar lights glinted off the tears welling in her eyes. She sniffed and wiped them with the back of her hand.

"Yeah. You could say that. We got together for dinner and drinks at least once a month. And I saw Dan around town all the time."

Jan sensed Kathy was holding back, downplaying their relationship. But, rather than alienating her, he switched gears.

"Sandy didn't want to sell?"

Kathy shook her head. "No way. I heard them argue about it once. Dan, I thought, was pretty reasonable. With no income, how would they live? Sandy just kept saying they had 'plenty' to ride it out. Finally, she said, 'The only way I'm leaving is in a body bag.'"

"Wow. That's pretty definitive."

Kathy nodded. "And it was the last time I saw the two of them together. I had coffee with Dan about a week later, and it was weird. He was much more upbeat. Told me about plans he had to expand the place."

"Where would they get the money for that?"

Kathy shrugged. "Good question. I asked him and he got pretty defensive and vague, saying something about an 'angle' he was working that would solve all of their problems."

"An angle?"

"Yeah. He wouldn't tell me what it was. Maybe he was courting an investor or something." She shrugged again and lifted her beer.

Jan nodded along with that train of thought. "And when the deal fell through …"

Kathy licked the beer foam from her upper lip. "He realized it was hopeless and he couldn't convince Sandy to sell, so he took off, I guess."

Jan thought for a moment. "That story ought to be pretty easy to check."

He wondered if she would take the hint, but she leaned back on the barstool and eyed Jan with a frown.

"I'm not investigating my friends. Dan talked about leaving, and then he did. Case closed."

Jan wasn't ready to let it go. "All it would take is a check of his credit cards or his phone records. Or even just a phone call to his family."

Kathy shook her head violently. "No, no, no. Stop right there. First of all, I know for a fact that he doesn't have any family, so there is no one to call. Plus, you need a warrant to check phone and financial records. It's not like on TV, where some geek hacks into phone company computers to track someone's movements."

She slid off her barstool and pulled a money clip with folded bills from her pocket.

"I got this," Jan said, but Kathy very deliberately slid a ten off the clip and slapped it on the bar.

"Around here, we keep our noses out of other people's business," she said, looking him straight in the eye. Then she turned and in three strides she was out the door.

It's never good to piss-off the local cops, he thought. *But then again, she did kind of overreact.*

15

Why did I let him push my buttons like that?

Kathy knew she had overreacted, and it bugged her as she drove through town to her apartment.

It's these damned double shifts. They're exhausting. He was just curious about Dan's departure, which, to an outsider, could look kind of suspicious.

The same thought that had nagged at her since Dan left popped into her head again.

Maybe not just to an outsider.

She tucked her hair behind her ears as she got out of her car and climbed the outside stairs to her second-floor apartment. She waggled her fingers at her landlady, Mrs. Druesmiller, who always seemed to look out her window just as Kathy walked past.

Nosy old bitty, she thought, flashing her brightest fake smile.

Grabbing a beer from the fridge, she sat at her kitchen table and replayed the encounter with Jan in her mind. Using a technique her father, a retired cop, had taught her, she started asking herself questions.

First, why did you wear your hair down?

Frowning, she pulled her silky, jet-black hair into her normal ponytail.

Thank you, Mom.

She got her hair, skin tone, and even the planes of her face from her mother. When her father, whose roots ran deep in Wayne County, brought fellow student Shwetha Subramanian home from college, the gossip flew around town like a bitter winter wind. But when they married and settled down in Dundee, the extensive tree of families, of which the Jensens were a thick branch, simply adopted Shwetha as one of their own and made it their mission to turn her into a Jensen.

For Kathy, though, growing up the only brown kid in her class was a struggle. Being the butt of unending racist jokes was her daily norm. The fact that she could outrun every other lacrosse player, out-kick every other soccer player, and out-skate every other hockey player only made the epithets worse. After she finally put her weekly Tae Kwon Do lessons to good use and kicked the shit out of her main tormenter, Tommy Spatz, Deputy Spaz's younger brother, everybody just left her alone. She figured the three-day suspension from school was well worth it.

And when her dad, well out of earshot of her Mom, smiled and said, "It's about damn time you stood up for yourself," her vindication was complete.

The rest of her high school days she mostly spent alone, even though her gangly tomboyishness gave way to a mature beauty well beyond her years. A few boys sniffed around, so she always had a date for the school dances, but she never offered more than a goodnight peck to her suitors. In truth, she couldn't wait to get out of the confines of small-town Dundee.

It was a surprise to everyone, most of all herself, when she moved back there after college and the police academy, having applied for and gotten a job as a Wayne County Sheriff's Deputy. Ten years later, she was still alone, still bored, and still getting crap—now about being a gay, Indian-American, female cop—from the same assholes she knew in high school. At least she had learned to give as well as she got.

Why did you react so strongly to talk about Dan's departure?

That one made her think.

It's not about Dan leaving. It's about people accusing Sandy, she decided.

They had become fast friends soon after Sandy and Dan bought the Mackey House. And their friendship had grown into something more since Dan left.

That's what set me off—people with nothing better to do, making up lies about other folks' troubles.

She knew that was part of life in a small town.

And I chose to live here.

She looked around the kitchen, its decor frozen at a point in time before Kathy was born, probably before her parents were born. Cracked linoleum floor, painted pine cabinets, a big, white farm sink, and a round-top refrigerator that rattled away in the corner.

Staring at the yellow and blue tile of the 1950s kitchen counter, she took a long pull of her beer.

If Dan would just turn up and make contact, all the rumors would stop. Those rumors, at least.

She raised the beer bottle to take another swig, but froze halfway there.

Or, if I found out where he went, then he wouldn't have to come back here or even contact Sandy. I don't think she could handle another rejection. She smiled. *Plus, finding him might convince the Sheriff to make me a detective and get me off patrol.*

Nodding, Kathy finished lifting the bottle and downed the rest of her beer in one long swallow.

16

Jan sat in an overstuffed club chair in the Mackey House parlor. It was too late in the season to use the fireplace, but he could imagine the room, dimly lit by a roaring fire in the hearth and the two Tiffany-style lamps on small side tables. He remembered many such scenes over the years. The dark craftsman style wood paneling, wrought iron light fixtures, and intricate moldings seemed to him the perfect setting for a cozy mystery, or maybe a ghost story.

He snapped out of his reverie when Sandy walked into the room and perched herself on the arm of his chair.

"Any plans for dinner?" she asked.

"I was going to get something at the Tavern, but … that didn't work out."

She didn't seem to notice his hesitation. "I'm throwing a burger on the grill. I can make two just as easily. And I bet it will be a lot more satisfying than one of Tony's." She grinned down at him.

She's not coming on to me, is she? His thoughts swirled for a moment. *No way. I'm old enough to be her father. Just wishful thinking.*

"The company will be more satisfying, that's for sure." Realizing his fleeting thoughts had escaped his mouth, he gulped. "Ah, the burger that is … more satisfying."

Unoffended, Sandy giggled and stood up. Reaching back for his hand, she said, "Come on, you can set the table while I make dinner."

***

"That's the best burger I ever had. And the grilled veggies and corn. Oh, my God." Jan sat back in his chair.

Sandy leaned her chin on her fist and looked at him across the table. "Satisfied now?"

Her raised eyebrow and the huskiness in her voice made him draw breath.

Holy crap! What is happening here?

"Culinarily," he said without thinking.

Sandy burst out laughing. "Is that even a word?"

Jan smiled and shrugged. "It is now. That's the only superpower a writer has—making up new words." He raised his wineglass to cover his embarrassment.

"Oh, I bet you have other powers." Sandy sipped her own wine.

I need to change the subject, Jan thought.

"Any new reservations coming in?" His question had the desired effect. Sandy sat back in her chair and a decided chill fell over the table.

"No. Whenever somebody Googles us, the first several pages are all posts about the murders and stupid posts about the damned ghost."

Ghost? Maybe I can learn something more about this supposed ghost.

"Excuse me. Ghost?" He feigned surprise. "What ghost?"

Sandy looked at him with a mixture of surprise and exasperation.

"God, you really are disconnected, aren't you? The ghost is the spirit of that girl who died in the fire, Flora James."

"Oh, she haunts this place?"

Jan's voice reflected his amusement at this revelation as he looked up at the ceiling. His reaction drew a shrug from Sandy.

"Well, that's what people say, though I've never seen her," she said with a defensive edge to her voice.

"People who've stayed here have seen her? I've never seen her."

Sandy gulped her wine, spilling a bit on her blouse. "Last September, right after the—thing—Dan said he saw something at the top of the stairs. A kind of silhouette, but not quite. Something like a shadow, but there was nothing to cast the shadow. That was the first time. He said he saw her more and more after that, always at night.

"Then, a couple weeks later, we had our first guests after—you know. They were staying in the Raven's Nest— your suite. Everything was fine the first night they were here, but on the second, I was cleaning up in the kitchen before going to bed. Dan was already asleep when we heard screaming. Such horrible screaming coming from upstairs. I thought we had another murder, so I was afraid to go up, but Dan woke up and ran upstairs straight away, and I followed him.

"The two of them were huddled in the corner of the room, butt naked. The man, John I think his name was, lay there staring at the window, and the woman just screamed and screamed and wouldn't shut up."

Sandy paused long enough to finish her glass of wine and refill it from the bottle on the table.

"We finally got them covered and calmed down enough to tell us what happened."

Sandy's eyes took on a faraway look, and Jan had to prompt her to go on.

"So, what happened?"

She refocused on Jan, sipped her wine again, then continued. "Apparently, they were, you know, 'doin' the do' as they say around here."

She paused to make sure Jan understood.

"They were fucking."

Sandy's eyes blazed at Jan's crudeness. Her eyes met his.

"Yeah, they were fucking."

Where Jan's word had been casually tossed out, Sandy said it deliberately, with a guttural undertone.

That's the sexiest thing I've ever heard her say, he thought.

"Anyway," Sandy lowered her gaze, but Jan noticed a flush to her cheeks, which made his own burn. "While they were—fucking, the woman saw a jet black something hovering over her husband while he was—you know." Jan nodded his understanding. "This shadow thing reached around them like it was giving them a hug. They both felt a heat, like being scalded, they said. When she started screaming, the shadow darted through the window, probably back to her namesake."

Jan sat mesmerized. He reached out to take Sandy's trembling hand, and she gave it a welcoming squeeze.

"The couple packed up and left that night. The next day, posts started appearing on our website, our social media pages, everywhere. Apparently, they're some kind of social media 'influencers.' TravelTubers who posted scathing videos on YouTube about the Hotel. The cancellations started rolling in the next day."

"That's a shame. Couldn't you get somebody to take their posts down, or turn off their access?"

Sandy gave him another what-planet-are-you-from look.

"Once it's on the Internet, it never goes away. Plus, it's great click-bait for their channel."

She reached her other hand across the table, offering it to Jan, who took it anxiously.

He thought for a moment, then asked, "You said the ghost was probably headed 'toward her namesake.' What did you mean by that?"

"The statue out on the front lawn. You must have noticed it."

"Of course. It intrigued me the first time I came here."

"Well, that is Flora, the Roman goddess of flowering plants. Ephraim Mackey placed it there after he built the house to honor the human Flora who died in the fire. The hotel was much bigger than the house and extended another twenty or thirty feet out towards the road.

Supposedly, the statue sits right above the spot where Flora died."

They chatted a bit more, but every time Jan tried to steer the conversation toward the ghost, Sandy changed the subject. He had more luck getting her to talk about Dan, though.

"You've managed to keep the business going for nine months with no revenue coming in. I guess Dan was wrong, huh?"

Sandy looked confused. "Wrong about what?"

"Didn't Dan leave because he thought you would have to sell the place?" She still looked confused. "But you wanted to stay, so he … left."

The scenario had sounded feasible, even reasonable, when Kathy spun it in the bar. But when Jan repeated it, the logic didn't make sense. Sandy's reaction also told him he and Kathy were way off base.

Shaking her head, Sandy said, "That's just the story I told the Sheriff's deputy."

Jan sounded incredulous. "You lied to the cops?"

Sandy crossed her arms and sat back in her chair. "I couldn't hardly tell them the real reason."

Jan's heart quickened.

Are Barb and Jim right? Is she going to confess to me?

His expectant look asked the obvious question, and her response was harsh.

"Dan left because he was scared. Plain and simple. He said he was afraid of Flora and terrified … of *me*."

The last word came out in the harshest tone Jan had ever heard her use. Her hands balled into fists and she gave him a steely eyed stare.

"I won't—" she paused to steady her voice, which trembled with rage. "I won't be driven out of my home. Dan didn't understand that, I guess. He showed his true colors, his cowardice … when I needed him most."

Her voice broke on the last word and she dropped her chin to her chest. Jan sat in silence. He found this side of Sandy, her fierceness and determination, incredibly attractive and, he had to admit it, damned sexy.

I'm almost old enough to be her father. Get a grip.

He wanted so badly to kiss her, but the conflicting paternalistic and animalistic needs gave him pause, and while he hesitated, Sandy lifted her head and met his eyes.

"Thank you," she whispered. "Thank you for letting me be weak by being strong for me. I've had to be so strong on my own for so long. It feels good to be able to relax and let things out."

"You're anything but weak," he said, pouring all of his admiration for her into his words.

She drew back, breaking the spell of their momentary intimacy. Jan took his cue and stood, but when Sandy took his hand again, instead of returning to his seat, he pulled one of the other chairs next to hers and sat down.

"There's more to tell," she said.

"It's good to talk about things. Helps clear the cobwebs."

"Cobwebs?" She cocked her head to the side and studied him for a moment. "Funny you should mention cobwebs. The day after Flora scared the shit out of the

YouTubers, Dan spent the day puttering around in the basement. There are old storerooms down there just full of them—cobwebs, I mean. It's spooky. Anyway, his shop is down there, and I figured he was working on some project, but when he didn't come up for lunch, I went down to check on him."

She paused, looking a little embarrassed.

"One thing led to another, and we ended up …"

She nodded toward the bedroom in the owner's apartment.

"We started to, you know, make love when Dan got this terrified look on his face and started yelling, 'Get away, get away!' at something behind me. He threw me off and when I turned around, there was nothing there, but Dan was already scrambling out of the bed."

Jan felt a jolt of jealousy, but pushed it down. When he responded, his voice was hushed. "He saw Flora."

Sandy nodded. "That's what he said. Apparently, she was reaching out to me when he, ah, broke contact."

"He saved you from what happened to your last guests."

"He claimed he did. But that was the last kind act he would do for me. Our marriage effectively ended that moment."

Sandy hung her head, and she looked to be balanced between anger and sorrow, between curses and tears. But she gathered herself and looked him in the eye.

"He never touched me again. God, I can't believe I'm telling you this. No sex, no kissing, not even a hug. The more I asked—then begged—for anything like we had before, the angrier he got. Finally, we had a huge fight. I asked him why didn't he just leave, at which point he said, 'Thank you' and packed his bags and left."

"He said 'Thank you?'"

Sandy nodded, looking bewildered.

"I guess he had been thinking about leaving me and just needed permission. But I just said that in the heat of the moment."

Silent tears finally broke free from her eyes and made tracks down her cheeks.

"I told him I didn't mean it, but he didn't say anything else. He just packed and left."

"I'm so sorry, Sandy. That's just horrible."

She nodded with a resigned smile.

"The next few days are a blur. I don't really remember how I got through them. I tried calling him and texting him over and over, but I got no answer. I haven't heard from him since."

"So, you don't know where he went?" She shook her head. "Does he have family somewhere?"

She shook her head again. "Not that he knew of. Dan was an only child, and his parents died when he was a toddler. He thought they died in a car crash but was never sure. He grew up in one foster home after another until he turned eighteen. Luckily, he worked construction part time and during the summer, so he could get a job and move out on his own. Eventually, he started his own business and hired me to run the office."

"How did you end up here?"

Sandy took a deep breath. "That's a long story for another time."

She stood and looked at the dishes scattered across the table. Jan watched as her demeanor changed from that of a wounded little bird to Mistress of the House. "I've got to clean up."

Jan stood, as well.

"Here, let me help."

She scooped up plates and silverware.

"No, I'll take care of it," she gave him a friendly smile. "You go write. Or is my story too unbelievable?"

Without another word, she carried the dishes into the kitchen.

17

Kathy came in early for her midnight shift. The squad room contained a dozen or so low-walled cubicles with old computers and cheap, uncomfortable desk chairs. Most of the desks held family photos and a couple even had the occupants' favorite toys—Lego mini-figs or Hot Wheels cars. Two desks had pride-of-place in front of the only windows. They were the domain of the department's two detectives and were littered with file folders and surrounded by stacks of cardboard boxes with case numbers written on their sides.

Kathy sat at her bare desk. Firing up her ancient PC, she headed for the coffee machine. While her computer finished booting, she looked longingly at the detectives' desks.

Those two couldn't find their dicks with both hands.

The number of open cases represented by the ramparts of cardboard boxes making up their fortress proved her point.

Lardass Lewis is too lazy to get out there and do a proper investigation, and Old Man Stevens is 'retired in place.'

The network login prompt finally flashed on the screen and Kathy turned her attention to her task. A plan had formed in her mind that evening while she lay in bed trying to sleep. If she could track down Dan's whereabouts, she could accomplish two things. First, she would put to rest all rumors surrounding his disappearance, and second, she would show the Sheriff she was detective material.

Her fingers hovered above the keyboard.

This is it—the point of no return. If I do this, I'll either get promoted or fired.

They descended and typed Detective Stevens' username and password, which he conveniently taped to his computer monitor every three months when IT gave out new ones. She held her breath until the department's welcome screen popped onto the display.

Her own username and password didn't allow access to the websites and menus she would need to find Dan, hence her highly unethical and possibly illegal use of Stevens' credentials. Luckily, she had made a point over the years of clandestinely watching how the detectives navigated those sites.

Thank God the County's too cheap to upgrade the security around here. Facebook's got better security, for Christ's sake.

A couple of mouse clicks brought her to the cellular provider interface. A complete pull of Dan's cellphone records—calls, texts, and locations—would require a warrant. She guessed that filling in that field with garbage would satisfy the application, but that was illegal and would probably get the DA, another chauvinistic prick, involved. Instead, she just checked the box for location data, filled in the dates around Dan's departure, and hit the Submit button.

Apparently, where you take your cellphone when out in public is not private information, so the website didn't ask for a warrant. The busy wheel spun for a few seconds, then a PDF report appeared on the screen. With a quick look over each shoulder and with trembling hands, Kathy sent the report to the department printer and fidgeted in her chair, waiting for the printer to come to life.

It was still sitting idle when headlights streamed through the window as two cars pulled into the patrol car lot. The clock high on the wall read 11:40.

Of course. Those lazy-ass bastards never get midnight shifts like I always do, and they're still knocking off early.

She hurried to the still-quiet printer against the far wall of the squad room.

Where is my printout? Why is this damned printer just sitting there?

Then she saw the blinking "Paper Out" message on its display as the headlights blinked off and she heard car doors slam.

Shit, shit, shit. No time.

Running back to her workstation, she pulled up her weekly schedule and sent it to the printer as well. Taking a deep breath, she waited until she heard the outer door open, then walked back to the printer.

"Fuckin' thing's out of paper again! I bet their toilet paper roll is empty, too," she said to the empty room as the two deputies came through the squad room door.

"Hey, Spaz, do you smell curry?"

Standing with her back to them, Kathy bent at the waist to load paper into the printer.

"No, but I see a meal, and it ain't vegetarian."

Kathy straightened up, and the printer hummed to life. "Keep dreamin'," she said without turning. She knew her tight uniform would keep their barely adolescent minds occupied while the incriminating report printed.

Sure enough, when her schedule popped out of the printer on top of the two-page cellphone report, she plucked the papers from the bin and turned to the two deputies who still stood watching her.

She glanced at her watch.

"You two are knocking off early. You gonna put that down on your timesheet?"

The one called Spaz glared at her, while Gheringer walked over to the refrigerator next to the printer. Looking Kathy in the eyes, he pulled two cans of beer from inside while counting, "One. Two." She was coming on duty while they were finishing their shift, so she hadn't expected him to offer her one. Still, the message was obvious, and she agreed.

We'll never have a beer together, not that I'd want to.

After logging off her computer—she was still logged on as Stevens—she slung the backpack with the printouts nestled inside and headed for the door. As she passed Spaz and Gheringer, who lounged at their desks with their feet up and beers in their hands, she dropped her right hand to belt-level behind her back and extended her middle finger. The appreciative snicker and snort told her exactly what they were looking at as she walked away.

Spaz's mumbled, "Yeah, you wish," confirmed it.

18

Sunday, Late Spring

Kathy was dragging. Another overnight shift after a day with only a few hours' sleep added to her growing exhaustion.

You should stand up for yourself, she thought as she pulled a beer from her fridge. But the voice in her head wasn't her own. *Tell them you need a break, Silly Girl.*

"Yes, *Maan.* You know, we talk more now than we ever did when you were alive."

And whose fault was that? You were either working or asleep.

Kathy nodded. The memory voice of her mother was right on both counts. She pulled the folded cell phone report from her pocket.

"And now I've committed a felony. If I'm caught, I'll have plenty of time to relax."

Silly Girl, you will talk your way out of it like you always have.

"I'm not so sure."

She carried her beer to the living room and stared for a moment at the miniature shrine on the top of the bookshelves. An incense burner flanked the framed picture of her *maan* and a small carved sandalwood idol. The four-armed figure with its grinning elephant head returned her stare.

After lighting an incense stick, she picked up the wooden Ganesha figure. The details of the familiar carving still stood out in sharp relief after all these years. Her *maan* gave her the idol after a particularly difficult episode at school. Raising it to her nose, she inhaled the clean sandalwood scent.

"Ah, Ganesha, Remover of Obstacles, help me out here."

You do not need the resurrected son of Shiva and Parvati to fix your problems. You, Kaveetha, have the power in yourself.

Kathy tenderly reached out to touch her mother's picture. Her lessons in the Hindu religion came rushing back. She felt, as she always did when touching her mother's *murti*, a closeness to her spirit that she never did when her *Maan* lived. It was that feeling, rather than the hours silently studying the many gods, demigods, spirits and demons of Hinduism, which convinced Kathy that she touched the spirit of her *maan* through her image.

"Thanks for the pep talk."

The memory voice in her head fell silent, but Kathy felt the calming warmth of its presence.

At least I've answered some of the questions around Dan's disappearance, she thought. Maybe not all of them, like where he ended up, but I've cleared Sandy, thank God—or Ganesha.

Kathy spread the cell phone location report on her kitchen table and grabbed a notebook and pen.

8:00 PM Jan. 21: Dan leaves house

8:45 PM Jan. 21: Stops in Stroudsburg

10:00 AM—3:32 PM Jan. 22: Drives around
Stroudsburg

1:32 AM Jan. 23: Leaves Stroudsburg

4:14 AM Jan. 23: Arrives close to JFK
airport in NYC

10:32 AM Jan. 23: Heads for the airport

11:24 AM Jan. 23: Plane takes off

1:02 PM Jan. 23: Phone turns off

Writing it down wasn't nearly as satisfying as she expected it to be. Her subconscious nagging continued.

19

When Jan came down for breakfast, he found a buffet laid out on the sideboard in the dining room. He felt guilty but relieved that he might avoid any awkwardness this morning. He really didn't know how to feel about the personal confidences Sandy shared the previous evening. Her attentions inflated his masculine ego, but his more rational mind kept returning to the fact that he was old enough to be her father.

Still, the protectiveness that filled his heart while she cried had felt so good. It had awakened in him feelings that had long been dormant, feelings of intimacy, of shared emotions and shared pain. When those romantic emotions mixed with his physical reaction to her touch, they created a strange brew of desire. She was so obviously vulnerable, but also strong and determined. It was because of his appreciation for that combination, fueled by his own feelings of inadequacy, that he resolved to be there for her when she needed him, but otherwise to keep his distance.

The emasculation he had suffered at the hands of his ex-wife, followed by the monkish life he had lived for the past two years left him bereft of confidence in his own virility. Fear of failure leads to real failure in sexual situations, and Jan's mind overflowed with those fears, born out by the events of his failed marriage. Best to be the father figure Sandy seemed to need, rather than the lover he so desperately wished he was.

The hot eggs and bacon on the sideboard, along with the pot of steaming coffee waiting on the table, were a pretty clear sign that Sandy needed her space, too.

Jan ate heartily but quickly and slunk out of the house. Not sure where to go, he tossed his ever-present laptop satchel onto the passenger seat and climbed into his SUV. His problematic next novel forgotten, he thought about the list of questions he had written out the night before:

1) Why did Dan leave?
2) Where did Dan go?
3) Who and where are the last guests?
4) ~~Is there really a ghost?~~

He had scratched out the last one, thinking it unanswerable and silly. Surely these sightings were nothing more than people's imaginations running wild. To him, the idea of an actual ghost was preposterous. But he did find the notion of a vindictive spirit, bent on extracting retribution for a horrible death, to be a great premise for a story. Add in the genuine mystery of Dan's disappearance, and he had the makings of a real pot-boiler, one that was much more interesting than the fluff he had planned to write.

Where to start?

Many more questions danced in his mind on the short drive into Dundee. The coffee at breakfast was good, but he hadn't stuck around to have his usual three cups.

Crossing Main Street, he swung into a parking space in front of the Fae Feine, a cute little coffee shop in an old storefront. Busy spots weren't his normal hangout. He preferred the quiet of a library over the hustle and background noise of a coffee shop. But the Fae Feine had the bad luck of serving excellent, finely roasted, and expensive coffee three doors down from the Sheetz Mini Mart with its cheap thirty-second coffee machines. To Jan, the struggling little shop was the perfect combination of caffeine and quiet.

Sitting in the back corner with a steaming extra-large double-hulled cup, Jan connected his phone to his laptop and uploaded the photos he had taken at the Historical Society. Over three dozen separate documents transferred to his hard drive. One by one, he stuck them in folders for a more-detailed examination.

He was so focused on trying to read the slightly out-of-focus pictures that his coffee had gone cold, and he never heard the bell above the door jingle or the barista say, "Morning, Deputy. The usual?"

It was the voice that trickled into his consciousness. "… thanks, Jimmie. How's your Mom?"

"Hangin' in there, I guess."

"Tell her I said hello," Kathy said as she walked to Jan's table.

She set a fresh Costa Rica blend in front of him. He looked up and smiled as she sat down and tossed a handful of creamers and sweeteners onto the table.

"I didn't know how you take it, so…"

He pointedly lifted the cup of unadorned black coffee, sipped it, and leaned back, grateful for the chance to stretch his back.

"Thank you, Deputy Jensen. How are you this morning?"

"Just fine. Doing some writing? Or is it research?"

Jan put on his best blank look. "What would I be researching?"

Kathy frowned. "Don't be coy, Jan. Barb told me last night that you took 'tons' of pictures of their documents. She said Jim was positively in heaven. You spent more time listening to them tell stories about this place than all of their other visitors this year combined."

They shared a chuckle. "So much for assurances," he muttered. Kathy raised a questioning eyebrow, but Jan waved it off. "So, you've been checking up on me?" He wasn't sure how he felt about that.

"No, don't get a big head. Barb and I are in a book club. We meet at the library one Saturday a month. You should come by sometime. You could even donate advanced copies of your next one to review," she teased.

"That would be … incredibly scary, I think."

"You don't think it would tweak your ego a bit?"

"First, my ego doesn't need any 'tweaking,' and second, I'm afraid it would get more pricked than tweaked."

"You won't get pricked by me." Kathy gave no sign she intended a double *entendre*, so Jan took it as a compliment.

"Why, thank you, Deputy—"

"Come on, call me Kathy. I thought our relationship had progressed beyond formalities."

Jan pretended surprise. "Frankly, I didn't know we had a 'relationship,' Kathy." He smiled.

She smiled back. "OK, Mr. Writer, how would you describe—" she wagged her extended thumb and forefinger back and forth between them, "—this."

"Hmm." He put on his best high-brow voice. "I would call it a 'bantering series of *tête-à-têtes* characterized by a grudging mutual respect and tinged with just the faintest hint of sexual tension.' How's that?" he said, grinning.

Kathy laughed so hard she had to wipe tears from her eyes.

"Oh, my God! What a load of crap, especially that 'hint of sexual tension' part. Besides, you never wrote a line like that in your life."

Jan chuckled. "You got that right." They both sipped their coffees. "It is good to see you again, though. Our last little get-together ended on a kind of sour note."

Kathy nodded, her smile gone. "Yeah, sorry about that. I guess I'm a little overprotective of Sandy. She's a good friend who's been through a lot."

"No worries. Sometimes my writer's brain forgets that, although conflict is crucial to a good story, it's best to avoid it in real life."

She thought for a moment. "I don't know. In this job, I see more conflict than most folks. Sometimes conflict is the crucible that melts down somebody's story so you can separate the truth from the lies."

Jan sat back, impressed. "Wow, that's quite the metaphor. You should be a writer."

"Maybe I am," she said with a twinkle in her eye. But, before Jan could pursue this revelation, she continued. "Anyway, our 'bantering *tête-à-tête*' aside, I thought about our last conversation and I can see how an outsider might be curious about Dan's sudden departure, so I, ah, talked to one of our detectives about how to find him. It turns out you don't need a warrant to track a cellphone's location. The detectives had already done it back in November when they opened a missing persons case."

Nothing in Kathy's demeanor belied her lie.

"Dan was reported missing? By whom?"

"I, um, haven't gotten a look at the whole file—I'm not a detective, so I'm not authorized to access it. But I assume it was Sandy. He left unexpectedly. Maybe she thought something had happened to him."

Jan frowned and shook his head but remained silent.

That doesn't fit with what she told me, he thought, but he kept that bit of information to himself.

He looked at Kathy expectantly. "So, what did they find out?"

She pulled a folded sheaf of papers from the thigh pocket where she kept her notepad. "This is the data they got from the cell provider." She unfolded the papers to reveal a map of the northeastern U.S. The map had a thick line running along highways from Dundee to New York City, then from there on an arc to Illinois, where it stopped.

"Where is this?" He pointed to the end of the arc.

"Doesn't matter." He was a bit annoyed but waited for her to continue. "Look at the shape of the first part of the path versus the last part."

It took him a few seconds, but then he looked up at her with admiration.

"He was on a plane."

"Exactly. The wiggly part of the path ends at JFK airport. And the smooth part is a great circle route to LA.

We figure he either turned off his phone somewhere over Illinois, or the battery died."

"And he bought a new phone in LA." They both nodded. "So, he doesn't want to be found."

"Exactly. Case closed."

That answers a couple questions, he thought, *but there are still more.*

Before he could ask any of them, Kathy stood up with her coffee in hand.

"I'm tired—had a lot of paperwork to do after my shift. Sorry if I ruined your story," she said with a smile.

Then she turned and headed for the door, leaving Jan with the distinct impression that he had just been warned off.

That might answer the 'where', but not the 'why.'

20

Jan sat back and admired his work. He had organized the photos and articles into a virtual timeline. The text was all scanned, indexed, and stored in a database that let him choose a topic and get summaries of all references to that topic. Or he could generate a table of how often every keyword was mentioned. Despite the many analyses available to him, something nagged at him.

This is great, but what do I do with it? What questions can it answer for me? What am I missing?

Not sure what his subconscious was chewing on, he stood and stretched. His back was sore from sitting on the small wooden chair for—he checked his watch—six hours!

Jimmie, the barista, looked over and laughed. "I was going to offer you a cot to sleep here."

Jan picked up the four large coffee cups that littered the table and dropped them in the trash bin on the way to the men's room. Timelines. His stretched from the first newspaper advertisement that appeared in the *New York Guardian* and the *Philadelphia Record* in 1896 up through the truncated arc tracking Dan's phone across the country at forty-thousand feet. One hundred fifty years. How do you make sense of a century and a half of ephemera?

The same way I approached a tough programming assignment—divide and conquer—break it down into pieces.

His list of questions had grown, but at least he could check off the ones about Dan.

Let me write up the answers and put that to bed, he thought.

***

When he arrived back at Mackey House, he saw a pale green Prius parked in the driveway.

Annoyed but hopeful, he thought, *I guess I'll be confined to my room if Sandy has other guests.*

Given the emptiness of the place, he had come to think of the whole House as his own.

Climbing the sidewalk, he saw the statue, Flora, casting a long shadow across the front lawn. His pulse pounded in his ears as irrational anxiety drove up his heart rate. The enigmatic figure of Flora, with her arched back and upturned face, drew him near. He had initially interpreted her pose as joy or even sensual ecstasy, but in a certain light, it seemed much more sinister, her body contorted in tortured agony.

Today, though, the setting sun was behind Flora, hiding her upturned face in shadow, but illuminating the garland of granite flowers she wore across her shoulders. Blood-red light bathed the intricate folds of her gown and the stone roses that trailed behind her neck and down her arms. The contrast between her beatific back and unsettling front was markedly apparent and deeply unsettling.

When he passed through her shadow, a flush of heat ran through him and, despite the descending chill in the late spring air, he felt his face burning. He consciously dismissed the feeling, though the long-buried seeds of apprehension in his mind stirred as he climbed the steps and crossed the wide porch. The heavy oak front door was unlocked, and he pushed it open, intending to slink through and up the stairs to his right. When he peaked through the parlor into the dining room, though, he stopped short. Two figures were relaxing at the table, glasses of wine in front of them.

"'Bout time you got here, Jan," Sandy said with the faintest slur.

Kathy chuckled. "Yeah, where've you been? We thought we'd have to drink all this wine ourselves," which sent both women into a round of giggles.

Seeing the two of them together for the first time, it struck Jan how much alike, yet how different, they looked. They each had their hair—Sandy's blonde and Kathy's jet black—pulled back into ponytails, which accentuated their matching features. The curve of Kathy's cheekbones and jawline were more severe than Sandy's, thanks to Kathy's *maan*, but their nose and chin were a close match. Most of all, though, it was their eyes. That piercing blue that had somehow bred true down through the James line.

Jan's caffeine-fueled senses took in these similarities and differences in the blink of an eye. The flash of insight they provided let him see the underlying familial connection between them. He perceived Kathy, not as Sandy's sister, but more like her distant cousin.

Setting his satchel on the floor in the parlor while trying to keep from staring at the two women, each beautiful in their own way, Jan stepped into the dining room.

"This looks like fun. May I join you, or is this a ladies-only party?"

A knowing smile passed between the two women, which elicited another round of giggles. Still smiling, Sandy, who sat at the foot of the table, slid back the chair on her left and across the table from Kathy.

"Be my guest. Oh, wait, you already are." When Jan sat down, Sandy continued, "Jan Sorrensen, this is Sheriff's deputy Kathy Jensen." Neither offered to shake hands. They just smiled and nodded to each other.

"Do you want to tell her, or should I?" Kathy asked.

Jan pointed at his chest with his thumb and smiled.

"Deputy Jensen here has been following me all over Dundee."

"That's not true. There just aren't too many places to be in Dundee."

Jan chuckled. "Maybe that should be the town motto."

Sandy held up her hand. "So, you two have already met, obviously." They both nodded. Sandy smiled a half-smile. "Well, I'm glad to know my two best friends are also friends."

"Friends?" Kathy and Jan said together and laughed. Jan found it odd that Sandy considered him one of her best friends, but when he thought of the emptiness of his own existence, he reluctantly acknowledged the sad fact that she held the same role in his life.

Sandy picked up her phone from the table.

"Selfie time!" she said in a sing-song voice that was getting more slurred by the minute.

Kathy made a face, but Jan slid his chair to the right and Sandy waved Kathy to move her chair to Sandy's other side. Leaning her head on Jan's shoulder, she held the phone up in her right hand and slid her left hand across his thigh. He turned his head in surprise, making eye contact with Kathy, who was scowling at him just as Sandy snapped the photo.

"No, no. Look at the camera, you two."

Dutifully, they squeezed together into the frame and smiled. After the pseudo-click of the non-existent shutter, Kathy resumed her seat around the corner of the table, but not before throwing Jan a scolding look. Jan also started to move, but Sandy's grip on his thigh tightened, holding him in place.

As he had before, Jan felt torn between Sandy's ego-boosting attentions and his innate feeling of inadequacy, which was heightened by his lack of physical reaction to her warm hand in such an intimate place. He picked up her wine glass, took a sip, and set it down beyond her reach.

"Hey," she said, but didn't reach for the glass.

"My dad used to say that when you start speaking in *cursive*, it's time to quit drinkin'."

Kathy laughed and gave Jan an approving smile, then turned to Sandy.

"And you, my dear, are beyond cursive and into doctor scrawl territory." Sandy looked up at Kathy and swayed. Kathy shook her head. "Come on, kid. It's time for bed."

Kathy and Jan stood and helped Sandy to her feet. As the two women shuffled through the kitchen into the apartment beyond, Jan called, "Good night, ladies."

He only heard one reply, Sandy's "G'nigh'," as he crossed the parlor and climbed the front stairs to his suite.

***

Ten minutes later, after he had brushed his teeth and undressed, he heard a cop's knock on his door. Pulling on a pair of running shorts, he opened the door for Kathy, who stood in the hallway with a stern look on her face. Expecting the worst, he stepped back and waved her into the suite's sitting room.

"Look, Jan," she started, but he held up his hands, palms out.

"Kathy, believe me. I have no intentions toward Sandy. She's almost young enough to be my daughter, for God's sake."

Kathy considered this for a few seconds, searching his face as only a seasoned cop could. Finally, she nodded.

"I believe you. But I promise you that if you break her heart or take advantage of her fragile state, I will make your life hell."

"I have no doubt. And it would be well-deserved." They looked at each other for a moment, then he continued, "Are we good?" He held out his fist.

Kathy smirked and fist-bumped his. "Yeah, we're good."

"Good," Jan said as he turned to the mini-fridge. "You want a drink?"

"What've you got?"

He pulled out a round bottle half-full of brown liquor and held it up so she could see the horse and jockey perched on top of the cork. "Only the best bourbon ever made."

"Ah, Blanton's," she said in an appreciative tone. "I should have guessed."

Once the drinks were poured and Jan had donned a bathrobe and slippers, they sat out on the second-floor porch. The full moon and blustery breeze cast shadows that danced across the lawn like pagan revelers.

"All we need is a bonfire," Kathy whispered.

Jan turned his head. "A bonfire?"

She nodded slowly. Her voice was wistful when she spoke.

"When we were kids, teenagers, I guess, we'd build a bonfire in the woods and drink beer … and smoke a bit, too."

Something about the way she said "we" triggered a thought in Jan's alcohol-slowed brain.

"You know, you and Sandy look enough alike to be, not sisters, but cousins at least."

Kathy kept her gaze on the lake but gave him a wry smile. "I'm seven years older than she is."

"Oh. I never would have guessed that. Still, the resemblance is remarkable."

She finally turned to him, chuckling. "Genetics will do that." Jan's face went blank while he processed that bit of information, so Kathy continued, "We're cousins, well, first-cousins once removed, actually. Sandy's mother was my cousin."

"So, she grew up around here?"

He had the feeling that she was enjoying stringing him along.

"Sure. Right over there, in fact." She pointed to an empty lot across the road.

Jan looked in the direction she was pointing, but then shook his head. Scudding clouds shrouded the moon, sending the scene into deepest shadow. But Jan had stood on this porch and stared at that plot of ground so many times that the landscape was fresh in his memory.

"There's nothing there, now."

Kathy's voice lost all its teasing tone. "The house burned down when Sandy was twelve. Her mother," she cleared her throat, "Her mother died in the fire searching the house for Sandy, but she was already outside." Kathy's voice trailed off to a whisper.

Jan put a comforting hand on her arm and Kathy covered it with her own, their fingers interlocking. The warmth of her hand felt good, but Jan felt nothing like the spark that seemed to leap from Sandy's touch. He remained silent, letting Kathy gather herself.

"That's when Sandy … went away."

"To live with relatives?"

She shook her head. "No, to a—a hospital."

"Oh, I see. A trauma like that would make any kid need help."

Kathy gave him a penetrating look and an almost imperceptible shake of her head. "Yeah, she needed help."

Jan got the impression she was holding back. She took a breath and turned back to the lake. "I was at college in Wilkes-Barre at the time."

Jan caught another undertone in her voice. "You shouldn't feel guilty about not being here for her."

Kathy hung her head and whispered. "She's a good kid. A little too gullible, maybe, but basically a good kid."

"Gullible?"

She took a deep breath and raised her head.

"She was always fascinated, almost obsessed, with this place. Not the house so much, but the hotel that was here before, and its history. The story of how it burned down. And the legend of Flora."

She nodded toward the statue, barely visible in the moonlight.

"She was always talking about the fire."

Her voice trailed off, and she looked lost in her memories. Then, in a moment, she was back. She squeezed his hand, disengaged, and stood up.

"Remember what I said about how fragile she is." Jan nodded. "And what I told you I would do if you screw with her."

This time, he was sure she meant the double *entendre*.

21

Jan sat lost in thought after Kathy left. Wide awake despite the whiskey, he stood at the porch railing and looked out over the front lawn with its enigmatic statue. Somewhere in the night to his left, two foxes called out to each other. Their wailing cries, so much like a baby's screams, sent a shiver down his back. From his right came the squeal of a rabbit as it died in an owl's talons. A satisfied hoot followed, as the marauding mother returned to feed her fledglings.

As always, though, his attention returned to Flora's statue. A full moon shone down through wisps of clouds, zipping along on the high winds. The waxing and waning of the moonlight animated the shadow Flora cast across the lawn. Jan stood mesmerized by its seeming struggle to break free from its mistress until movement of the statue itself caught his eye. As he watched, Flora slowly lowered her head from her upward gaze and straightened her arched back. Then, with languorous slowness, she turned, the hint of a mysterious smile on her face, and met Jan's eye.

He stumbled backward as if pushed by an irresistible wind, hiding Flora from view below the railing. His rational mind floundered in the tempest of fear that commanded his muscles without conscious thought. He felt his heart thudding in his chest and heard every beat pulsing in his ears. But after a moment, logic and rationality reasserted itself.

A trick of the light. That's it. You saw how the shadows faded in and out. It must have been the moonlight.

With control of his muscles again, he crept back to the railing. Sure enough, the statue stood as it always had, frozen in a posture that appeared to be ecstasy one moment and tortuous torment the next.

What a story that chunk of granite represented. A story that deserved to be told. A story he knew in his bones he could tell.

First things first. Do your research, he thought as he hurried into his room to relieve his recently terrified bladder.

***

Back on the porch, Jan sat hunched over his laptop. The documents Jan photographed at the Historical Society included a full set of architectural plans for both the Mackey Hotel and current house. The House matched the old Hotel's width, but was not as deep. About twenty feet had been cut off at the front, which in the Hotel included an English basement, first-floor library and billiard room, guest rooms above that and guest servants' quarters in the attic. The basement was a warren of kitchens, storerooms, and live-in staff quarters. At the very front, beneath the grand portico, were five small rooms opening off a short hallway.

Using the Hotel's basement floorplan as a background, he overlaid the current building's first floor on top of it. With a few adjustments to the overlay's transparency and to get the scaling right, he could see how the architect had added a basement wall to the foundation, which cut the footprint by a third. He added an 'X' to the diagram where he estimated the statue to be. Sure enough, right underneath where Flora stood was a small, six-foot by eight-foot room labelled "Servant Guest Room."

So that part of the story is true, at least. I wonder what really happened down there on that night a century ago. He looked again at the now-immobile statue and thought, *I wish you really could come alive. I'd love to hear you tell your story.*

After confirming the placement of Flora's memorial, he added more questions to his list and checked off others. Something still nagged at his subconscious, but he knew not to force it. That part of his brain worked at its own pace and would notify his conscious mind when it had something to say. He had more holes to fill in on his timeline, so a visit to the library's archives of the local newspaper was in order.

22

Monday, Late Spring

Breakfast was late. Jan had worked late into the early morning processing his collected data, so before going to bed he left a message for Sandy, telling her he was sleeping in and she should do likewise. He figured she needed it after the previous evening.

He awoke in the late morning, around ten o'clock, to the smell of frying bacon. After a quick brush of his teeth and shower, he bounded down the front stairs, following the delicious mixture of breakfast smells and freshly brewed coffee. Sandy was just finishing laying out omelets, bacon, rye toast, and fresh blueberry muffins for two people.

"I hope you don't mind if I join you for breakfast," she said a little hesitantly.

"Of course not. I'd love the company." He gave her a knowing smile. "Rough morning?"

She nodded sheepishly. "Thanks for the text. My alarm went off at six, as usual, but I slept right through it. I woke up again at eight and was panicking when I saw my phone blinking. I thought you were asking what happened to breakfast." Jan shook his head. "But then I was so relieved when I read it."

"We both needed a sleep-in," he said as he poured them coffee.

They ate in silence for a minute, then Sandy said, "Kathy told me you've been looking into the history of this place."

Jan nodded. "I have been. I've never written a ghost story before. I think it'll be fun."

"A ghost story?" Sandy sounded nervous.

"This house, it's history, even the town is the perfect setting for something gothic." Then he saw the look of concern on Sandy's face. "Oh, don't worry, I'll change all the names so no one knows I'm writing about Dundee or your place."

She didn't look relieved. "The town will know." Her voice was flat.

"Probably true, but they know the history already, although even Barb and Jim seem reluctant to talk about it."

"Nobody wants their dirty laundry aired in public."

Her voice had gone cold, but Jan was so excited to talk about his new story idea that he didn't notice.

"A lot of places make up a ghost story to attract interest. People like to feel 'safe scared.' It's good for business."

Sandy was shaking her head and her voice dropped to a lower register.

"It might be good for business when it isn't true," she spread her arms indicating the empty chairs at the table, "but not so much when it's real."

Jan blinked in surprise. "You think the ghost of Flora is real?"

"I don't know what to think. All I know is strange things have been happening in this house lately." Her eyes pierced his. "I bet you've noticed them, too."

"Well," he took a deep breath, not yet ready to voice his suspicions. "Old houses have their own squeaks and—oddities."

Sandy nodded. "And this one has plenty of those. But do old houses also have fires and murders, and—" her voice cracked, "broken marriages?"

Jan waited for the tears to come, but Sandy lifted her head defiantly, so he said, "A lot of houses have broken marriages."

He tried to make a joke out of it, but the words even sounded bitter to his own ears.

It elicited a chuckle from Sandy, though. "Aren't we a pair?" she said, and they both fell silent while finishing their breakfast.

When Sandy stood to clear the dishes, Jan offered to help, but Sandy waved her hand dismissively.

"You go and do your research." The words came out harsh, but then her tone softened. "Where do you think you'll go?"

Jan stretched and said, "I think I'll head to the library and look up old newspaper articles about the hotel and the construction of the house. I'm curious why Ephraim Mackey built this house instead of rebuilding a hotel. He was too young to retire. Hell, he lived here for another sixty years, right?"

Sandy nodded, then shrugged. "Maybe he had made enough money to retire," she offered.

"But enough to live off of for the next sixty years? He must have had some other income. Anyway, that's my mission for today."

Before turning toward the kitchen with her armload of dishes, she looked at his stomach.

"You need to stop eating Tavern burgers. I'll make you a healthy dinner, say six o'clock?"

Without waiting for an answer, she turned and pushed open the kitchen door.

Well, alright then, he thought.

23

Kathy walked into the station at the end of her shift. She was dragging, having gotten only a couple hours' sleep over the last few days. Tired as she was, she still caught the strained look on Cindy's face when she signed in her keys.

"Hey, what's up."

Cindy frowned. "The Old Man wants to see you 'as soon as the little shit gets in.'" Her fingers made air quotes.

Fuck! If I get fired, how will I explain that to Dad?

Despite the foreboding sense of doom she felt and the shame at being caught, she gave Cindy a tight-lipped nod and headed for the Sheriff's office. Her mind raced through one implausible explanation after another as she walked down the hall to his closed door. Sheriff Eric Peterson was famous for his interrogation skills, having a near-perfect record of extracting confessions, whether for shoplifting or murder. Deciding that sticking to the truth was her only shot at keeping her job, she politely knocked on his door.

The response was immediate. "Get your ass in here, Jensen."

No 'Deputy.' I guess his mind is already made up.

Kathy stepped into the small office and stood in front of the desk. The two guest chairs had been moved to the sides of the room, leaving the area she stood in as empty as the tight confines of the room allowed.

Sheriff Peterson didn't offer her a seat. Instead, he stared hard at her for what felt like an eternity, making her feel like a steer being prepped for slaughter. Finally, with a shake of his head, he spoke.

"Well? What do you have to say for yourself?"

Kathy swallowed hard and felt a bead of sweat run down her back.

"About what, Chief?"

His face darkened, and she knew she had made a mistake.

"Don't play coy with me, Jensen." He held up a sheet of paper. "Since you asked, I'll tell you. Every day IT gives me a report of who logs into the system and when."

Kathy felt the blood drain from her face. The Sheriff continued, "Usually, I use it to make sure you sons-of-bitches are on time and do your paperwork. Imagine my surprise when I saw Stevens logging in at," he glanced at the paper, "11:36 Saturday night."

Kathy didn't move and managed to keep her face neutral, even though she could see her last ten years and any future she had in law enforcement going down the drain, along with her relationship with her father.

I'm going to have to move away. I won't be able to stand the judgmental, self-righteous looks I'll get. That is, if I don't end up in jail.

She knew what she had done was a federal offense and could label her a cybercriminal. Her legs felt like jelly and she almost glanced at one of the guest chairs.

Sheriff Peterson put down the sheet of paper he was holding and picked up another one.

"So, I checked out what *Stevens* was doing here so late."

Kathy felt a glimmer of hope that there was a way out of this mess, that the Sheriff might be playing along with her charade. She remained silent as he made a show of reading from the second paper.

"*He* seems to have run a report on Dan Adams' phone location from way back in January. Why do you suppose *he* did that?"

She saw three paths forward from this moment. Two of them led to dismissal and possible charges being filed. The third and slimmest possibility, which required her to go against her very nature and bite her tongue, just might save her job. So she just shrugged.

Peterson, who was well aware of her typical smart-ass attitude, just nodded ever so slightly. She had passed the first test. Here came the second.

"Maybe I should ask him?" he said.

Taking a deep breath, Kathy knew it was time to come clean, but she also saw that just maybe this was an opportunity she had been waiting for.

"There's no need to ask him, Chief. I hacked his account and ran the report myself."

Peterson looked surprised by her response. "Are you sure you want to tell me that?"

She realized her mistake.

He was going to sweep it under the rug! Why couldn't you keep your mouth shut! Shit, I'm in it now.

"Yeah, Chief, I'm sure. Dan's *departure* has bugged me since the day he disappeared. I thought," she hesitated a second before going all-in. "I thought if I could figure out where he went, or what happened to him, you might be inclined to recommend me for Detective."

Peterson sat stunned by this, but he quickly gathered himself and sat back in his desk chair. He folded his beefy arms across his broad chest.

"Why in God's name would I recommend you for Detective?"

"I've been on patrol for ten years, and unlike most of the other deputies, I still work full shifts and I still care about the work." Peterson raised an eyebrow. "I have a lot more to offer this county than patrolling its back roads late at night."

The Sheriff's face was unreadable. "I already have two detectives. I don't have budget for any others."

Kathy scoffed before catching herself. "Chief, Stevens will hit thirty years next fall. He's already retired-in-place."

Peterson's lip curled into a half-smile.

"And Lard—Detective Lewis won't pass his next physical."

That brought a rueful smile to the Chief's face.

"So, as I see it, you'll have at least one, and probably two, openings in the next few months. Time to start training their replacements."

She had kept her voice confident throughout this speech, even though her heart pounded in her chest.

Peterson nodded his agreement with her assessment of his detectives.

"I know I have personnel issues, but Spaz and Gheringer have seniority."

Kathy just raised her own eyebrow in response as if to say, "Really?" which got a chuckle from him. He stared at her long and hard for several seconds, then he nodded to one of the chairs against the wall. With a sigh of relief, she dragged it back to its normal position and plopped down as if her legs had given out.

"OK," he said when she sat. "Here's the deal. You have two weeks—you have at least that much vacation banked, right?" Kathy nodded. "Good. Use those two weeks of 'vacation' to try to find Adams. I'll tell IT to give you detective privileges so you don't have to steal Stevens's password anymore. If you can find him in two weeks, I'll sign a letter of recommendation to the Promotion Review Board. That'll get you on the list for the next test seating."

Kathy smiled and started to thank him, but he held up a hand to stop her.

"If you can't find him, you'll go to the bottom of my list." He tapped the side of his head. "And these two reports," he tapped them where they lay on his desk, "will go in your file. Whichever way this detective thing goes, they'll stay in your file for a year. If you keep your nose clean, I'll shred them a year from now. If not…" He spread his hands in a you're-screwed gesture. "Do we have a deal?"

Kathy could hardly believe she had danced through this minefield. Taking a deep breath, she nodded and said, "Deal."

Proving that word spreads quickly in a small town, the mistress of the Dundee Public Library, a typical Carnegie-built neoclassical building on Main Street, was expecting Jan and had been for two days.

"Jim and Barb down at the Hysterical Society filled me in on your research project," Miss Elizabeth Gheringer, Head Librarian, said after Jan introduced himself.

He smiled and asked, "Did you say, 'Hysterical Society'?"

Miss Gheringer smiled in return. She could have come straight from Central Casting, with her grey hair tied up in a bun and an actual pencil stuck into it like a Ticonderoga hair pin. Half-glasses, strung on a silver chain, perched on the end of her nose.

"Jim and Barb are nice people, but they tend to— exaggerate things a bit."

Her dry sarcasm drew a chuckle from Jan. "You mean like stories of the ghost of Flora James?"

"Florence James, yes. She was only called 'Flora' by her family and closest friends."

Jan was intrigued. "You seem to know a bit of the history yourself."

Elizabeth—known only as Elizabeth, not Liz, Betty, or Eliza, even to her close friends and family—sniffed. "Indeed, as well I should. Flora was my great-aunt."

"Really? You're from Philadelphia?"

She scoffed. "Of course not. I grew up three blocks that way." She jerked her thumb over her shoulder. "My great-grandparents had seven children, two sons and five daughters. Flora's mother, Stephanie, moved here with her other four daughters a few years after the fire, so many residents of Dundee and the surrounding area are related to the James family. All of Stephanie's children being daughters, the James name died out in these parts, but the family flourishes."

"Wow. I wonder why Barb and Jim didn't mention that."

"Well, they are my second cousins—each from different branches of the family, mind you, and folks around here like to keep their family foibles private."

She delivered the last statement with a hint of warning, which Jan was getting very used to.

"You're afraid I'll write some scandalous tell-all, aren't you? Don't worry, that's not my style. Like I told Sandy this morning, I write fiction, not history. The story of Flora—Florence—and the Mackey Hotel is just research."

The story brewing in the creative regions of Jan's brain was much closer to the truth than he let on.

This town and the people in it are way too interesting to leave in backstory.

Elizabeth's skepticism showed in her raised eyebrows. "But the folks of Dundee will know."

"That's exactly what Sandy said."

"As well she should, given that she is my niece."

Jan felt the warm air being sucked out of the room and replaced with a cold north wind. Speechless, and not wanting to let on that he hadn't known that bit of information, he just nodded and offered his best harmless smile.

Elizabeth looked at him over her reading glasses for a moment, then sniffed and said, "Anyway, I have retrieved boxes of microfilm and microfiche archives of the two newspapers which merged to form the *Dundee Gazette* in 1910, along with the *Gazette*'s issues up through 1926. They are all stacked in chronological order next to the machines in the basement, which you can access through *that* door."

She nodded to her left.

"Of course, they are."

He meant it as a compliment to her organizational skills, but his tone of voice was more sarcastic than he intended. With a withering look, she pointed to an old wooden door that stood open to the left of the circulation desk. A dim yellow light illuminated a set of narrow stairs. A rusted padlock hasp laid back against the doorframe.

"I assume you know how to work the machines." Jan nodded. "The library closes at five o'clock. I will lock the door at four fifty-five."

And I'll have to spend an uncomfortable night down there if I'm not out by then, he thought.

Without another word, he headed downstairs.

"You're welcome," he heard her mumble as he descended the creaking stairs.

By three-thirty, he had skimmed and photographed every article that mentioned Ephraim Mackey, the Mackey Hotel, and Mackey House. His back was stiff, and his head hurt from squinting at the blurry pictures of smudged newsprint captured on the tiny negative films. Sitting back in the old metal desk chair, Jan reviewed his notes.

There was a big surprise which he intended to investigate further. It was a few mentions of the "Mackey Hoard," which Jan at first attributed to the accumulated wealth from Ephraim's stock trading schemes, but the articles were dated between the fire and the building of the house.

They referred to lawsuits claiming that several wealthy guests had lost their families' treasures, gold and jewelry, in the fire. Responsibility for reimbursing those guests fell to the insurer of the property. Reports of Pinkerton agents combing through the burnt ruins of the hotel told of a few half-melted pieces which were recovered. The general belief, however, was that the vast majority of the guests' finery had melted in the intense heat.

Still, local legends grew up around this lost "Mackey Hoard" with some reporting to the press that they had seen Ephraim sifting through the rubble many times before the Pinkertons arrived. Jan decided to find out why Barb and Jim hadn't mentioned this Hoard during their chat two days ago.

The last piece of interesting news was a detailed account, documented in several articles, of how Ephraim Mackey had commissioned the sculpting of the statue of

Flora in the Mackey House front yard. He hired an Italian artist-in-residence who lived at the house for almost a year, making one version after another of the figure.

As was common practice, the preliminary sculptures were destroyed, but a clever reporter had gotten a look at the artist's sketchbook, probably through the Italian's affinity for the local moonshine. Several of the trial sketches were reproduced in the newspaper.

The sequence of drawings showed the subject figure evolving from a demure, almost adolescent girl to the nearly erotic final version.

When it was unveiled to the public in 1925, it was scandalous. The use of pagan imagery, especially the garland of flowers that flowed across her shoulders and down to the ground, seemed to be more disturbing to the locals than the obvious sexuality of the statue.

Amid the hubbub and scandal, Ephraim retired from his Telegraph Master position and cut the telegraph relay line between the train station and the house, symbolically cutting himself off from the world. He lived as a recluse for the next sixty-seven years, growing vegetables and raising chickens in his backyard.

The house was well-maintained throughout those years, and the garden surrounding Flora's statue was in constant bloom from the last frost in the Spring to the first one in the Fall. It was also noted that regardless of how much snow piled up during the winter, the statue remained clear even during the worst blizzards.

Having been invited to the unveiling of the memorial to her daughter, Stephanie James, by then a widow, was persuaded by Ephraim to stay on as his housekeeper and cook. Thus, was planted the root of the James family tree in Wayne County.

"Why didn't you tell me about the Mackey Hoard when I was here the other day?" Jan tried to keep his tone neutral, hoping to gauge Barb and Jim's reactions. He wasn't disappointed.

"Just local legend."

"Yes, utter nonsense."

Jan gave his best disbelieving expression, one eyebrow raised and a wry smile. Barb looked like a deer caught in the headlights while Jim slowly sank down into one of the mismatched chairs surrounding the long worktable in the Society's reading room.

"That's BS and you know it." His voice was firm but still light. He figured he'd keep his stern voice in reserve. "I've been to the library and searched through the Gazette's back issues." He paused. "But you probably know that already, given it took me all of *four minutes* to get from there to here. I bet 'Miss Grundy' over there was on the phone the second I left."

Hoping for an abashed admission, but Barb's chuckle and Jim's laugh surprised Jan.

"Actually, she called as soon as you went down to the basement," she said.

"You didn't expect her to keep news like that to herself, did you?" Jim finished.

Jan couldn't keep a straight face listening to Dundee's version of George and Gracie.

"I should've figured." Then he got serious. "Look, I'm not here to write an exposé of your ancestors' dirty laundry. I'm a novelist. Whatever you folks tell me about your history, gossip, or even rumors, is going to get filtered and twisted until it's unrecognizable."

"And exaggerated," Barb said. "Filtered, and twisted, and exaggerated."

"Ah, sure. I write fiction. I'll exaggerate the good stuff."

"Therein lies the problem," Jim fired back. "Once stories get exaggerated and expanded, they can't ever go back to being rumors and gossip."

Jan was starting to see their side of things.

"I told you that I'll change all the names, and I can even put the story in Maine if you want. Everybody expects weird stories to come out of Maine."

He smiled at his own joke, but neither Barb nor Jim seemed to get it.

"You might fool everybody outside of Wayne County," Barb answered. "But nobody *inside* the county will be fooled. And we live here."

Jan finally understood their reluctance to discuss local legends with him, despite their initial enthusiasm during their first meeting.

"And, from what I understand, you're all related to each other somehow." Jim shrugged and nodded. "So, you had a bout of 'buyer's remorse' over voicing your suspicions about Dan's disappearance, perhaps?"

This time Barb shrugged, so Jan looked at Jim, who again nodded.

"Well, let me lay those fears to rest. Dan headed to California."

Both of his listeners' mouths fell open. "What?"

"How do you know—"

"Where in California—"

Jan held up both hands, palms outward.

"Stop. Let me tell you what I know." He waited for quiet before continuing. "Cell phone records confirm that Dan drove to Stroudsburg, spent the night, then continued on to JFK airport, slept there, then got on a flight headed for Southern California the next day. After that I don't know where he went. His cell phone went dead over Illinois."

The three fell silent for a minute, then Jim asked, almost to himself, "Why would he spend the night in Stroudsburg? It's only another couple of hours to the city."

It was Jan's turn to shrug. He consciously wanted that part of his story to be resolved, but his subconscious, which had been nagging at him for days, wasn't ready to give it up.

"It was late, and he had just left his wife. I'm sure he was upset."

"Where in Stroudsburg did he stay?" Barb asked.

"I don't know …" This discussion was reopening a chapter that he thought had been closed, so he let Barb and Jim talk.

"If Dan was tired, he would have slept in his car along the Interstate."

"Yeah, he was too frugal to spring for a hotel."

"Did he sleep in the airport?"

"He never would have sprung for two hotel rooms just to get to JFK."

An idea bubbled up from Jan's subconscious. "Maybe he had a girlfriend in Stroudsburg—"

They both turned to him with anger burning in their eyes.

"No way! Dan was totally in love with Sandy."

"Yeah, he gave up a booming contracting business to move out here in the sticks for her."

"There's no way he would step out on her."

"He'd never leave Sandy for some floozy in *Stroudsburg*."

"Or take off for California, of all places."

Jim was shaking his head, and his voice became more and more vehement. "And he wouldn't just leave his truck at the airport."

"Abandon it, you mean."

Jan jumped in. "Maybe he sold it in New York. That could take a day. He might have made his plans on his way east and stopped in Stroudsburg to figure out how to sell his truck to somebody in New York."

Both Barb and Jim were shaking their heads before Jan even finished.

"No way."

"Uh-uh. He loved that truck."

"He called it 'Helen Wheels.' You know, like the Beatles song."

"It wasn't the Beatles, it was after Paul went solo."

"Whatever. The point is that he never would have sold that truck."

"In fact, if he was going to the West Coast, he would have driven there."

"That's right! He said he hated flying."

"Too cramped, with someone else in control."

They both stopped suddenly, and stared at Jan, who had sat down during their tag-team rant. He was speechless, astounded that in just a few seconds, they had blown Kathy's solution to Dan's disappearance out of the water. Finally, he found his voice.

"Then how do you explain the cell phone tracking data?"

They both shrugged, satisfied that they had, in their minds at least, vindicated their friend. Finally, Barb said, "Cell phones aren't the people who carry them."

26

Jan was lost in thought as he walked down the sidewalk to his car. Barb and Jim had finally come clean and told him all they knew about the Mackey Hoard. Unfortunately, they couldn't really add anything to what he had learned at the library, other than the rumor that Ephraim never hired a night watchman to guard the property after the fire, even though many thrill-seekers and thieves came snooping around. Many claimed they were attacked by a malevolent black shadow. That was how the legend of Flora's ghost standing guard over the Mackey Hoard was born.

They did relate, though, that after the fire that took her mom's life, Sandy became near catatonic and was sent to a state mental hospital. When she recovered enough, she was shuffled off to live with distant relatives in Philadelphia. But when Jan asked why none of her local relatives took her in, Barb and Jim clammed up.

Poor Sandy. Orphaned by the fire, they orphaned her again emotionally when none of her relatives would take her in. Maybe they blamed her for the fire? What a messed-up story of family secrets, land ownership, lost jewels and an angry ghost.

All this information was running through Jan's head as he walked along the street in the gathering dusk. He was so lost in thought that he didn't notice the Prius pull to the curb behind him, or Kathy step out of it.

"You're getting pretty predictable, Jan," she said as she strode toward him.

Startled, he turned to face the glowering woman. She was dressed in tight jeans, a light jacket over a button-down shirt, and her hair was pulled back into a high ponytail.

"Hey, what's up?" he said before the look on her face registered. "Ah, what's wrong?"

"Don't you have your damned phone on you?" she growled.

He patted his pants pocket. "Yeah …"

"Then why didn't you answer it?" Her tone was biting.

"I don't know. I was busy. Why?" He was truly bewildered, but his heartbeat ticked up a notch.

What happened?

"You were supposed to be at dinner half an hour ago. Sandy's worried and upset."

"Oh, shit. I completely forgot." He ran to his car, which was still parked in front of the library across the street. "Tell her I'm on my way," he called over his shoulder.

27

Sandy was sitting at the head of the dining room table, wineglass in hand, when he slunk into the room.

"I'm so sorry, Sandy. I was in the middle of doing some research and I didn't notice the time."

"Yeah, right."

Her tone was sarcastic, and Jan noticed the bottle of wine on the table was half-empty.

"'Research.' Is that what you call gossiping with those two tongue-waggers?"

Clearly, Kathy told Sandy where she had found me, he thought, which angered him for some reason.

"Yes, they were telling me all about your family and the terrible things you've had to live through." He saw her face soften a little. "It gave me a new appreciation for how strong your spirit is."

He pulled out a chair on her right and sat down.

"I'm truly sorry for what you've had to live through. It's almost Shakespearean."

He instantly regretted the last statement when he saw her face harden again.

"And great fodder for your story, eh?"

"That's not what I meant. I just mean that you, personally, have suffered a great deal, as has your family, going back for what, four generations?"

He studied her face, but saw no softening this time.

"If I had known the story of the Hotel—and this house—was your family's story, I guess I would've tread a lot more lightly."

Sandy's furrowed brow smoothed out, and she closed her eyes. Her fragility in that moment overwhelmed him with a feeling of masculine protectiveness. Without thinking, he stood behind her chair and placed both hands on her shoulders. Under his soft kneading, he felt the tension in her muscles relax, and she rested first one cheek, then the other on his hands.

When she opened her eyes, her penetrating stare bore into him and pierced the shield that had held back his desire. In an instant, she was out of her chair and into his arms as their lips met in a crushing kiss.

The instantaneous pleasure of her mouth on his, her tongue probing his own, gave way in a moment to an increasing mixture of pleasure and pain. He felt a burning heat that numbed his lips and scalded him where Sandy's tongue met his. Her hands went to the back of his head, pulling him deeper into the crucible of her kiss.

When the pain overtook the pleasure, he jumped back and thrust her away with both hands on her hips. For a second, her hands interlocked behind his head, held her mouth inches from his, and he felt the searing heat of her breath. Then he ducked his head and, with all his strength, threw her onto the floor. She drew herself up onto her haunches like a wild animal ready to pounce. Her dilated eyes were deep black with no white visible, and her mouth was drawn into a rictus smile of feral ferocity.

Frozen in horror, Jan could do nothing but raise his hands, hoping to fend off her attack. But then, her head snapped to the side and Jan, too, heard the front door opening. When he turned back, he glimpsed Sandy darting for the kitchen.

Unfrozen, he headed for the stairs, meeting Kathy in the parlor.

"Jeez, it's hot in here," she said, then stopped when she saw the look on his face. Jan could feel his lips swelling and blisters rising in his mouth, as if he had bitten into a too-hot slice of pizza. Kathy put a hand to his flushed face and her demeanor became threatening.

"Did I interrupt something?"

Jan pulled her hand away from his face and mumbled, "Yeah, but not what you think."

As he pushed past her, she said, "What the hell happened?"

"Ask *her*," he said, barely moving his sore lips and climbing the stairs.

28

Tuesday, Late Spring

Jan barely slept that night, having barricaded both the suite's hall door and the slider to the balcony. Every neuron in his hindbrain, the seat of the fight-or-flight response, screamed for him to pack his things and get the hell out of there. But his conscious mind tried to make rational sense of what had happened. He told himself that his sore lips weren't as swollen as he thought they had been, and they were simply sore because of the passion of their kiss. The blisters on his tongue faded quickly, leaving only a mildly pleasant warmth that, by the time he did finally fall asleep, had convinced him he had imagined the pain. How, his rational mind thought, could she have burned him with a simple kiss? His baser instincts agreed, and by the time he drifted off, he had convinced himself he owed Sandy an apology.

His fitful sleep was populated with dreams of a female figure shape-shifting between a completely opaque black shadow, a bashful-turned-feral Sandy, and the statue of Flora come to life. Their erotic attentions culminated in his first full erection in years, and his first wet dream since puberty.

Jan awoke late the next morning and, unsure of the reception he would receive, he showered quickly, dressed, and tried to creep down the front stairs. Even keeping to the sides of the stair treads, though, his footsteps nevertheless sent out loud creaks.

When he reached the bottom, he halted when Kathy's voice called out, "Yo! Get your butt in here."

Resigned to facing Kathy's wrath for what almost happened the evening before, Jan hesitantly crossed the parlor into the dining room.

Putting on a devil-may-care air, he said, "You're here awfully early."

She studied him for a moment. "Actually, I'm here awfully late. Sandy needed a shoulder, so I spent the night."

"Oh, I see."

He tried, unsuccessfully, to hide the smirk her comment implied. She either didn't notice his expression or ignored it.

"Anyway, I wanted to talk to you this morning."

That was the last thing he wanted, so he tried deflecting her.

"Don't you have to be at work?"

She gave him a withering look.

"It's Tuesday."

"There's no crime on Tuesday?"

"What are you, my boss? If you need to know, I'm on … vacation starting today. Not that that's any of your business."

Jan just shrugged.

"So, like I was trying to say," she glanced at the closed kitchen door, from behind which came the sound of Sandy faintly singing to a song on the radio. "Sandy told me what happened last night."

She took a deep breath and Jan prepared himself for the onslaught.

But it stunned him when she said, "I want to thank you for what you did, er, didn't do."

This statement was so unexpected, he just plopped down in a chair. In the silence that followed, he thought through possible responses, but every flippant or serious remark that came to mind seemed inappropriate, and he wasn't in the mood to be graciously demure, so he just stared.

Not getting a response, Kathy continued, "When she practically threw herself at you—"

Practically? he thought.

"—she said you were the perfect gentleman. She wanted me to apologize on her behalf since she's too embarrassed to tell you herself."

Jan regained his mental footing.

"I told you, she's young enough to be my daughter. She's very lonely. I get that, 'cause so am I. But, as I told you before, I will behave myself." He looked Kathy straight in the eye. "I promise."

That seemed to satisfy her, so she sat back and changed the subject.

"We need to chat about some things."

She checked her watch—9:30—then again looked furtively at the kitchen door.

"How about the coffee shop at eleven?"

Jan nodded, curious to hear what Kathy had to say, but when he was about to press her, Sandy backed through the kitchen door, arms laden with steaming plates.

They lingered over breakfast, all awkwardness over the previous night's events seemingly forgotten. Jan couldn't forget, though. Every bite of his French toast left a strange, not-completely unpleasant tingle on his tongue. Both Jan and Kathy offered to help with the dishes and cleanup when they finished, but Sandy would have none of it. She shook her head and told them in no uncertain terms to "get lost."

As they left the house together, Kathy turned to Jan.

"Feel like some coffee?"

Not really, he thought.

But he felt like he needed more information, so he nodded and climbed into his car. Turning right out of the driveway toward Dundee, he noticed Kathy turn left and head in the opposite direction. Wondering if he had misinterpreted her cryptic offer, he headed into town anyway and parked on Main Street.

29

He sat at his usual table in the back corner of the Fae Feine when Kathy came in carrying a laptop satchel.

After a bit of bantering with Jimmie the barista and acting surprised to see Jan again "so soon," she sat at his table and pulled out a laptop. It came awake immediately and Kathy turned it so Jan could see the screen. Displayed there, was the cell phone track she had shared with him before. This time, though, the red squiggly line was overlaid on top of a satellite view.

"I understand that Barb and Jim blew the idea that Dan flew to California right out of the water."

Is nothing secret in this town?

Jan said, "Well, they certainly knew him better than I did, and they wouldn't believe that he spent a night and a day in Stroudsburg before going to JFK, where he spent another night before taking a flight west. They claim he would have just driven to California or wherever he was headed."

Kathy nodded throughout Jan's explanation.

"I have to agree with them," she said. "This meandering path has been nagging at me."

"Me, too. Especially spending the day in Stroudsburg. What was he doing there?"

Kathy gave him a teasing smile. "I may have an answer to all of that."

She paused for effect until Jan finally twirled his hand, meaning "let's go."

Satisfied that she had built up enough anticipation, she zoomed in the image on the screen as she followed the cellphone track along Route 390 south into Stroudsburg. Zooming in more, the overlay that represented the triangulated cell phone position spread out into a wide area covering several blocks of downtown.

"Somewhere in here, the cell phone spent the first night."

Jan consulted his notes.

"From 8:45 on the evening of February twenty-first to 10:00 AM on the twenty-second."

Speaking those times out loud started to form connections from his subconscious to his conscious brain. He looked up from the display to Kathy.

"Have you ever known Dan to go to bed that early or sleep that late?"

She shook her head and pointed back at the screen.

"And where did he sleep?"

The laptop showed wide streets lined with buildings labelled with business names in the downtown district of Stroudsburg. Of all the names that tagged the buildings, none represented a hotel.

"Barb and Jim claimed he would have slept in his car," Jan offered, though he didn't believe that himself.

"If he was sleeping in his car in this part of town, he would have been rousted by Stroudsburg PD. I checked their logs and there is no mention of someone sleeping in their car."

She panned the display a bit, moving one of the street corners to the center of the screen.

"What do you see?"

All Jan saw was a normal intersection of two downtown streets. A few cars sat at the curb, and one or two that were frozen in the traffic lanes. While he watched, Kathy panned a little more and zoomed in to the maximum. In the center of the now fuzzy and pixilated image was one of the four corners of the intersection, its sidewalk curb cuts clearly visible, along with three blue…

"Mailboxes!"

A line of public mailboxes stood twenty feet from the intersection, the yellow paint on the curb in front of them clearly visible.

Kathy zoomed out until the tag "Stroudsburg Central Post Office" popped up on the building across the sidewalk.

"She mailed the phone." Jan whispered.

"Whoa! What do you mean 'she?' Don't jump to conclusions. Dan probably mailed it himself before taking off for who-knows-where."

Jan looked at Kathy incredulously.

"Are you serious? Why on Earth would he do that?"

"To throw off anyone looking for him." Kathy's voice trailed off.

"Wouldn't leaving it at home have made it a bit, I don't know, easier?"

He gestured to the papers and laptops strewn across the table.

"Besides, he was running away from the house—and Sandy, maybe—but not the police. Why not just turn it off and throw it away?"

When Kathy didn't answer, Jan continued. "Where does it go when it leaves the Post Office?"

Jan was pretty sure he knew the answer, and Kathy confirmed his suspicion when she zoomed out a bit and followed the phone's path to a massive building in Queens, New York labelled "USPS Distribution Center" sitting adjacent to JFK airport.

Kathy sat back in her chair with her left arm across her chest and her right hand covering her mouth. Her eyes flicked between Jan and the laptop as her expression grew more and more concerned.

Finally, she mumbled, "I need to have a conversation with my cousin."

But Jan shook his head. "No. I wouldn't just yet. As illogical as your explanation may be, there are a lot of other possibilities. And if Sandy did mail his phone, the implications of why she felt the need to leave cellular breadcrumbs for someone to follow is … significant."

Kathy snorted at his choice of words. "The word you're looking for is 'suspicious,' damned suspicious."

"And damned dangerous. If she did what we're both thinking and she thinks we're on to her, that's dangerous for both of us."

"Especially for you," Kathy responded, and Jan nodded. "And if she didn't do what we're both thinking, any accusation will stick to her like a scarlet letter around here."

"Maybe you should talk to the detectives in your department."

Kathy snorted. "Are you kidding? They think I'm a hayseed cop who just hands out traffic tickets to tourists and rousts drunken kids on Saturday nights."

They sat in silence for nearly a full minute while
Kathy's face hardened.

Finally, she said, "I've got to find his truck."

30

After Kathy went off to continue her under-the-radar detective work, Jan ordered another coffee to replace the one that had gone cold and set to work outlining his novel. The writer's block that plagued him when he'd arrived just a few days before was forgotten, along with the story he had planned to write. In its place was the beginning of a very different one. It was a story that paralleled what he had learned about the real Mackey Hotel and House. He could spin the history into a wild tale of tragedy, madness, and murder. He would let his agent worry about the legal ramifications of portraying characters and events that skirted reality. For now, simply capturing these strange experiences into a first draft was exhilarating.

Several hours later, with eyes burning and back aching, he finally paid Jimmie and headed for the House. The afternoon had turned blustery and giant cumulous clouds climbed high above the western horizon. Though they blocked the setting sun, it backlit them with a fiery glow that faded from deep red at the horizon to a pale pink almost at the zenith. Their relentless approach felt like the gods were drawing closed a curtain over the world.

As always, when he parked his car at the foot of the Mackey House lawn, his eyes found Flora, frozen in a pose of ecstatic torment. As he closed the car door, the clouds parted just a crack and bathed her in a beam of crimson fire. The powerful sight pulled him, in a daze, across the lawn until he stood before her. The direct light turned her features fiery red, then faded to the color of blood where it fell more obliquely. Where the light cast shadows, the stone looked like charred, blackened flesh.

Mesmerized by the horrific beauty of her, he could believe that the gusting winds whipped her gossamer dress and pressed it even more tightly against her stunningly beautiful body. A chill ran through him as a cold gust swept across them. His breath caught in his throat when he saw that her granite body also felt the chill, raising her nipples to proud points. Unthinking desire overtook him, and he raised his hands to cup, then grasp her perfect breasts. Her nipples became burning points of heat beneath his palms, and that inhuman warmth flowed through his body, causing an almost forgotten stirring of his cock.

He leaned forward, relishing the warmth she radiated. Unbidden, a thought born of his irresistible desire formed, then consumed him. If only she were alive, if only this stone was flesh, he would take her right then and there. Beneath his hands, the hard granite of her breasts melted into the softness of a woman. He stepped even closer to press against her warm, seductive flesh. Then, he nearly burst with joy and need as Flora lowered her head and met his gaze with hooded eyes and parted lips.

Beyond conscious thought, Jan leaned in to taste that perfect mouth as a prelude to what he now realized he had wanted since the first time he had seen her. As their faces slowly came together, though, he saw her eyes flare red with an internal fire and her mouth open to reveal a black abyss. In an instant, temptation turned to terror. He imagined he felt his very essence being pulled toward the black emptiness inside her. For a heartbeat, the threat of losing his soul balanced against the promise of her burning pleasure. Then, reflexively, he shoved himself away from her and fell backwards onto the ground.

31

The sun had set, and the dew had formed when he regained his senses. In the gathering gloom, with heart pounding, he hesitantly looked up at the statue in its never-changing pose. The cold, wet ground and springtime air chilled him to the bone. Climbing to his feet, the memory of Flora's heat tugged at him, but he hurried past her to the house, glancing back to be sure she didn't follow.

He found Sandy in the parlor. She had a fire burning in the fireplace, and the two lamps standing in the corners gave the room a cozy, inviting feel. Jan stepped to the fireplace, soaking in its warmth and fighting the shivers that rippled through his body. When he had control of himself again, he rubbed the gooseflesh on his arms and turned around. Sandy sat in a club chair by one of the lamps. On her lap was an open notebook, and she clutched a pen in her hand.

"Is it raining out there? You look wet."

Jan shook his head, not sure how to explain the state he was in.

"No, I was admiring Flora and I guess I lost track of time."

Sandy's eyes opened wide. "How long were you out there?" She sounded genuinely concerned. "Let me get you something. Tea? Coffee?" she said as she stood and set the notebook on a side table.

"Coffee would be great, thanks."

She hurried through the dining room into the kitchen. In a moment, he heard the coffee maker start its gurgling magic. His eyes, which had followed Sandy from the room, returned to where she had been sitting, then onto the closed notebook. He had never seen her show any interest in writing, and it piqued his curiosity.

His eyes still lingered on the notebook when she returned to the room, carrying a mug in one hand and a bottle of brandy in the other. When he looked over at her, he saw her looking at the notebook as if checking to make sure he hadn't touched it.

She handed the steaming mug to him and held up the brandy bottle by way of invitation. Jan nodded and smiled as she poured a healthy portion into the black liquid.

"Thanks. This'll help."

Sandy returned his smile, then added a dollop of liqueur to her own mug sitting on the table. When she sat back down, she placed a hand protectively on the spiral-bound book.

Jan interpreted her gesture as an invitation to ask about it, so he did.

"Are you writing your own novel?" he asked with a teasing lilt.

Sandy chuckled in response, but shook her head. "No. This house is only big enough for one novelist's ego."

Jan laughed out loud, and Sandy joined him.

"So, what's in the notebook?" he asked as he sat in the other club chair.

"If you must know, it's my journal." Jan nodded appreciatively. "I've been keeping one since I was a kid." She got serious. "I, ah, had some issues when I was a kid and the only thing that my therapist suggested which helped was to write down my thoughts and fears. Now it's just become a habit."

"It's a great habit to have." Jan's eyes and tone were sympathetic. "In a lot of ways, my novels serve the same purpose. Most people don't know, but most of what a writer puts down never makes it to print."

Sandy looked startled. "I find that hard to believe."

"Oh, you can believe it. By the time the first draft is edited and revised and whole sections rewritten, then sent out to beta readers who all give you feedback, then revised again, copy edited, yada, yada, yada, the end result usually bears little resemblance to what started up here." He tapped the side of his head.

"I don't feel so bad now. I can't bear to go back and re-read any of what I wrote before," she said with a small smile.

"But you don't throw them away."

It was a statement, not a question, and Sandy shook her head in surprised agreement.

"Believe me, I know. I have every version of every story I've ever written tucked away on backup hard drives and in desk drawers."

Sandy nodded her understanding. "These are my thoughts." She patted the notebook. "I can't imagine throwing them away, even if I don't believe them anymore."

"*Especially* if you don't believe them anymore."

They sat quietly drinking their laced coffee for a few minutes. Sandy reopened her journal but didn't resume writing.

"This has been a pretty horrible year," she whispered. "I still dream about all of that blood. Nobody's slept in the Veranda suite since that night." Sandy was thoughtful for a moment. "They wanted to stay in your room, but you were already booked." She met Jan's eyes. "I don't get it. It's pretty creepy up there."

"'Pretty creepy' is part of the attraction." His voice trailed off.

She scoffed. "You writers. Anyway, I'm glad I put them in the Veranda Suite instead."

"I'm glad, too. That might have been too creepy, even for me."

She looked at him with her head tilted to the side. "Nothing spooky so far?"

He flinched, then smiled.

If I tell her I almost made out with the statue that came to life, I'll sound like a fool.

"Ah, nope. I have had some interesting dreams, though."

Why did I bring that up?

"Oh? Good 'interesting' or bad 'interesting'?"

"Just dreams. Probably my subconscious trying to process my research to turn it into a coherent story."

Sandy's eyes lit up. "Oooh. Tell me about your story."

Jan wagged his finger. "Oh, no. Not unless you read me your journal."

Sandy's teasing look darkened, and she clutched the notebook to her chest.

"No way. You'll think I'm crazy. Crazy dark."

"Nah, we're all a little crazy." His tone was light, but he studied her intently. "We'd all be pretty crazy if we had to endure what you have this year."

She gave him a tight smile. "I know what you're trying to do, and I appreciate it. But I'm not ready to talk about any of it, yet." She paused and took a deep breath. "When I am, though, I hope you'll be *here* to listen."

Jan didn't get the implication right away.

"Whenever you're ready, I'll be ready to listen."

"Jan, I hope you'll be here to listen." Her voice cracked.

Jan hesitated, not sure if he had really heard her invitation.

"Sandy, are you inviting me to stay? Like, move here?"

He tried to be as gentle as possible, but her face fell. That was enough to lift him out of his chair. Without considering the consequences, he crossed the room and dropped to one knee on the Persian carpet in front of her.

"Sandy, I can't—I can't just up and leave my home." He saw tears welling in her eyes. "But I promise you, I can be here in a couple hours whenever you need me."

She shook her head and wiped the tears with the back of her hand.

"I'm sorry. I can't ask you to give up your life in Philadelphia to move up here to no-man's-land. I'm just being stupid."

"No, you're not stupid. Not at all." He laid his right hand on her arm, welcoming the spark he felt. "Look, let me think about it. Really, I can work anywhere. And my apartment there certainly isn't much." He stopped, realizing he was talking himself into uprooting his life on a whim.

Sandy took his hand in her own and laid them both on her lap.

"I appreciate you humoring me when I'm just being silly."

Jan started to object, but she squeezed his hand to stop him.

"I'm being silly and incredibly needy." He returned her squeeze in reply.

"Not silly," he teased, which had the desired effect. Sandy smiled and relaxed. She raised his hand to her lips and kissed it lightly.

"Thank you for putting up with me," she whispered.

Seeing where things were headed, Jan stood up to the sound of his knees cracking and popping and returned to his chair. Sandy, reluctantly it seemed, relinquished her grip on his hand.

As Jan sank into the soft cushions, he felt the quality of the air change. Warm air wafted in from the hallway, where he sensed movement. Thinking it strange, since he hadn't heard the front door open, he strained to see—nothing. Or, as he thought of it, "A Nothingness."

The wrought iron pendant light hanging in the front hall cast a yellow glow from its Edison-style lightbulbs. Barely bright enough to illuminate the stairs and entry foyer, its light couldn't reach the kitchen end of the hallway visible from Jan's chair. That end was a black emptiness that seemed solid yet formless.

While his mind tried to make sense of this utter nothingness, it moved. Eyes wide and mouth open, Jan sat frozen in place. What remained of conscious thought was drowned out by his thumping heart and a buzzing in his ears. Slowly, the Nothingness emerged from the shadowed hall and passed under the archway into the parlor. Blacker than any shadow of the physical world, it was an animated, opaque silhouette, a Nothingness with substance, an interloper from another realm.

Confirming its substance, the old oak floor creaked with each of its steps, a sound Jan had heard on the stairway many times late at night but had dismissed as the house "settling."

Surveying the room, the Nothingness turned first to Jan, who remained in his chair, frozen in terror. Its movement confirmed what Jan's mind struggled to understand.

This Nothingness had form and substance, but its form occupied some negative space carved out of the reality of our normal existence. Where its face should have protruded forward, exposing forehead, nose, mouth, and chin, those features extended backwards along a dimension beyond the three of our world.

His mind, grasping for some real-world analogy to represent this phenomenon, finally formed the concept of negative space as a multi-dimensional Rubin vase, those optical illusions that look alternatively like a vase or two faces peering at each other. With this mental pattern, he could see the figure as both a hole in the normal world and an extension into another. He could resolve features of the Nothingness: its flowing garment, its voluptuous torso, its—no, her—beautiful face. Flora's face. A whimper escaped his lips as Flora smiled, clearly pleased that he recognized her.

Jan's heart hammered in his ears. A cold sweat, born of fear and Flora's radiant heat, burst from his pores, soaking his clothes again. As Flora continued to stare at him, Jan's breathing became shallower and more labored. Then a quiet snore intruded on this tableau.

Both he and Flora turned to Sandy, who sat slumped in her chair, fast asleep. The notebook lay closed on her lap, her pen tucked within its pages. Without even another glance at Jan, Flora took two strides across the room and merged with the sleeping woman. Flora's negative form slid into Sandy as if she were putting on a mask.

Immediately, Sandy's eyes flew open and her back and neck arched in imitation of her statue's ecstatic pose. With practiced familiarity, Sandy-Flora opened her notebook, picked up the pen, and began writing.

Emotions flooded Jan: protectiveness for Sandy, fear for her safety, confusion, and abject terror. But somehow, curiosity won out and his mind regained control of his body.

Rising slowly, intending to peek at what this combination of friend and possessing spirit was trying to communicate, he crept toward her chair. Sandy's hand flew back and forth across the page, but before he could see what it wrote, her head snapped up and he again froze in place. Sandy-Flora's eyes flared red, and her mouth opened, revealing the same black abyss he saw earlier when the statue came alive. A shout assaulted him. Not a shout heard by his ears, but rather a shout of pure psychic energy whose message was clear:

"GET OUT!"

The force of that psychic blow threw him backwards across the parlor and into the hall. His heel caught on the carpet runner, sending him toppling backwards and slamming his head into the corner of a staircase tread. All was blackness before his body hit the floor.

32

"Jan! Jan, are you alright?"

Sandy's voice faded in and out, trying to wake him, but the comforting coolness of the rag on his forehead held him in limbo.

"I called 911. The ambulance is on its way."

That spurred him into wakefulness. Even in a semi-conscious state, something told him that the last thing he wanted was to be incoherent when asked what had happened. His eyes fluttered open to see Sandy, her disheveled hair backlit by the yellow lightbulbs forming a halo around her flushed and worried face.

"Wh-what happened?" he stammered.

"I don't know. We were talking, then I fell asleep. There was a thump and when I woke up, you were lying here on the floor. Did you trip?"

He struggled to sit up, but Sandy placed a firm hand on his chest.

"You should lie there until the paramedics check you out."

But he shook his head, which sent the world spinning.

"No. I need to sit up."

He sounded like he was about to vomit. This time, Sandy didn't object and helped him to a sitting position. His head pounded, and he thought he was going to black out again, but he closed his eyes and took a couple of deep breaths, which lent him a bit of equilibrium. Reaching up to the back of his head, he felt a large lump, but his hand came away dry.

"No blood, thank God," Sandy said. "You must have tripped, probably on this damn carpet runner. I told Dan it needed to be replaced. It's almost threadbare and sometimes the edges curl up."

Her words came out in a rush, getting faster as the wail of sirens drew closer.

"Yeah, that must be what happened," he said, unsure whether to believe her.

The moments right before his fall were, at best, fuzzy in his memory, but he was sure he didn't just trip. He slowly turned his head toward the dark end of the hallway, which brought one of those fuzzy memories into focus.

There was something—no, not something. It was Nothing, pure emptiness.

One memory triggered another, which triggered another, like a line of dominoes falling.

That Nothingness was Flora. And it had possessed Sandy!

Was the story she wanted him to tell the paramedics a cover-up, or was she unaware of the possession? Or was it all a fever dream his mind concocted while he was unconscious?

Shit, I can't even trust my own memory now.

But the impression left by that hole in our universe felt very real.

His eyes looked past Sandy into the parlor, where her notebook lay on the floor. That was the evidence he needed to sort out. What she wrote in those pages would tell him if what he remembered had actually happened, or if he was losing his mind.

Sandy followed his gaze, then looked back at him. Her expression changed from concern for him to panic. They sat, frozen for a second or two, until a firm knocking on the door, followed by a key in the lock, captured both of their attentions. In another second, Kathy burst into the hall.

"Oh, my God. Are you two all right?"

The EMTs bustled in behind her with their bags of medical equipment. The hallway suddenly became very crowded.

Jan tried to nod his head, but pain and nausea followed in a rush, and he had to close his eyes again to stop the world from swirling.

"He tripped, and he hit his head on the staircase," Sandy blurted as a paramedic gently but firmly moved her out of the way.

Kathy, having responded to similar incidents many times, took up a position on the stairs overlooking the scene. The EMTs quickly assessed Jan's injuries and strongly recommended he spend the night in the hospital for observation.

"No, I don't need to go to the hospital," he said in response.

"Don't be a douchebag," Kathy said, taking up the paramedics' cause. "You're on vacation. What difference does it make where you sleep?"

Jan's head had stopped spinning and he could now focus his eyes, so he gave her a withering look.

"But I'll miss Sandy's breakfast in the morning."

His attempt at humor fell flat as Kathy simply frowned in response, and Sandy just stood in the doorway, wringing her hands. Another wave of nausea forced his eyes closed again, and he realized he probably had a concussion.

"OK," he said, "let's go."

After a failed attempt to stand, the two paramedics, both beefy members of the local volunteer fire company, wheeled in a transport cot and practically lifted him onto it.

Kathy's focus was on this procedure, but once Jan was down and secured, she turned to Sandy, who was no longer watching the procedure. Instead, her head was turned to the parlor, and she appeared to be studying the corner of the room where her notebook lay face up on the floor.

"Sandy," Kathy said with a police officer's voice of command.

Sandy's head duly snapped around to face her.

"Why don't you ride with Jan to the hospital? I can lock up here."

Kathy's words clearly were not a question or a suggestion, and they seemed to break through to Sandy's attention.

"Um, sure. Let me get a coat." She looked down at her slipper-clad feet. "And some shoes."

Rather than walking down the hall to her apartment in the back of the house, though, she turned and hurried across the parlor to her notebook, scooped it up, and closing it against her chest, she then cut through the dining room and disappeared into the kitchen. A minute later, she returned from her apartment and followed Jan, now tightly strapped to the wheeled stretcher, out the door.

Kathy stood on the porch, holding the door for the entourage as they emerged. Sandy grabbed Kathy's arm lightly and whispered, "Thank you."

It sounded more like a plea for help than a statement of gratitude.

Watching the ambulance drive away, Kathy turned to the door, but instead of closing and locking it, she stepped inside.

What the hell is going on here? Kathy thought as she closed the door and looked into the dim hallway. *Why was Sandy more concerned about the damned notebook than about Jan's head?*

After a moment's hesitation, she walked down the hall and through the door into the kitchen. Directly in front of her, a window overlooked the back garden and below it was the deep, white porcelain farm sink. The sink was flanked by the Stainless-steel appliances Dan and Sandy had installed as part of their renovation. To her left, a swinging door led to the dining room, and to her right, three doors stood closed.

The one immediately to her right led down into the basement under the stairs in the front hallway. It was locked with a heavy-duty padlock. Across from it, another door opened into a pantry, but it was the third door that drew Kathy's attention. It stood at the end of the kitchen and led into the apartment where Dan and Sandy—now just Sandy—lived.

Three strides and Kathy stood in front of that door, fingering the spare keys that Dan had asked her to hold for them shortly after they moved in. It was a full set since, "You never know which ones you might lose," as Dan had said.

If I go snooping around in there, will I be violating Sandy's trust?

Kathy knew the answer before she finished the question in her mind.

Of course I will be. So, am I willing to cross that line?

She looked down at the ring of keys and absently flipped through them. She knew which ones opened which doors, but still she hesitated. Her mind drifted back to all the good times she had shared with Dan and Sandy. Drinking beer, watching Sunday football, riding ATVs in the woods, playing nickel-ante poker. After several seconds of mental paralysis, she still couldn't bring herself to insert the key in the lock.

Who do I owe my loyalty to? A guy who probably lit out and left his wife with a failing B&B, or my emotionally fragile cousin?

Put in those terms, her decision was an easy one. She turned, hurried out of the house, and pocketed the keys after locking the front door.

33

Wednesday, Late Spring

The morning sun streamed through the window blinds, casting angular bars of shadow across unadorned walls. The light did nothing to soften the sterility of the hospital room. Jan sat up in bed, trying to focus on his phone, but without his reading glasses, he held it at arm's length and cursed under his breath. His need for their aid was a jealously guarded secret, one of his few vanities. So, he was relieved when a knock came at the door. He looked up as it opened to see Kathy poke her head in.

"OK, if I come in?"

"Sure," he said. "I'm happy for the company." He looked past her at the closing door. "No Sandy?"

Kathy looked momentarily flustered. "I imagine she'll be here shortly. I didn't tell her I was coming, since I wanted to chat with you alone first."

Intrigued by this bit of subterfuge, he pushed himself more upright in the hospital bed.

"OK, what's up?"

She gathered her thoughts for a moment, then seemed to decide. She sat down on the edge of the bed.

"First off, how are you feeling?"

He shrugged. "I've still got a goonie back here," he gingerly touched the back of his head, "but other than that,

I'm fine. They say if all the tests come back OK, I can go home this afternoon."

Kathy nodded and smiled. "That's good. If you need a ride, give me a call."

"Thanks. I imagine Sandy will be hanging around today, though."

Kathy pursed her lips. "She's what I wanted to talk to you about." Jan raised his eyebrows but remained silent. "What can you tell me about what happened last night?"

"The same thing I told the EMTs and the doctors. I remember sitting in the parlor chatting with Sandy and, ah, reading, I think."

He wasn't about to tell Kathy everything he remembered about his encounter with Flora's ghost. She'd probably have him involuntarily committed.

"Anyway, I noticed after a while that Sandy had fallen asleep, so I got up to go to my room. The next thing I remember is coming to with Sandy hovering over me."

Kathy nodded throughout his recounting.

"That's what you said last night. You don't remember anything else this morning?"

Jan's suspicion radar started pinging.

"No, that's it. Why all the questions?"

Kathy, who had been leaning forward intently, sat back and let out a long breath.

"I don't know," she admitted. "Something is bugging me about this."

"Like what?"

Jan's tone was defensive, which Kathy responded to in kind.

"Like how you fell over backwards if you were walking out of the parlor?" Jan opened his mouth to respond, but Kathy plowed ahead. "And the *fact* that there was no book in either the hall or the parlor for you to have been reading."

Her eyes bore into his, but he kept his face blank, since he knew she was looking for a guilty eye flick or some other poker tell.

Getting nothing back, she continued. "Or why Sandy seemed much more interested in her precious notebook than in *you*."

Trying to deflect the questioning, he responded casually, "Well, her journal is very important to her, and very private."

His tone was light, but he felt a pang of jealousy that she was more concerned with it than with his wellbeing.

"Have you ever gotten a look at it?"

Kathy's tone had turned conversational, but Jan knew the interrogation wasn't over, and he didn't like where it was headed.

"I didn't even know about it until last night. She seems very protective of it, which, as a writer, I fully understand. Believe me, I know what a terrible invasion of her privacy it would be to read it without permission."

"Yeah, I guess it would be," Kathy mumbled.

The events of the previous evening replayed themselves in Jan's mind in the ensuing silence. He realized Kathy had hit upon the key to the whole puzzle, namely the journal. As he replayed his memories for the first time—he must have been subconsciously suppressing them—he kept coming back to the Sandy-Flora shadow thing writing furiously in it.

Bringing his thoughts back to the present, he lifted his head and saw Kathy staring intently at him.

"What is it?" she asked, genuine concern in her voice.

"Just trying to remember anything else," he lied.

Maybe I should tell her at least some of what happened, he thought. *But what can I tell her that wouldn't make me sound like a nutcase?*

Kathy leaned forward and her voice came out in a whisper.

"If it's any help, I know weird shit happens in that house."

This got Jan's attention, but he still said nothing.

Kathy continued, "I've seen stuff myself. Strange shadows where they shouldn't be. And that statue … that's creepy beyond words. And," she paused for emphasis, "it's gotten worse since Dan left. Sandy has gotten … odd, too."

Relief washed over Jan. Someone else had experienced at least a little of what he had. Kathy's admission erased all the doubts about what he remembered.

He had been suppressing the importance of his experiences since returning to Mackey House: the shadows, the footsteps on the stairs, the mesmerizing and incredibly erotic statue, and even Sandy's new sultry looks and attempts at seducing him. His rational mind was suppressing these bizarre experiences, but Kathy's admission unlocked the floodgates and granted him permission to examine them and speak them out loud.

He opened his mouth, ready to pour out all the pent-up confusion and fears, just as the hospital room door opened and Sandy popped in, a bouquet—the first blooms of the season from Flora's garden—in one hand and an insulated thermal bag in the other.

"Hi! Oh, Kathy, you're here already."

The moment of revelation shattered, Kathy stood and Jan shut his mouth.

"Yeah, ah, something came up this morning, and I could only stop by for a minute."

"Oh, OK."

"You have to go?" Jan asked, disappointment obvious in his voice.

"Yeah, busy day today," she said as she leaned forward to give Jan a quick hug. With her cheek next to his, she whispered, "Call me," then straightened, gave another quick hug to Sandy, and waved goodbye on her way out of the room.

Sandy watched her go, then turned to Jan with a frown. But her face quickly brightened as she set the flower vase on his bedside table. "I got just enough from the garden."

"They're beautiful," he said. "Thanks, but I hope I'm going home today."

"That's OK, I'll just put them in your room at home," she said lightly.

Then she held up the thermal bag.

"I also brought you breakfast so you don't have to eat hospital food."

She unzipped it and the wonderful scent of bacon and eggs wafted from the bag.

"That smells fantastic. Will you be joining me?" he asked. With a big grin in response, she pulled two plates, napkins, and sets of silverware from the bag.

Sandy kept him company all morning and into the afternoon, telling him all her plans for improving the house and stepping up her marketing efforts to bring in new, or any, guests. Jan mostly just listened and nodded, occasionally offering a piece of advice or an encouraging comment about her ideas.

When the nurse pronounced him well enough to leave, Sandy walked alongside, carrying the flowers while they wheeled him, against his protests, to the entrance.

When they got to the house, Jan announced he was wiped out and just wanted to take a pain pill and go to bed. Sandy agreed that was a good idea and followed him to his suite. As he got undressed and swallowed an Oxy in the bathroom, she placed the bouquet on a bedside table and pulled the window shades down against the late afternoon sun.

They were both surprised when Jan emerged from the bathroom in his underwear. He hadn't expected her to still be there.

"Oh, my!" she said, laughing and hiding her eyes behind splayed fingers that nonetheless allowed her a clear view.

Without an ounce of self-consciousness, he just shook his head at her, then chuckled despite himself.

"I'll see you in the morning," he said firmly as he climbed under the covers.

Sandy, who had dropped her pretended shyness, bit her lower lip and looked at the empty space next to Jan in the king size bed. When their eyes met, he slowly but deliberately shook his head. She sighed.

"Sleep tight," she said, and left.

Sleep came quickly, and he fell into a dreamless sleep for the next fourteen hours. It was the best rest he had in days. Before drifting off, though, he noticed how the gloom of the sun, filtered by the window blinds, lent the brightly colored flowers from Flora's garden a sinister air, like they were silently watching him.

34

Thursday, Late Spring

The strong need to empty his bladder woke him before sunrise the next morning. With the shades drawn, the room was lit only by the dim glow of a nightlight outlining the door to the bathroom. The pain in his head was reduced to a dull ache, and he briefly considered popping another Oxy and going back to bed, but the oblivion of opiate-induced sleep had never appealed to him. So he dug a Tylenol out of his toiletry kit instead.

Shivering a bit from the early morning chill, he pulled on sweatpants and a matching shirt and took his laptop and a towel to wipe the dew from the chair out on the porch.

He opened the document where he captured his notes and started to write down what he remembered of the Nothingness and Flora's possession of Sandy.

How do you describe an entity that is present but has no substance? Something, in fact, with a kind of negative substance that creates a dimple in space-time?

How much of what he saw and remembered was real and how much was his rational mind trying to make sense of it? But Kathy had seen the shadow, too. Maybe she saw more than a shadow.

She did ask me to call her, he thought, and he reached for his phone.

The time, 6:15, glowed from the otherwise black screen. Too early to call, he sent her a text.

I'm up finally. Call me when you get a chance.

Within a minute his phone buzzed with a response.

Don't talk there. Coffee at 8:00?

Puzzled by her response, he nevertheless wrote back.

CU then.

Why would she want me away from the house? Or did she want me away from Sandy?

If it was the latter, she must have her own suspicions. Either way, he needed to find out why.

Sitting lost in thought, he noticed the familiar scent of coffee brewing. The Tylenol having done its job, he was suddenly famished, so he went back inside to shower and shave.

Sandy hovered over him at breakfast like a mother hen. She eyed his laptop satchel suspiciously and tried to insist that he return to his room and relax for the rest of the day. But Jan assured her he felt fine, which he did, surprisingly. At 7:45, he stood to leave. Sandy huffed her disapproval when he slid the satchel's strap over his shoulder.

"You've been more than kind, Sandy. It was my clumsiness that gave me this bump." He gingerly fingered the back of his head. "All you've done is help me, and I really appreciate it."

He leaned over and kissed the top of her head, trying to appear fatherly. The lavender scent of her hair was intoxicating, though, and he lingered a bit longer than a father would, giving Sandy the chance to turn and meet his eyes just inches away.

"Don't be late," she purred.

How he wanted to lower his head just a bit to taste her lips again. This time, though, Sandy broke the contact, turning her head with a teasing glint in her eye.

Out of habit, as he descended the front walk, his eyes were drawn to Flora. From this vantage point behind her, he could study her back, which he hadn't really done before. The details of her flowing robe, the waves of hair cascading down her back, and her delicate hands were stunning. But these details paled in comparison to the intricate work the artist had done rendering her flower garland.

Each of her hands held an end of the long string of roses which swept up the back of her arms and formed a loop through her thick, flowing hair. Each rose of the garland was perfectly formed and seemed to be opening as he watched the early morning light play across them. Flora was positioned facing south, so her upturned face was bathed each evening in the fiery red of sunset, while in the morning, the newly risen sun highlighted her youthful beauty and innocence.

From behind her, with her ecstatic face and voluptuous features hidden from view, the interplay of morning light and an accompanying breeze seemed to bring Flora to life in an almost childlike way.

No, not a child. From this view she looks like a young girl, barely past adolescence, running through a meadow full of wildflowers—wild roses that have been strung together into a royal crown and mantle.

He could see, as clearly the breeze ruffle her hair, as if she were flesh not stone, as it sent ripples through her gown.

The motion he imagined highlighted the artist's subtlety in the rendering of the folds in her gown as they flowed from her slight shoulders to her fine-boned hands. From her shoulder blades, those folds formed small angel's wings.

The poignancy of this detail brought tears to Jan's eyes as he thought about how Flora was taken from this world just at the dawning of her adulthood. How ironic that this rendering of virginal purity shared the same block of granite with the immodest image of Flora as a fully seductive woman.

Jan stood mesmerized by Angel Flora until the sun, which had helped induce his stupor, highlighted a flaw in the rendering. Once he noticed it, his mind broke free of its captivity. The low-angled light cast sharp-edged shadows which flowed uninterrupted across the many intricate peaks and valleys of the sculpture, except in one spot. The incongruity of a tiny part of the otherwise perfect pattern of light and dark drew his eye like a magnet.

Stepping into the danger zone of the now-clipped flower bed surrounding the statue, Jan could see the cause of the discontinuity. A petal on one of the roses behind Flora's right shoulder had been chipped away and subsequently repaired with tinted cement. The repair was quite good, and the color matched almost perfectly. So finely was the repair made that it would have been invisible in any other lighting.

Jan reached up and lightly touched the tips of his fingers to the broken rose. While the natural stone of the original carving gave forth its now-familiar internal warmth, the repaired part felt cold and dead.

Bringing his other hand up, Jan rested both on the garland, absorbing not only their gentle heat but also the peace and contentment they radiated. With both hands he caressed the remaining flowers down to Flora's right hand, then retraced his path up her right arm and across her shoulder, careful to avoid the repair, which he sensed was as painful to her as an unhealed wound.

Tracing his fingers across the roses that held her hair coiffed down her back, he felt the faintest vibration, as if a train were approaching from far down the tracks. Or, no, more like the purr of a contented cat curled on one's lap.

As the fingers of his left hand slowly traced the petals, his right stroked the intricate waves of her hair. His hand brushed them, and in response, the strands seemed to part between his fingers, and he again caught the faint scent of lavender.

Continuing his reverent examination of Flora's garland, he traced it to where it ducked behind her hair—which he again stroked just to evoke her delicate scent—then emerged to run down her back and out to where its end was held by her equally delicate left hand. As he ran his hand along the strand, his hands were protected from the chilly morning air by the warmth the stone roses radiated.

Intertwining her delicately carved fingers with his own, he closed his eyes and felt her fingers become supple as they returned his light squeeze. The comforting softness of her touch held him mesmerized.

When his phone buzzed with a text, he was finally able to break free of her spell, but the feeling lingered on his fingers as he reluctantly climbed into his car.

`Where RU?`

How long was I standing there?
His loafers were stained from the dew.

35

Kathy was already sitting at their corner table when Jan entered the Fae Feine. She made a point of checking her watch as he sat down.

"You're late. Your coffee's cold."

He shrugged. "I was distracted."

She frowned and shook her head. "It was that damned statue again, wasn't it?"

Jan stared at her. "How the hell did you know that?"

She scoffed. "You were pretty out of it once they put you on the morphine drip in the hospital. All you kept talking about was Flora."

She looked like she was trying not to smile.

"Shit. What did I say, exactly?"

"Lots of incoherent crap about how sexy she is. And how her nightgown flutters in the breeze."

She gave up trying to suppress her smile.

"Well, in my defense, it is a pretty revealing pose."

"Oh, please!"

They both laughed.

When he could talk again, he said, "I may be losing my mind." His tone cleared the smile from Kathy's face. "I've seen stuff in that house that I can't wrap my head around."

"Like empty black shadows."

"Was I babbling about that, too?"

Kathy shrugged. "A little, but you're not the only one." Kathy paused to sip her coffee, but Jan could see she wanted to say more. Finally, her voice dropped to a whisper, and she said, "I've seen it, too."

He was not surprised, and he felt a great relief that maybe he wasn't going nuts.

"When?" he asked.

Kathy kept her eyes fixed on the tabletop.

"A couple weeks ago, I was drinking with Sandy one night, pretty late. We both fell asleep, but I woke up when I heard her mumbling in her sleep. While I lay there, still half asleep, something came into the room and *covered* her. I nearly jumped out of my skin and when I reached over to wake her up, I burned my hand. Then she looked at me and growled."

"*Get out!*" Jan tried to imitate the ghost's snarl.

Kathy's head snapped up and her eyes met his.

"Yeah, you got that, too?"

He nodded, and her next words came out in a rush.

"I got out of that bed as fast as I could, but I was all twisted in the covers and by the time I got off the floor and turned around, Sandy was sleeping peacefully again. I figured I must have been dreaming—but I didn't get back in bed. I dressed and got out of there." Kathy paused. "I hadn't been back to see her until just the other day."

Realization startled Jan. "Wait. You and Sandy were in bed?"

Kathy's revelation, and the way she casually mentioned it, was shocking to him, and his reaction made him feel like an old fart, while he pushed down a stab of jealousy.

She ignored his surprised expression and plowed ahead as if sleeping with your same-sex first cousin once removed was no big deal.

"There's something there—a presence—"

Recovering, Jan said, "I call it a Nothingness."

Kathy slapped the table and gave him an appreciative look.

"I guess that's why you're the writer," she said, then her voice hardened. "It seemed so empty, yet terrifying. And it's got control of Sandy."

Yes, that's the crux of it, Jan thought. *And probably the reason I've been sticking around, despite all that's happened.*

"We've got to save her."

The words came rushing out of him.

Kathy stared at him for a few seconds, then nodded.

"Whatever this ghost is, whether it's the spirit of Flora or something else, there must be some way to get rid of it. Some way to send it on to wherever it belongs."

Jan sat back in his chair. Now that his fears had been confirmed as more than his imagination running wild, he saw Flora as a problem to be solved, and he had spent a career solving problems. Granted, they were problems solved with software, but the process, the methodology ought to work for malevolent ghosts, as well.

"OK, so the problem is how to get rid of Flora." He held up a finger, "One: how to disconnect her from Sandy." then another finger, "and Two; how to move her out of this realm and on to the next."

"Or just destroy her somehow."

How do you kill a ghost? Or a demon? They're already dead. Shit, I can't believe I'm seriously discussing ghosts and demons.

Kathy's eyes were wide, but she otherwise looked determined.

He said, "If we manage to destroy it, what will that do to Sandy? They're linked together somehow. Destroying Flora might destroy Sandy, too, or at least some part of her. How do you destroy a ghost, by the way?"

Kathy's voice was low. "What if she's a willing participant in the possession? Or, maybe she's just given up?"

Jan shook his head. "I don't think so. From what you said and what I saw, Sandy seems to be asleep when Flora possesses her. She may be too weak to resist anymore, but I don't think she invites Flora in." He shook his head in frustration. "There are too many 'what ifs' to go around. We need to figure out exactly what we're dealing with. Break the problem down into questions that we can answer."

"Like why you're so obsessed with that statue?" Kathy's tone was light, but with an edge.

Jan's cheeks flushed. He was too embarrassed to tell her about how intimate he and Stone Flora had become. He needed some assurances first.

"Look, the only way we're going to succeed is if we're perfectly honest with each other, right?" Kathy nodded. "So, if you two were sleeping together, either before or after Dan left, it could be important."

"And if you and she were fucking, that could be very important!"

Jimmie glanced over from behind the counter, and Jan held up his hands.

"Whoa, I just mean that we need to share any relevant information. As a sign of good faith, I'll start. No, we were not 'fucking,' although I have to admit we've come close. I don't know if you've seen it, but Sandy can go from being the sweetest innocent girl to a sultry temptress like that." He snapped his fingers. "And she has almost seduced me a couple of times."

Kathy chuckled. "'A sultry temptress?' Is that how you describe the women in your books?"

Jan chuckled in response.

Kathy's voice dropped to a whisper. "To answer your question, yes, but that was the first night Sandy, and I … spent together."

She waited for any recrimination from Jan, but he just nodded.

"And I've seen the other thing happen, too—her turning into a wild woman." She paused and continued in an even quieter whisper, "That's how we ended up in bed together when Flora showed up. And that's why I warned you off when you first got here."

"And I took your warning to heart. One minute I feel like she's my daughter, and the next she looks at me and I forget all the warnings and promises I've made. If Flora hadn't shown herself, well…"

"How many times have you seen Flora? Sounds like more than once or twice."

Do I take the plunge? Oh well, in for a penny…

"OK. Full disclosure, but we'll need more coffee."

Over the next half-hour, Jan related each of his encounters with Flora, including both episodes at the statue, how he got his head injury, and even his wet dream. By the end, their coffee was cold, and he was mentally exhausted, but a great weight had been lifted from him.

When he finished, Kathy said, "There are some basic questions to answer, I think."

She thought for a moment, then checked off the ideas on her fingers as she said them.

"Flora the woman: what was she like? What's her side of the story?" She ticked another finger. "Then there's that damned statue: why was it made? What is its source of power?"

Jan interrupted, "Or is it all in my head? Am I just imagining that she is being tortured or, or …"

"Having an orgasm."

"Yeah. And why is the back so different from the front?"

Kathy held up her third finger. "And what's up with the ghost? What does it want? Why is it pissed off? Why now, after all these years?"

"And how do we get rid of her?"

"Right. How do we get rid of it?" Kathy paused a moment. "You could just ask it."

Jan smiled, but then realized Kathy wasn't joking when she continued, "I mean, next time she appears, try to talk to her."

"Did she feel like talking when you met her? Or did you, for that matter?"

Kathy shook her head. "But maybe it was jealous, like maybe Sandy was cheating on her."

It was Jan's turn to shake his head, but only because he didn't want to admit that talking to Flora was actually a pretty good idea.

When she didn't get a response, Kathy held up her hand, now with four fingers extended.

"Don't forget Dan. What happened to Dan?"

Jan swallowed hard but wasn't ready yet to voice his doubts about ever finding Dan at all, let alone alive. From Kathy's downcast look, he figured she was thinking along the same lines.

"I think we should start with facts. What questions can we answer with facts? Like the questions about Dan. Can you use police stuff to find him?"

Kathy grinned. "'Police stuff'? Is that a technical term?"

"No, it's a literary one from a writer who only knows about police *stuff* from reading novels and watching TV. Besides, didn't you say you want to be a detective someday?"

Kathy nodded but didn't tell him that finding Dan was her try-out for the job.

"OK, I'll see what I can dig up. What are you going to tackle? An interview with Flora?"

She smiled, but her tone told him she was serious.

"I won't try to summon her, if that's what you mean. But, if she does appear, I guess I could try to talk to her."

Then I'll have to change my underwear, he thought, and shuddered.

"In the meantime, I'll see what I can learn about the statue," he said.

"Can you get a look at Sandy's journal?"

Jan hesitated. "She guards that like the Crown Jewels."

"I know. She took it back to her apartment even before getting in the ambulance with you. But, if Flora was writing in it, reading what she wrote would be even better than talking to her, wouldn't it?"

"Okay, Okay. But the door to her apartment is probably locked."

Kathy held up a ring of keys. "I have spares to all of them."

"We'll need to get her out of the house. How about a Girls' Night Out? That would give me plenty of time to snoop around."

Kathy took a deep breath, then nodded. "I'll ask her out to dinner tonight." She clutched the spare keyring. "This is breaking and entering, you know," she said. "Seriously, if you get caught, we'll both be going to jail."

Jan slowly nodded, then snatched the keys from her hand, put away his laptop, and headed for the door.

Kathy sat for a few seconds, lost in thought. Then, as if she had reached a decision she didn't like, she slowly rose and left.

36

The sun was high in the sky when Jan and Kathy, now co-conspirators, parted ways on Main Street. Jan walked to the library where he asked Miss Gheringer if she had any information about the statue in front of Mackey House. She insisted that the library did not keep records of such frivolous things as half-naked statues and that the only sources which might have mentioned it were in the newspaper archives, to which he had plenty of access the other day.

Feeling stonewalled, Jan walked to the other end of Main Street and popped in on Barb and Jim at the Historical Society. Barb greeted him with a smile.

"Hi, Barb. I'm curious what you or Jim can tell me about that strange statue in front of Mackey House. I find it kind of intriguing and thought there must be a story behind it."

Barb's face darkened while Jan spoke. "Oh, that thing. Do you want the facts, or the superstition?"

"Better start with the facts," Jim's voice came from behind him, startling Jan. "Ephraim Mackey commissioned an Italian artist living in New York City to carve a memorial statue honoring Flora, who you know died in the fire. After months of sending sketches back and forth,

Ephraim got so frustrated, he created a studio in the basement of the house and coerced the artist to move into Mackey House until the statue Santori finished it to Ephraim's satisfaction."

"He 'coerced' him? How?"

"With money," Barb said. "Lots and lots of money according local legend."

"The artist, a fellow named Santori, I believe, liked his drink and was used to the speakeasies in New York—this was during Prohibition, of course. All the Tavern here in town served in those days was 'near-beer', so Santori ended up buying moonshine from some local bootleggers who kept stills up in the mountains. They claimed he was their best customer, paying exorbitant prices every week."

"He said he needed it to sleep at night—to keep 'the demon' out of his dreams," Barb said.

Jim gave Barb a scowl. "At least that's what the moonshiners said. I thought we were sticking to the facts, first."

"Oh, posh," Barb said. "Facts are boring."

"Anyway," Jim continued, "Santori worked on the statue for over a year. Ephraim had to order at least three additional blocks of granite before it was finished."

"Santori tried four times?" Jan said.

Jim nodded. "We have copies of the quarry's sales records. He had the stone shipped in from Vermont."

"I would have thought Mackey would want to use Italian marble, or something finer than granite."

Jim shook his head. "Marble wouldn't stand up to the winters we have here. Besides, the statue is essentially a grave marker. Somber."

"Except it ain't so 'somber,' is it?" Barb said. "When they unveiled it, they had a funeral service and everything right there on the front lawn. It caused quite a scandal. People were shocked."

Jan was eager to get more of the legend surrounding the statue. "It is quite a striking pose. She appears from the front to be—"

"Having a 'Big O'," Barb said with a note of disgust.

Jan chuckled. "I was going to say 'ecstatic,' perhaps spiritual ecstasy rather than physical."

Jim jumped in. "It's interesting you should say that, because some people see her as being in torment, like she's being tortured."

"Or burned alive," Barb said.

"I can see that, too. But why is the back of the statue so different from the front?" Both Barb and Jim looked confused. "Look," he pulled up pictures on his cell phone. "The front is, well, borderline erotic, while the back is almost angelic. See how the folds of her gown form wings?"

"I'll be damned," Barb said. "I've never noticed that before. You're right, there's nothing sexual about her from the back. She looks like an innocent angel."

"Hang on a second..." Jim hurried through the door leading to the building's attic archives. In a minute or two he returned with a thin file folder, whose contents he spread out on the room's worktable. After shuffling through what looked like work orders and invoices, he laid out three photographs.

"Each time they delivered a new block of stone, Ephraim had the quarry men haul away the pieces of

Santori's failed attempts. Before dumping them on the tailings pile, they pieced the faces back together and took pictures."

Jim laid the photos out in a row showing a progression from a beautiful angel, head bowed in repose, to a scowling demon's face with flared nostrils and a rictus snarl.

"Wow," Jan said.

"That's terrifying," Barb whispered.

Jim pointed to them in order. "I suspect this one was the first, and it just wasn't anything special. This one," he pointed to the middle picture, "is closest to what she looks like now."

"For some reason Ephraim didn't like it, though."

"It's not so overtly sensual," Barb said. "But she looks more mature than the first one."

Jan nodded. "It's actually quite lovely."

"The last one looks like Santori was going mad," Jim said. "But somehow he got it together enough to create what's out there now, a work of art that, for all its controversy, is really quite stunning."

Barb eyed him sideways. "Should I be worried?"

Jim just laughed as Jan's phone buzzed. The text was from Sandy telling him he was on his own for dinner, since she was going out with Kathy.

"Mind if I take pictures of the pictures?" he asked. Jim nodded and Barb said, "That's what we're here for."

After Jan had snapped photos of all the documents in the folder, he asked, "Any other info about the statue?"

Jim and Barb shared a nervous look. "No more facts," Barb said.

"Well, let's hear the gossip, then."

They both started at once, but Barb waved Jim to silence.

"Like I said, a lot of the townsfolk were shocked by the statue and wrote letters to the Gazette, trying to get it removed. The strange thing is, though, the neighbors around the Mackey House were quite pleased with it. Including Flora's mom and sister, who were living across the road by then."

"Really. Why were the people who had to look at it every day happy about it?"

Barb was silent, so Jim picked up the thread.

"The story goes that before the statue went up, there were lots of strange things goin' on at that house. But once the statue was there, everything just sorta calmed down."

"What kind of 'strange things'?"

"Ghost sightings," Barb said, and Jim nodded. "People, especially Flora's sister, Sophie, claimed they saw and felt a terrifying presence that haunted the place."

"Sophie called it the 'Black Thing.' She was so afraid that she ran away from home several times. Ephraim finally built them their own house, but even that didn't help much."

Jim paused and Barb continued, "It wasn't until the statue went up that things settled down. It's stayed that way ever since."

Until now, Jan thought.

"People figure the statue appeased Flora's ghost enough that she 'moved on,' as they say."

Jan, who had listened intently through the tag-teamed story, put on a fake smile and thanked them for sharing a great story. But his mind was racing with these new revelations and what they implied.

Why did she wake up after so many years? Did she somehow know that Jeff Tomlin was a descendant of Jennifer Smythe? Was it just his presence that brought her back, or did he do something to piss her off?

"Thanks for sharing that bit of local lore," he said as calmly as he could. "I'm not sure how any of it fits into my novel, but it's a great backstory."

Remembering the text from Sandy, he took his leave and headed home to do some snooping.

Kathy looked out over the boats bobbing in the marina.

"Looks like a storm's coming," she said.

Sandy turned to look out the large windows as well. Captain Joe's restaurant overlooked the small marina on Lake Wallenpaupack. Its ambience was a typical resort town pub—a ship's wheel on the wall, duck decoys on the windowsills, fish nets and buoys hanging from the ceiling, and a flat-bottomed dory serving as the bar. From there in the upstairs dining room, they could look straight north, up the length of the lake. The shoreline on either side contracted toward the vanishing point in the gathering gloom.

Without turning her head, Sandy said, "Why did you come back here?"

Kathy gave a half-laugh. "I admit the food's not that great here, but—"

"No, no, I mean, why did you move back to this area? To tiny little Dundee, for God's sake."

Kathy was surprised by the turn of the conversation, which gave her pause. She faced Sandy.

"That was when Maan first got sick. I was almost finished at the Academy and the County had an opening, so…"

Her excuse didn't even sound convincing to herself, and Sandy wasn't buying it.

"Yeah, right. I don't know why you gave up your life in New York to become a cop in the first place."

Kathy turned back to the darkening view outside the window.

"Life in the Big City ain't all it's cracked up to be. Besides, I think I was trying to impress Dad. Anyway, now I'm here and I guess this is where I'll stay."

Sandy nodded her understanding.

Anxious to change the subject, Kathy asked, "So, how's it feel to have a guest again?"

Sandy remained silent for a moment.

"It feels good. Jan's a regular who apparently doesn't use Facebook. At least not to follow us."

"He didn't know about the 'incident'?" Kathy made air quotes with her fingers.

"No, but he probably would have come, anyway. As a writer, I think he's intrigued by the place and its history—including its recent history."

It was Kathy's turn to nod knowingly. To the rural folks of Wayne County, someone who came all the way up to the backwoods of the Poconos just to write must be a strange person indeed.

"Ah. That explains a lot, then."

At that point, their drinks arrived, and they each took a tentative sip before proceeding.

"A lot?" Sandy asked.

"Hmm?"

"You said 'that explains a lot.' A lot of what?"

"Oh. Liddy Gheringer at the library and the Donnellys at the Hysterical Society—" Sandy giggled at the common mispronunciation, "—both say he's been asking about the history of your place."

"That does make sense. I think he's going to write a book about it."

She didn't sound too enthusiastic about the idea.

"Maybe it'll be good for business. But make sure you get to read it before it gets published."

Sandy nodded. They both knew from experience how hard life in a small town could be if the locals turned against you. Her face broke into a sly smile.

"He is kinda cute, though—in a nerdy kinda way."

"Euww. He's so old."

They both broke into laughter.

"Listen to us. We sound like a couple of high schoolers."

Sandy said, "He may be older, but we're no spring chickens, either. And it gets lonely as Hell in that big place all by myself."

Their smiles disappeared.

"Still no word from Dan?" Kathy's voice dropped to a near-whisper.

Sandy just shook her head. "It's the not knowing that's the killer. If I just heard *something*, maybe I could move on."

Kathy saw the tears glistening in Sandy's eyes and reached across the table to take her hand.

"Do you think you could poke around a little?" Sandy asked. "You know, do your cop stuff?"

Kathy frowned. *Do I tell her I'm already looking into it? I can't if I find out the worst and she becomes a suspect.*

She shook her head. "Not without an active missing person report. You can file a new one. That would at least get the ball rolling again."

Sandy sat back in the booth and crossed her arms.

"No. He told me he was leaving, so he's not really 'missing', ya know?"

Kathy nodded. "What about finances? Bill collectors might be able to track him down."

Sandy shook her head again. "Everything's in my name. The house, the business, everything except that damn truck. And he took that with him."

She covered her face with her hands and seemed to shrink into the corner of the booth. Kathy saw her shoulders begin to shake, feeling helpless. After a minute of quiet sobs, Sandy got control of her breathing and headed for the Ladies Room.

Kathy pulled out her phone and texted an all-clear to Jan.

38

The house was empty when Jan let himself in. As he entered, his phone buzzed with a text from Kathy confirming that she and Sandy were having dinner at Captain Joe's in nearby Pine Hills.

Plenty of time, then.

He pushed through the kitchen door at the end of the hall and crossed to the locked door that led to Sandy's apartment. With a shaking hand, he tried three times to insert the key in the lock before he managed to turn it. When the door finally swung open, he still hesitated to cross the threshold.

This will make me a criminal, he thought. *This threshold is my Rubicon—a point of no return.*

With a shrug at his own melodrama, he stepped into Sandy's domain. The apartment was a slightly larger version of the suite he occupied upstairs. A sitting room held a television, stereo equipment, and a closed laptop sitting on a rolltop desk. An overstuffed chair and a mismatched loveseat flanked by two end tables made for a tight, cozy arrangement.

Jan went immediately to the desk and tried the drawers. The long top drawer slid open to reveal the standard pens, paper clips, and assorted office supplies.

The top drawer to the right of the knee well, however, was locked. None of the keys that Kathy had given him fit, so he opened the long drawer and took out two thin paperclips. Back in the kitchen, he found a pair of pliers in a cabinet drawer and set about shaping the paperclips into a lock pick set.

Several years before, he attended a security conference in Toronto where he learned the basics of picking simple barrel locks like the one on the desk. He was hoping this one had no more than three pins, since he was long out of practice.

Returning to the desk, he inserted one clip and twisted it slightly to keep tension on the cylinder so friction would hold the pins in place. The other clip, the one with a small hook on the end, he inserted fully and slowly drew it back, feeling for each of the pins. When he felt one, he eased it up into its receiving slot.

On the first attempt, he successfully positioned two pins, but then lost tension on the cylinder. With no friction to hold them in place, the spring-loaded pins dropped out of their slots. The same thing happened on his second and third tries. Finally, despite shaking hands and sweat running into his eyes, he felt the last pin slide into place and the cylinder turn.

Hoping his efforts had not been in vain, he slid open the drawer to find a stack of notebooks. Before touching them, Jan snapped a photo of their positions so he could put them back in exactly the same way. Then he picked up the one on top, which had writing on the cover. The others in the stack were new and unsullied. Opening it, he was disappointed to find nothing but blank pages. Confused, he flipped it closed and looked at the writing on the cover. It was today's date, followed by a dash.

She hasn't started this one yet. Where is the one she was writing in yesterday?

Although he had plenty of time before the women returned from dinner, standing in Sandy's inner sanctum made him decidedly nervous.

As he carefully replaced the notebook and relocked the desk, Jan suddenly felt the temperature in the room climb, and he sensed another presence behind him. Turning slowly, eyes wide with fear, he saw the Nothingness between himself and the door to the kitchen. His eyes darted between the doorframe, which was his only escape route, and the writhing abyssal blackness. That horrible emptiness-which-wasn't stepped closer. With no escape and balanced on the razor's edge between fight and flight, panic and reason, he gathered his courage and stood up straight, turning to fully face Flora's ghost.

"What do you want?" he said with a much firmer voice than he expected.

The spatial emptiness that had once been Flora stood motionless.

"Why are you doing this? Why possess Sandy and terrorize me?"

Slowly, the Nothingness took a step closer, and Jan instinctively stumbled backwards into the desk.

I've got to stand up to her, or she'll consume me.

Gathering his mental strength, he again stood up straight, and when Flora took another halting step toward him, he stood his ground. The heat that radiated from her broke sweat out of every pore of his body, soaking his clothes.

"What do you *want*?" he said, louder this time.

Flora turned the negative space her head occupied toward the desk and pointed. When seen in profile, her non-face was not the statue's ecstatic expression. Neither was it that of the half-finished demon Santori had started, then abandoned. Rather, it was the childlike face of an innocent angel—Santori's first attempt.

Jan turned to look where she pointed, and realization dawned.

"The notebook?"

Flora folded her hands and bowed her head.

Is she praying? No! She's reading.

"You want me to read it?" The heat that had threatened to burn him a moment before became a welcoming, comforting warmth that enveloped him and somehow relieved his fear.

"But this one is empty. Where are the others?"

Then, without turning within our three-dimensional world, the Nothingness folded in upon itself and a different figure emerged from the abyss. It wore Santori's demon face, a snarling three-dimensional silhouette. Heat exploded from the figure, and Jan was forced back a step. The sweat that had drenched his face a moment before evaporated in a flash, and he felt his skin begin to pucker.

Demon Flora stepped closer, but she halted mid-step and screamed in anger. Her demon persona retracted, snarling, and Angel Flora reemerged. The struggle between Flora's two manifestations continued for a few seconds, as they flickered in and out of existence. With each turn, the temperature in the room rose, forcing Jan to retreat further until he was bent backwards over the desk. With every blink, his eyelids felt like sandpaper on his eyes, and his lips cracked and split from the heat.

Then, as quickly as the struggle began, it ended and Jan recognized the figure occupying the space before him as the angelic back of the statue, complete with flower garland and folded wings. Angel Flora then opened her arms in a protective gesture, and with her gown flowing down to the ground, she left the apartment. Taking his cue, Jan followed her into the kitchen where she paused by the basement door, then flowed through it.

I'm not following you down there, Sister.

After quickly relocking the apartment door, he ran for the relative safety of his suite.

39

Friday, Late Spring

"Why are you still sleeping there?" Kathy said. "I'd be on my way back to Philly by now."

"That's just it. Last night was the best night's sleep I've had since I arrived."

Jan had just finished relating the previous evening's clandestine, yet fruitless, snooping and his encounter with Flora over lunch in the Tavern.

"Wouldn't matter to me." Kathy bit down on her burger and a drop of ketchup stuck to her chin. "So, you actually think Flora's ghost has a good side?"

Jan nodded and pointed to his own chin, but she didn't notice.

"I do. She transformed from a menacing demon to a protective angel right before my eyes. I feel like she's watching over me or something."

Kathy looked unconvinced. "I think you're giving her way too much credit. One night's sleep versus everything else she's done? Doesn't seem to balance out to me."

"Maybe not."

This time, he pointed at her chin.

"But now that you mention 'balance,' I think there are two sides to Flora, kind of like two personalities."

225

He waggled his finger at her chin again.

"You mean like schizoid? A ghost with multiple personality disorder?"

He picked up Kathy's napkin off the table and handed it to her.

"Wipe your chin. God, you're a slob."

"Jeez, OK, *Dad*."

Jan shook his head in exasperation. "Anyway, I saw her switch back and forth between Angel Flora and Demon Flora until Angel Flora won out."

Kathy considered this while she swigged her beer. "You need to be careful. Why would Angel Flora have this change of heart?"

"Good question, but I think it was because she truly wants me to read her journal. Why else would she hold off Demon Flora, especially when I was violating Sandy's personal space?"

"That's harsh." Kathy scowled at him. "But true, I suppose. And the difference last night, of course, was that Sandy was with me."

"Ah, right. Any sign of Flora on your side of things?" Kathy shook her head. "So, we can check that off. Flora can't leave the House."

"I think it's more than that. Flora should have been pissed at you. You were looking for her secret journals, for God's sake."

"She wanted me to read them."

"Maybe last night she did, but not the other night when she was writing in one."

Jan was silent for a moment. "You remember how you felt when Flora kicked you out of Sandy's bed?" Kathy nodded. "What I felt last night was exactly the opposite. As terrifying as Demon Flora is, Angel Flora is just as comforting."

"You're talking about two different—things? Entities? Spooks?"

Jan shrugged. "Don't overthink it. Flora is clearly not of this world. The way she turned from front to back was like ... I don't know ... like she was a three-dimensional shadow of a four-dimensional thing."

Kathy looked confused, so Jan pushed his plate to the side.

"Think of shadow puppets."

He held his hand over the table, palm-down and fingers splayed.

"Your three-dimensional hand makes a two-dimensional shadow. As you move your hand—"

He rotated his hand until the shadow became a line, then he turned it palm-up and closed his fingers.

"—the shadow shrinks and grows and changes. If my hand had four dimensions, its shadow would have three dimensions, like Flora."

"I get it."

Kathy held up her own hand, palm facing Jan.

"Angel Flora is like the front of your hand."

She flipped her hand around with just her middle finger extended.

"And Demon Flora is like the back."

Jan smiled, proud that his explanation was clear and impressed that Kathy understood it so quickly. She wasn't finished, though.

"So, what happens when they come together?"

She formed a fist and slammed it down on the table, making their beer glasses jump.

"I take your point. Let's just hope that doesn't happen."

"You have to do more than hope." She dropped her voice. "Don't get attached to this Angel Flora. We can't trust her."

Jan nodded and they both silently drank their beers. Around a mouthful of club sandwich, he asked, "Did you have any luck finding Dan?"

Kathy frowned and set her beer glass down.

"Nothing positive, only negative results."

She ticked them off on her fingers.

"No credit card activity, no phone activity, no use of his Easy Pass on any toll roads, no traffic stops, and no reports of his truck being abandoned."

"Airports?"

Kathy shook her head. "I could only check with airports in the state, but no, nothing."

"I guess he could have kept to back roads and gone completely off-grid."

"But why? Who would he be running from? Not Flora. She can't leave the House, apparently."

"That leaves Sandy," he said. "She's the key."

Kathy stared into her empty beer glass. "Maybe he didn't leave at all."

"Don't think I haven't considered that."

"Maybe we should do more than just consider it. Maybe we should investigate the possibility that Dan never left the House, that he—or his body—is still there."

They both were leaning across the table, voices barely above a whisper. Jan sat back in the wooden booth and swirled the last swallow of beer in his glass. He wasn't sure he wanted to hear the answer to his next question, but he asked it anyway.

"And how do you propose we do that?"

"You're staying there. Snoop around."

"Looking for what? I'm not a detective. I can't even write a detective story, let alone be in one. You're the one who wants to be a detective."

He didn't mean to hurt her feelings, but he could see his words really touched a nerve.

"Sorry. I didn't mean…"

She gave an annoyed shake of her head.

"I can't go snooping around the House without probable cause and a search warrant."

"And what will you be doing while I'm risking life and limb from a possessed murderer and her malevolent ghost?" Kathy looked startled. "Don't look so shocked. That is what we're talking about, right? If Dan didn't leave Mackey House and his truck is nowhere to be found, there's only one conclusion you can draw."

Kathy nodded slowly. "She must have killed him and disposed of the truck."

"So, I ask again: what will *you* be doing?"

Kathy met his eyes, and a tone of resolve filled her voice.

"I'm going to do my own 'snooping,'" she said.

40

Saturday, Late Spring

"You look like hell," Sandy said as Jan sat down to breakfast.

"Good morning to you, too. Cut me a break. I was up all night working."

Sandy slid an omelet out of the pan she carried onto his plate.

"Making progress?"

"I am. It's turning out to be a very interesting story. A tragedy, really."

"Yeah, there's a lot of that going around."

Her tone of voice encouraged him to ask a question he never would have asked her before this trip.

"Are you going to be able to keep this place? With so little income coming in? How are you paying the mortgage?"

He stopped, afraid he had strayed too far into the personal.

"I know it's none of my business, and if I'm prying, just tell me to butt out."

He hesitated. The fact he had betrayed her trust by breaking into her apartment had him feeling awkward.

Sandy didn't seem to notice, though, as she shook her head.

"It's OK. I know you care about me, and I appreciate that."

She reached across the table and squeezed his hand.

"There is no mortgage, actually. I own the place outright."

Jan looked up, surprised. Sandy smiled and continued,

"I inherited it from my mother. I never knew she owned this place the whole time we lived across the street. She inherited it from her grandmother, who inherited it from Ephraim Mackey himself." She sipped her coffee. "I should say that there isn't a mortgage *anymore*. Dan and I took a loan to rehab the house when we decided to move up here. Business was so good for the first ten years that we were able to pay it off just last year and put away a nice nest egg." She paused a moment, lost in thought. "That won't last forever, though."

Her voice trailed off, and they ate in silence for a few minutes.

"What are your plans for today?" she asked when they had finished eating and were sipping fresh cups of coffee.

"I'm going to bed," he said, then eyed his coffee mug and set it down. "And you?"

"Not much. I have some errands to run and some shopping to do. I'll be gone most of the day, so it should be quiet around here."

Jan carried his dishes into the kitchen, then nodded toward the apartment door.

"Why do you live back here when you have the whole rest of the house?"

Sandy's expression said the answer was obvious.

"Most of the time, the rest of the house is full. Or at least it used to be."

She handed Jan a towel as she started washing their dishes.

"Here, make yourself useful."

"So, Ephraim must not have had any family of his own if he left this house to your great-grandmother."

Sandy nodded and handed him a plate.

"But nobody before me wanted it. Too many … memories, I guess."

Jan had the distinct impression she was going to use a different word. *Ghosts* perhaps?

"Anyway, that's why it sat empty for so long until Dan and I moved in."

A few minutes later, Sandy rinsed the suds off the last dish and handed it to Dan to dry. As he turned to stack it in the cupboard, he felt Sandy's hands slide around his neck. He froze for a moment, unsure whether they would tighten across his throat. He turned within the ring of her arms, and Sandy pressed her body against his, setting off that now-familiar tug-of-war between rational thought and irrational desire.

"I need to go to bed," he said as he inhaled the intoxicating scent of her hair.

She turned her face up to meet his, their lips only inches apart.

"May I join you?" she whispered.

All resistance crumbled when he saw the desire in her eyes matched his own. She placed her hand on the back of his head as if to keep him from running away again, but instead, he met her open mouth with his own.

Sandy pulled him into her apartment, as Jan's performance anxiety, born of years of celibacy, set in.

Things had better work down there. But not too fast!

They tore at each other's shirts, dropping them in a trail through the sitting room.

Shit. Nothing's happening.

Their mouths were locked together, their tongues dueling, while they stumbled into her bedroom.

Come on, damn it. This is what I've been dreaming about.

With a shove, Sandy pushed him down on the bed and, reaching behind her back, unsnapped her bra. Jan's mouth opened and his tongue touched his lower lip. Stepping out of her shoes, Sandy slid her jeans over her hips and down her legs. When she kicked them free, she hooked her thumbs in the waistband of her panties and slowly slid them off.

Jan tried to wet his lips and reach for her perfect breasts as she bent forward, but she caught his wrists and pinned them to the bed as she knelt between his legs. Instead of excitement, though, he felt a debilitating fear.

Oh my God. She's going down on me and I'm as limp as that dish towel.

His heart pounded as Sandy undid his belt and fly and yanked his own jeans down to his ankles. Before she bent her head down, though, she met his eyes. Instead of a look of disappointment or the emasculating sneer he expected, her eyes burned with a black fire, and he saw Angel Flora embracing her. His eyes darting between Flora and Sandy, he gave in to the ultimate temptation and nodded. Sandy opened her mouth as Flora flowed into her.

She gasped, and the heat of her breath accomplished what no amount of kisses alone could. His erection strained against his boxers.

41

Jan awoke to the insistent buzzing of his cell phone. Momentarily disoriented, he realized he was alone in Sandy's bed. Pushing aside thoughts of what happened there, he searched the pile of clothes on the floor for his phone. The buzzing stopped before he found it and he saw three, now four, missed calls and six texts from Kathy.

Shit, it's 3:30 in the afternoon.

Hitting redial, memories of that morning came flooding back, but he pushed them away again when Kathy's shouting voice came through.

"Where the hell have you been? I've been trying to reach you for over an hour."

"Sorry, sorry. I was sleeping dead to the world since I was up all night."

He tucked the phone between his ear and shoulder as he started to get dressed.

"What's up?"

There was only silence from Kathy's end of the connection for several seconds.

Finally, she said in a deliberately calm voice, "Meet me at the Tavern. We need to talk."

The beep when she hung up felt like she had slammed a landline phone into its cradle.

Jan would have preferred meeting over coffee, but Kathy hadn't given him a chance to object. He asked for coffee when he got to the Tavern, but Lloyd made a face and told him it had been cooking all day. He ordered Maker's and water instead and made his way to Kathy who sat at a table in the corner behind a tall glass of amber Lager.

"Don't you ever work?" he joked when he sat down.

She didn't smile. "I told you, I'm … on leave this week."

"Oh. Sorry I didn't answer. I, ah, went to bed after breakfast."

She eyed him for a second. Suspicion was obvious on her face.

"Right. Whatever." Her eyes bore into his. "I think you lied to me."

"I didn't lie to you. About what?"

"About not finding anything in her apartment. I think you found something that incriminates Sandy."

"What the hell are you talking about? Why would I lie about that?"

"Why would she hide her latest journal?"

"Maybe she filled up the latest one, or maybe she doesn't want a confession written in her own hand read in court."

"I hadn't thought of that.

Jan frowned. "Still, I find it hard to believe that she could have done anything to Dan."

"Killed him, you mean." He looked startled. She continued, "There's no sense sugar-coating it. If she 'could have done anything' to him, that 'anything' would be killing him."

"She still loves him, though."

Sandy shrugged. "Is that lost love or guilty regret?"

Jan shook his head, and his words came out harsh. "I don't believe it. She's too gentle, too nice—"

"I spoke with her earlier today. About you."

"Oh?" Jan didn't like the idea of these two women talking about him.

"Yeah. She was … chipper. In better spirits than I've seen her in months. Practically glowing. She wouldn't stop talking about you. How gentle and kind you are."

Kathy's eyes flashed with anger.

"You slept with her, didn't you?"

Jan tried to sink back through the wood of the booth. He knew she would see through a lie.

"We're both adults. She's thirty-six, for Christ's sake."

He could feel his own anger rising. Kathy slapped the table, making their glasses jump.

"I told you what I would do."

"You'd better do it to her first because she was a very willing participant. And to yourself, too."

As the words left his mouth, he mentally tried to grab them and shove them back in. Kathy's reaction was immediate. With a quick swat, she backhanded her half-full beer into his lap.

His testicles retreated from the cold wetness, and he started to protest, but she was already on her way to the door. As he gingerly followed her out, Lloyd threw him a fresh bar towel.

"Keep your car from smelling like beer," he said with the hint of a smile on his careworn face.

I guess this isn't the first time he's seen that, Jan thought.

42

When Jan arrived back at the Mackey House, Sandy was nowhere to be found.

She did say she would be gone all day, he thought, *but that was before…*

But he still wasn't ready to process what had happened that morning.

After rinsing the beer out of his shirt, jeans and underwear, he showered and tried to objectively assess the last few hours. He'd broken his pledge to both Kathy and to himself and had taken advantage of Sandy's fragile state—.

No, that's bullshit. If she was in a fragile state, I'd hate to see her at full strength.

There was no sign of either version of Flora when he came downstairs. Standing in the empty parlor, he took a moment to gather his thoughts. What had been a pretty boring life of emotional solitude had become, over the last few days, a whirlwind of conflicting emotions.

Where is this relationship with Sandy going? Could it be long term? If so, would I somehow be cheating on Dan? Or on his memory? And if he is dead, did I just sleep with his killer? Shouldn't I care more about whether he's dead or alive? But I believe Sandy. He just dropped everything and took off. At least I want to believe her. Because if she is a killer, I've put myself in a very bad spot.

He started pacing back and forth in front of the fireplace.

And that's just the Sandy side of what my life has become. Then there's Kathy. Smart, witty, no-nonsense. I like her a lot, in an intellectual partner kind of way. But now she's pissed—jealous, maybe. How do I make it up to her? Win her over again? She really wants to find Dan, and she asked me to keep snooping around.

He felt the extra keyring in his jacket pocket.

Maybe if I find some clues ... the garage. Dan spent a lot of time out there. Maybe he left a note or something.

The question of Dan's disappearance burned like a beacon in his mind.

Yeah, that's the key. Finding evidence to vindicate Sandy will get me back in Kathy's good graces. And ease this guilt I'm feeling. He abandoned Sandy, so he doesn't deserve her anymore.

Nodding, he headed for the door.

He crossed the backyard to the large outbuilding that was the house's garage, and using a key stamped with the word "Master", he popped open the heavy padlock with a satisfying click. Opening the door just enough to slip through, he stepped inside the dimly lit interior. Double windows were set in both side walls, but the sun, hidden behind the house, did little to light the space.

Pulling the door shut behind him, Jan turned on his phone's video recorder so he could reexamine the space later. The app helpfully lit the flashlight function as well, so, with glaringly bright phone in hand, he started scanning.

The area for the missing truck was obvious, just inside the two large doors. Even though the interior was big enough to hold both Dan's pickup and Sandy's car, the couple's "toys" occupied the second bay. Two kayaks hung upside down from the rafters just above head-height. Below them, at the front of the garage, sat Sandy's ATV and Dan's dirt bike. Beyond them, deeper into the gloom, a bass boat sat on its trailer.

The walls were hung with ladders, a chainsaw, shovels, and various other tools. Two large hooks spaced about six feet apart stood empty.

Jan shone the phone into each of the kayaks, looking for blood or other clues, but they were clean, which wasn't surprising since he remembered how meticulous Dan was about cleaning off the gear before stowing it.

The dirt bike was similarly clean, its scratched paint more a badge of honor than a blemish. The condition of the ATV, on the other hand, made him pause. Dried mud was caked between the deep treads of the tires and splattered across its fenders. It had clearly been "ridden hard and put up wet," as his uncle used to say about his horses.

Jan was kneeling down, scanning the mud that had pooled beneath the ATV, when headlights flashed across the window facing the house.

Crap. Sandy's back.

Dousing his light, he scrambled to the door, but not quickly enough. Bright light streamed through the crack between the doors and the cement floor. In his mind's eye, Jan could see the big padlock hanging uselessly open from the lock's staple loop. Crouching by the side wall, he desperately looked for a place to hide.

The bass boat.

Its low sides wouldn't provide much cover, but he might avoid being detected by a cursory search.

He started duck-walking along the wall until he reached the windows. Torn between curiosity and fear of being caught, he peeked out the window when he heard a car door slam, followed by a string of muttered curses. He felt relief mixed with pangs of guilt when he saw Sandy crossing the backyard, struggling with armloads of grocery bags.

Returning to the front of the garage, Jan waited until he heard the kitchen door close, then he slipped out and turned to close the hasp and snap the Master lock shut. Thinking he had avoided being caught, another set of headlights turning into the driveway suddenly bathed him in their glare. His mind raced, yet his body remained frozen as the headlights kicked up to high beams, pinning him like a butterfly in a shadowbox.

Turning slowly and shielding his eyes, he was not at all surprised to hear Kathy's voice mutter, "Asshole." Then the lights turned off, leaving his eyes dazzled in the gathering darkness.

"What the fuck are you doin'?" she whispered, though her tone sounded more like a disappointed drill sergeant.

"What do you think I'm doing? I'm snooping around like you told me to."

"But I told you that before, before—"

"Before I slept with your girlfriend?"

The truth of Jan's angry response struck them both like a slap to the face.

Neither spoke for a moment, then Kathy said, "I have to get inside. Give me back my keys."

She held out her hand.

"No," is all he said in response as he walked down the driveway.

***

Twenty minutes later, Jan walked through the front door. Kathy and Sandy sat in the parlor, wine glasses in hand. He stood in the archway and repeated what he had said the last time they met in the Tavern.

"Don't you ever work?" He wore a smile, but there was no hint of humor in his voice.

"Jan, that's rude!" Sandy said.

"Oh, that's alright," Kathy interrupted, her voice tinged with sarcasm. "I could ask you the same thing, Mr. Writer Man. Where were you, and what were you doing there?"

"If you must know, I was taking a walk to work some things out in my head."

He hoped the honesty of this statement rang true. Sandy practically jumped from her chair and started for the kitchen.

"Well, you're here now. Come and sit down while I get you a wine glass."

She stopped and turned back.

"Or, would you like a bourbon? I got some of that today, too."

"Wine is fine, thanks," he said as he sat on the small couch that faced the fireplace.

"You need to give me those keys," Kathy whispered.

"Or what, you'll arrest me? But I don't suppose you want a police record of where I got them, do you?"

Kathy remained silent until Sandy returned from the kitchen with a full glass and a newly opened bottle of Syrah.

"There wasn't much left in the other bottle, so …"

She shrugged and sat on the couch next to Jan.

"Good, we're gonna need it," Kathy said.

"*Vino veritas*," Jan responded, lifting his glass in salute.

43

The rest of the evening was awkward at best, though Sandy seemed oblivious to the occasional sarcastic barbs and equally sharp retorts between her two guests. These flare-ups were usually precipitated by the increasingly intimate positions Sandy wiggled herself into, progressing from simply sharing the couch, through holding hands, and ending with Sandy fast asleep with her head in Jan's lap.

"I'm going," Kathy said. "I feel like I'm watching two high school kids."

There was no humor in her voice. Jan, who was himself conflicted by Sandy's escalating attentions, shook his head.

He mouthed, "We need to talk."

Kathy pointedly looked at Sandy and gave him a questioning scowl. In response, he lifted Sandy to a sitting position, awakening her.

"Hey," he said, "it's time for you to go to bed."

Barely opening her eyes, she whispered, "Will you join me?"

"Not tonight. Kathy's going to put you to bed."

Looking surprised but relieved, Kathy stood and helped Sandy to her feet.

"Come on, love. Time to hit the hay."

When Kathy returned ten minutes later, Jan handed her a full glass of wine. They sat in two chairs that flanked the front bay window, as far from the apartment as they could get. Kathy's hand shook when she took the glass and she immediately swallowed half of it. That's when Jan realized how pale she was.

"Which one was it, Angel or Demon?"

Kathy looked at him. "How did you know?"

He pointed to the wine sloshing in her glass, and she nodded.

"I felt her as soon as we got in the bedroom. It was Angel Flora, as you described her, 'a comforting warmth'. She stayed away from me, so I didn't feel afraid at all."

The sarcasm in her voice broke the tension, and they both chuckled.

"Anyway, she just hung out until Sandy undressed and got into bed. Then the strangest thing happened. I could have sworn Sandy fell right asleep, but as I turned to leave, she reached her arms up like she … I don't know, like maybe she wanted me to stay." Kathy blushed a little. "I was about to tell her, 'not tonight,' when Flora walked over and 'covered' her."

"Was she in pain?"

Kathy shook her head. "No, not at all. She had a blissful smile on her face, so I left them together. I'm not sure I should have, though."

Jan raised a questioning eyebrow.

"No, I didn't want a three-some with a ghost. Like you had. No thank you."

Jan chuckled, but then his mouth formed a worried frown.

"Yeah, I guess I did." Then, he shook his head and came back to the present. "Look, I know you think Sandy is this fragile shrinking violet or something, and that I somehow took advantage of her vulnerability."

Kathy started to protest, but Jan plowed on.

"But we're both adults. I'm older, for sure, but she isn't a debutante, either."

"You're old enough to be her father," she hissed.

"Maybe if I had gotten her mother pregnant in junior high school! But I didn't, and now she's a thirty-something woman who can make her own decisions."

"A thirty-something *married* woman," Kathy shot back, then stopped with her mouth open.

"Yeah, but that didn't stop *you,* did it?"

She clamped her mouth shut, so he continued. "Maybe we both took advantage of a situation, but that doesn't mean we took advantage of Sandy."

Kathy frowned but kept quiet.

Jan resumed in an even voice. "You do raise an interesting question, though. Namely, is she still a married woman? Or has she passed into widowhood?"

Kathy looked to be absorbing and processing Jan's words for a moment.

"So that's why you were in the garage. Find anything interesting?"

"I don't know. Maybe. We should watch the video."

"You took video? How could you be so stupid? What, so there wouldn't have to be a trial if you were caught?"

Jan's mouth flapped like a caught bass, which made Kathy laugh out loud. After a second or two, he joined in.

When they quieted down, Kathy said, "OK, show me the evidence," which set her off on another round of giggles.

When the video ended, Jan said, "I didn't get a chance to check out the boat, but I didn't, you know, smell anything."

"Yeah, if there was a body in there, it would be pretty ripe four months on. It might have been frozen for a while, but you'd've been able to smell it outside long before now. I had a call once, where I responded to a report of a foul smell at a house where this old guy lived alone--"

"Stop." Jan shuddered. "Let's stick to the point."

Kathy smiled at having scored a point and resolved to play the Gross Out game again sometime.

"Right. Anyway, you spent a lot of time looking at Sandy's four-wheeler. How come?"

"It's covered in mud."

"So?"

"Dan was a stickler for cleaning up his gear after using it. Everything else in there was sparkling."

Kathy nodded. "True. I saw him wash everything down many times. Maybe Sandy took it out on her own?"

The questioning tone of voice told Jan she didn't believe that either.

"Where? She couldn't get to any trails without the pickup to carry the ATV."

"People ride them on the roads around here all the time."

Jan shook his head. "I don't believe it. I bet she hasn't done anything fun, especially by herself, since Dan disappeared."

He had almost said "since Dan was killed," and it gave him pause when he realized his subconscious had already come to that conclusion.

Kathy apparently wasn't there yet, though.

"Mud on a four-wheeler isn't evidence of anything other than that it was used to do what it was made for—riding around in the mud. Maybe one of the guests took it out."

Jan was running the video again, and he paused it at a point when he had swung the camera past a shelf in the corner.

"What guests? Besides, would you let a stranger take your ATV up into the mountains alone? Something tells me my liability insurance wouldn't cover that." Kathy sat quietly. "Besides," he continued, "look."

He zoomed the picture until the fuzzy image of two helmets filled the screen. The black one was clean like the other items except the ATV and reflected the phone's light back at the camera. The other one, white with pink stripes, was splattered with mud.

"OK, so Sandy took the ATV out and didn't clean it up afterwards."

Jan panned the picture down to where a motocross-style jumpsuit lay crumpled on the floor. It, too, was covered with dried mud.

The apparent disregard for Sandy's cute jumpsuit must have tipped the scale for Kathy.

"So, Sandy went four-wheelin' somewhere and was either very preoccupied or in a hell of a hurry when she got back."

The implication hung in the air between them. Jan finally found his voice.

"Maybe to dispose of something?"

"You mean a body, right? You think she used a four-wheeler to dispose of Dan's body?"

When Jan thought of the logistics involved, he couldn't see anybody slinging a grown man's body across the back of the ATV when there was a perfectly good truck parked in the garage. That just didn't make any sense.

"I take your point," he said. "Just another bizarre mystery around here."

"There's way too many of them," Kathy agreed. "And we keep coming up with new ones."

Jan looked at his watch and was shocked to see it was well past midnight.

"You never answered my question."

Kathy stifled a yawn. "What question?"

Jan grinned. "Don't you ever work?"

Kathy looked annoyed. "That joke's gotten very old. Besides, it's the slow season and I have a shitload of leave accumulated, so I'm officially on vacation."

"Nice." He pointedly looked at his watch again. "Well, I'm officially exhausted."

Then he got serious and looked her in the eye.

"So, are we good?"

He held out his hand. Kathy looked down at it, then met his eyes.

"Yeah, we're good."

She grasped his hand and gave it a firm shake.

44

Instead of heading straight home to her apartment in Dundee, Kathy turned off the main road and drove into the mountains, making random turns. She couldn't get lost on these roads, since she patrolled them every day, and driving randomly with no destination in mind often cleared her head. But on that night, the sun was peeking over the horizon before she regained her mental balance and certain things clicked into place.

Yawning, and ready to head home and get some sleep, Kathy looked around, trying to get her bearings. She had been driving mindlessly for so long, hours actually, that she didn't remember all the turns she'd made.

The fog that had settled across the landscape obscured any obvious landmarks, making it hard for her to recognize exactly where she was. Feeling a bit embarrassed that she could get lost on back roads she had patrolled thousands of times, she pulled to the side of the road and opened her Map app. While it synced with the GPS satellites, she gazed out of her open window.

The road followed the crest of a ridge, which separated two farm fields just starting to show green sprouts—corn on one side and what looked to be soybeans on the other. The fields each ran down gentle slopes to lakes nestled in small valleys.

That part of the country, the Pocono Mountains of Pennsylvania, is famous for its ski slopes, honeymoon resorts, and outdoor activities. Lesser known are its hundreds of lakes, which are among the deepest in eastern North America—deep clefts left behind when the glaciers of the last ice receded.

As Kathy sat watching, a light breeze whipped at the fog, shredding it and sending its tendrils adrift on the promise of a warm spring day.

The rising sun painted the few puffy clouds on the horizon a fiery, angry red and their reflections on the lake to her right wavered and flickered with the breeze-driven ripples.

She remembered herself as a child running downhill toward a cold mountain lake just like that one. Enjoying the memory and letting her mind go where it wished, she suddenly was not running, but driving down the long slope, picking up more and more speed. Then she was no longer driving. Instead, she stood on a bluff and watched a blue pickup leap from a short cliff and swan dive into the lake.

Of course.

45

Sunday, Late Spring

"There're a lotta lakes." Jan was less than enthusiastic about Kathy's brainstorm. "It would take the National Guard to search them all."

He swirled the coffee in his cup.

"Well, maybe somebody saw or heard something. It's worth checking for noise complaints, or other police reports like that."

"Do you have access to those reports, *Deputy* Jensen?"

Kathy's face flushed, but she kept her voice neutral.

"I didn't want to say anything, because nothin' will come of it, probably."

"Nothing will come of what?"

"Well, I'm officially investigating Dan's disappearance—on a provisional basis. If I can find him, or find out what happened to him, the Sheriff will recommend me for detective."

Jan's face broke into a wide smile.

"That's fantastic. How can I help?"

Kathy smiled back at him. "I have a lead to follow up. I spotted something in your breaking-and-entering video."

Jan interrupted. "I looked it up. It's not breaking and entering if you're given a key."

"But Sandy didn't give it to you."

He just spread his arms, and she shrugged.

"Whatever. When I first watched it, nothing clicked, but now that I've thought about it, I'm positive."

"Positive of what?"

"Bring up the video," she said.

Jan duly started the video playing on his laptop. After about two minutes, she said, "There."

He hit pause on the wide shot, scanning across the interior of the garage.

"Yup, that's what I thought," she said.

"What are you talking about?"

In contrast to his growing frustration, Kathy seemed to enjoy knowing something he didn't.

"Look closely at the wall on the left."

"I don't see anything suspicious. Just tell me, dammit."

"That's just it," she said triumphantly. "It's what you can't see that's important."

Frowning, Jan leaned forward and scanned the image for something missing. Suddenly, he sat back in his chair.

"The ramp." He turned to face her. "The ramp is missing."

"You got it."

Jan flashed back to the time last fall when he went four-wheeling with Dan. They had loaded the ATV and dirt bike into the back of his pickup using a four-foot-wide ramp that hooked onto the tailgate. It was impossible to get the vehicles into or out of the truck without it. Dan kept it hanging on two large hooks screwed into the wall of the garage. Those hooks were empty in the video.

"Dan sure as hell wouldn't have taken the ramp and left his bike."

Kathy touched a finger to her nose. "Damn right." She waved at the video. "This whole scene makes sense now."

Jan let his subconscious process what he was looking at. When the pieces clicked into place, he ticked them off on his fingers.

"Somebody loaded up the ATV and the ramp, drove the truck somewhere remote, unloaded the ATV, left the truck and the ramp, and then they rode the ATV back here."

Kathy, who nodded her head at every step of Jan's explanation, shook her head when he finished.

"She. You said, 'they rode the ATV back here.' You should have said 'she' rode it."

Jan started to protest, but Kathy zipped the video forward to the closeup of the muddy helmet and jumpsuit.

"That's why I have to search the lakes around here. Find the truck, and I'll find Dan."

46

Jan returned to Mackey House in the late afternoon. The abnormal quiet that he had come to expect this trip was broken by tapping and scraping. The occasional high-pitched curse filtering up through the floorboards from the basement along with what sounded like muffled conversation. It struck Jan that he had never been in the basement, and he added it to his mental list of places to snoop around.

As he listened, he slowly crept down the hall, careful to avoid the squeaky middle. When he reached the kitchen, though, the century-old floorboards voiced their inevitable protest. He froze, listening for an interruption in the ongoing dialog down below.

The basement door was just inside the kitchen to his right. It was closed, but as he leaned close, the voices got louder and their tone grew angrier, but the words were still indistinct. The timbres were distinct, however. The voice uttering a stream of curses was clearly Sandy's.

The other voice, though, sent a jolt of fear down his spine. He heard that voice before, commanding him to "Get out." This time, it clearly directed its anger at Sandy, who pleaded with the monster that had possessed her.

Protectiveness for his murder-suspect lover won out over the terror that voice produced in him. He grabbed the doorknob, but reflexively yanked his hand back. The knob was hot and the pads at the base of his fingers throbbed.

The voices below dropped in volume, but using a dish towel, he threw open the door, anyway. The hauntingly familiar extra-dimensional emptiness of Flora met him. The void that should have been her figure stood just inside the doorway, facing the deeper region of the basement. She spread her arms wide. Her position and the gentle warmth she radiated identified the apparition as Angel Flora.

Jan, even more conflicted, took a tentative step forward, but Angel Flora reacted immediately. The heat, which a second before was a comforting, gentle warmth, grew in intensity. It forced him backwards, and his stumble causing the floorboard behind him to shriek. The muttering in the basement abruptly stopped.

Caught snooping, Jan called out, "Hello. Sandy, are you down there?"

His mind searched desperately for a reason to be in the kitchen, calling out to her.

"Yes, Jan. What do you want?"

Deciding to stick as close to the truth as possible, he stepped forward to the top of the stairs. Flora was nowhere to be seen, though her warmth lingered.

"I heard voices and swearing. Are you all right?"

Sandy's voice softened. "Yes, yes, I'm OK. I was just talking to myself."

"Sounded like you were struggling with something. Can I help?"

He stepped down onto the first step.

"No, no. I'm just finishing up. I'll be up in a minute."

"Don't rush on my account. I just wanted to make sure you were safe, that's all."

"It's all good. See you at dinner."

Since it was clear she didn't want him in the basement, he left the kitchen and made his way upstairs, stepping on as many squeaky floorboards as he could. Back in his suite, he wrapped his hand in a wet washcloth, poured himself a bourbon, and went out onto the porch.

Why am I still here? I haven't written a word since I've been here. Instead, I've been breaking and entering and fucking my friend's wife. I'm sharing a house with a schizoid ghost who routinely possesses my—girlfriend? Lover? Is that what Sandy is? And oh, yeah, she might have murdered her husband. Jesus, what a mess.

The notion that Dan might have dropped everything and taken off for parts unknown, leaving everything but his pickup truck behind, made a lot more sense to Jan.

Standing at the porch railing with these thoughts swirling through his head, he looked across the road to the empty overgrown lot where Sandy's childhood house once stood. Here and there, he could see parts of the house's foundation peeking through the weeds and brush.

In his mind's eye, he pictured a small cottage—a Cape Cod—standing there. A rope-and-board swing hung from the large oak tree that still stood on the property, just high enough off the ground for a small child to climb onto. He could see Sandy, her blonde hair pulled back in a cute ponytail, kicking herself higher and higher until the ropes went slack at the top of her arc, then snapped taut again.

The swing stopped and the girl in his vision stood and changed from Sandy to a young woman, taller, with darker hair and hardened features. She looked to be perhaps sixteen or seventeen. Still recognizable as Sandy's kin, she stared at Mackey House with hatred in her eyes, mouthing silent curses. The family resemblance was distinct, and Jan knew this must be Sandy's grandmother, Flora's sister.

Something behind her caught her attention, and she turned to face the cottage. As she did, Jan could see the baby bump that would become Sandy's mother. Hands curled into fists at her sides, her body shook with vehemence as she silently shouted at an older woman standing in the cottage doorway. Though no more than forty years old, she looked careworn and profoundly sad. Flora's mother weathered the storm of her daughter's verbal onslaught, with no reaction other than a deepening frown. The younger mother-to-be stomped off, disappearing into the gathering mist.

Then movement on the Mackey House front lawn caught Jan's eye as the statue came to life and reached out to the cottage like a child wanting to be lifted into her mother's arms. Jan felt an overwhelming sense of loss and longing radiating from her—the loss of youth and her life's potential, and a longing for the touch of family. Underneath it all, though, he also felt her dark need for vengeance.

Flora's mother broke from the doorway and ran across the cottage's front yard, but at the edge of the property, directly across the road from Flora's pleading statue, she stopped, unable to take another step. The two figures, mother and daughter, faced each other across an impenetrable barrier, a gap deeper than any physical chasm, forever unable to assuage their grief, desperate for a resolution to their eternal torment.

The moment, frozen in time for a full minute, was shattered by a delivery truck passing along the road, its engine revving and gears grinding. With the spell broken, Jan shook his head and wiped away the tears that had escaped his eyes and run freely down his cheeks.

That's why I'm still here.

47

"What were you working on in the basement?" Jan asked as he and Sandy ate dinner.

She glanced at him, then quickly looked back down at her plate.

"Nothing, really. Just trying to clean out some of the rooms down there."

"Rooms?"

She set her fork down and wiped her mouth.

"Oh, yes. Back when the Hotel stood here, the kitchen, pantry, workrooms, and storage rooms were down there."

"And the servants' quarters, too, I guess."

Jan's casual tone tried to cover the meaning of his question. Sandy fidgeted with her hair, tucking a stray lock behind an ear, before she answered.

Shaking her head, she said, "They weren't under where the House is now. The Hotel extended further out toward the road. Ephraim Mackey filled them in when the House was built."

Her voice trailed off at the end as she looked down at her plate again. The fork stayed on the table and her fingers tried again in vain to tame her wayward hair.

"So, like where the statue stands?"

Again, he tried to keep his voice conversational, afraid anything that sounded like an interrogation would shut Sandy down. He was afraid he had pushed too far when he saw her eyes widen and her hand, which still played with her hair, freeze.

To his relief, though, her face relaxed, and she lowered her hand to the table.

"Actually, legend says the statue stands directly above the spot where Flora, the young maid, died."

"That's a fitting tribute, I suppose."

Sandy frowned. "Pretty morbid, if you ask me."

"Especially since her mother moved in right across the street."

Jan said this quietly, but watched Sandy's reaction carefully. Her voice hardened.

"I see you've done your research. Why don't you tell me what stories the local gossips have told you, and I'll tell you what the real truth is."

Her eyes bored into his until he nodded.

"OK. I'd like to hear the details from you."

He took a deep breath, hoping to break the tension, but Sandy continued to stare.

"I only know the story in broad brush strokes. After the Hotel burned and the maid, Flora, died, Ephraim Mackey built this house on the hotel's foundation." He paused. "But not on the whole foundation, apparently. A couple years after the house was built, he hired an Italian sculptor to create a monument to Flora, which is what stands on your lawn. At some point, after her husband died, Flora's mother moved in as Mackey's housekeeper until he built her a house across the street. The house passed down through daughter to daughter until it, too, burned down. Tragically, your mother died in that fire."

He paused to gauge her reaction, but she sat stoically. Finally, she wiped her mouth and spoke.

"Roughly speaking, that's pretty close to the truth. Of course, it's the missing details that tell the real story."

"Like what details?"

"I'll dig them out for you tomorrow. They're down in one of those storage rooms in the basement."

"What other secrets are hidden away down there?" he joked.

Sandy didn't smile, though. "Lots of them, I'm sure."

Then a mischievous grin lit up her features. "I bet you don't know that there's a secret passageway in this house."

"I didn't know, but I'm not surprised. A back stairway, perhaps?"

Sandy frowned in mock disappointment, then smiled and nodded. "Now I can't sneak up to your room at night."

"You don't have to sneak."

The words were out of his mouth before he had consciously thought of them.

Once spoken, forever on the wind, as they say.

Sandy stood and flicked her wrist, signaling him to turn his chair, which he did without a thought. She then pushed his knees together and straddled his lap, her short, tight skirt sliding up above her hips. With a boldness only a determined woman can muster, she took both of his hands in her own, pulled them around her waist, then planted them firmly on her ass.

He felt her muscles twitching beneath the smooth, tight fabric of her panties as his fingers pressed into the flesh of her firm cheeks.

Sandy took her own hands and cupped the sides of his face. They locked eyes for a moment, each seeing their own desire reflected and amplified by the other. Then, as if some urgent telepathic message passed between them, they dove into each other's kiss.

Stoked by adrenaline and hormones, Jan lifted Sandy as he stood. She responded by locking her legs around his waist and hanging by her arms around his neck. Like a beast with two backs, with their mouths locked together, Jan carried her to the couch in the parlor.

This time was different, as second hookups often are. The passion was more intense, yet the pace was slower. A better understanding of each other's needs and desires led to a much more satisfying experience for both. Especially when Jan, feeling Angel Flora's presence hovering above, invited her to join them.

Sometime later, their passion at least momentarily sated, Sandy stood and stretched, her body still flushed and glistening with sweat. Seeing the reaction her display raised in Jan, she took his hand and led him back into her bedroom.

48

Monday, Late Spring

Rain kept Jan on the porch, but that motivated him to start drafting his new book. He could see the Tomlin murder/suicide as the inciting incident to kick off what could be either a cozy mystery or a gothic ghost story. After a couple hours of frenzied writing and an emerging ghost story, he texted Kathy.

```
        Can I see Tomlin
    mrdr/sucid polic rpt?
```

Her reply was nearly immediate:

```
No f-in way
```

Well, at least I tried, he thought. *I can use a break, anyway.*

Stretching his back, he heard Sandy's car start and back out of the driveway.

She said she was going to the gym this afternoon. That gives me time to snoop around the basement. Maybe I can find Flora's old journals down there.

Decision made, he hurried downstairs, unlocked the basement door, and gingerly touched the knob. It was just cool brass.

A plaster wall, painted white but long ago turned a dingy grey, flanked the stairway on the right. On his left, as he descended below the first floor's supporting joists, he saw a well-lit storage room lined with shelves and cabinets. The sheetrocked walls told him Dan had added this room during the remodel. The shelves were stacked with canned goods, napkins, toilet paper and the like. It was obvious that this room was the active storage area for the B&B.

Jan made a circuit of this room and found a door in the back wall, which led to a utility room with the House's oil furnace and boiler, an electrical panel, and in the back corner was the original coal bin. Opening a second door in the utility room, Jan emerged into a large open space.

Dan had set up his shop here, and the room contained all manner of power tools and a long workbench along the far wall. He remembered from his study of the original hotel floorplan that this area was mostly the working kitchen. Scars on the floor showed where cabinetry and plumbing fixtures once stood. A door at the back of the room opened onto a set of stairs leading to the first floor kitchen and the back exit. Scorch marks, probably from the Hotel fire, on the cement floor showed where walls had partitioned off live-in staff quarters.

Turning toward the front of the house, Jan faced a hallway flanked by four doors. The first on the left led back into the new storeroom and the front stairs. Just past it on the same side was a storeroom holding a collection of gardening tools—shovels, a wheelbarrow, and others. An exterior door in the outside wall afforded easy access to the side yard. A sledgehammer leaned against the wall next to bags of mortar, a cement mixing box, and hoe. Dried clay, cement dust, and masonry debris crunched under his feet as he examined the room.

A muddy trail crossed the room from the wheelbarrow to the door to the side yard. There were tracks in the mud from the wheelbarrow's single tire, but the trail of dirt was much wider.

It must have been full of dirt when they brought it inside, he thought.

Lumber, including a couple of six-by-six beams, was stacked against the other exterior wall at the front of the house. This wall, made of stacked cement blocks, differed from the poured concrete of the side and back foundation walls. Although newer than the original hotel foundation, this wall nonetheless showed its age to be close to a century.

This is where they cut off the front of the Hotel when they built the House.

Returning to the hallway, Jan found the source of the fresh mortar smell that permeated that end of the hallway. Freshly laid cement blocks formed a wall across the end of the corridor to his left. The new wall stopped two courses short of the ceiling joists. More construction debris littered the floor, and he had to step carefully around chunks of cement and globs of hardened mortar. Holding his cellphone light high, he could see behind the wall a heavy, steel door set in a rough opening in the century-old foundation.

I thought they filled in the unused part of the Hotel basement.

The blocks of the new wall were roughly set, the mortar unpointed. Jan stuck his finger into a joint. The mortar was still soft.

Somebody was in a big hurry. That explains the noises Sandy was making down here.

Turning, Jan opened the two doors on the other side of the hallway. The left-hand one revealed an old storeroom, whose inch-thick layer of dust looked to have been undisturbed for decades. The room behind the remaining door, however, was just what he was looking for.

Why is what you're looking for always in the last place you look? I guess because that's when you stop looking.

Racks of boxes, some made of faded cardboard an some of clear plastic, lined the walls. Jan wandered along the shelves, identifying the contents of some, either by handwritten labels or just by looking through the clear sides.

A box labelled "Santori" caught his eye. Inside was a stack of letters several inches thick. A quick scan showed that the artist and Ephraim Mackey had, at best, a contentious relationship. But the true treasure was a portfolio of drawings, each dated and signed by the sculptor and clearly annotated by two individuals. One set of notes, written in Italian, matched the artist's flowing hand, while the others were brusque notes in blocky printed letters. Jan snapped a picture of each.

Continuing down the row of shelves, he pulled out a box filled with spiral-bound notebooks. Some were old and tattered, while the ones at the top of the pile were much newer. Conscious of the time he had already spent exploring the subterranean warrens, he pulled out the newest journals and started a video recording of flipping through the pages.

He was so focused on his recording that at first he didn't notice the temperature in the room rising. When he finished filming all the notebooks, he shoved the box back on its shelf, straightened to stretch his back, and wiped beads of sweat from his forehead. That's when he noticed the heat on his back. Fearing that the House was on fire, he spun around. The heat became even more intense when he saw what stood in the room's only doorway.

Blocking his exit from the room, Angel Flora and Demon Flora struggled for dominance. As they had before, the negative space that was their shadows in the world of the living morphed between Demon Flora, her open-mouthed snarl baring sharp pointed teeth, and Angel Flora struggling to hold her twin at bay.

One aspect of the conflicted ghost gained the advantage, but then the other quickly became dominant. Their presence flickered like the shadow of a waving hand. With each oscillation between Demon and Angel, the heat intensified and the temperature in the small room rose.

Jan, having retreated to the wall of shelves, felt his exposed skin dry as his sweat instantly evaporated. His heart pounded in his ears. He felt his rational mind giving way to rising panic when he realized that with each flicker between Angel and Demon, Demon Flora held sway longer and inched closer to him. Could he somehow sneak past the struggling specters before Angel Flora, his protector, lost the battle?

As the other-worldly struggle crept closer, his skin began to sting. He raised his arms to shield his face when

Demon Flora took a full step toward him. The sting became intense pain as blisters rose on his forearms.

I've got to distract the Demon. Why is it attacking me? Sandy's not here. What does it want?

His breathing became shallow as the hot, dry air seared his mouth and throat. Ever closer, the mind-boggling display of writhing Nothingness reached out two arms, ready to pull Jan into its fiery embrace. Frozen in absolute terror, his mind became a blank wall on which no thoughts were written save one: *Distract. Distract. Distract.*

Into this mental fog, a new awareness dawned. Whether it was the faintest smokey scent, or the tiniest crackling sound, he never knew. More likely, it was some combination of those sensations that triggered an understanding, or at least an idea, of Demon Flora's motivation.

The journals. Flora's story was written, not to entertain, but to strengthen. To strengthen Angel Flora in her never-ending struggle with her Demon sister. In a flash of insight, Jan knew his only hope wasn't to distract Demon Flora, but to motivate Angel Flora.

Tearing his eyes from the approaching maelstrom, he saw the box of journals, their pages becoming singed at the edges, wispy tendrils of smoke curling up into the air. Commanding his terror-frozen muscles and locked joints to act, he kicked the box toward the battling half-ghosts.

The riskiness of his action nearly overwhelmed him. He had just bet his life that Angel Flora was trying to keep Demon Flora from destroying her story, told through her possession of Sandy.

What happened next left Jan struggling to understand. First came a scream of the purest terror, anger, and rage, all combined into an ear-splitting chord. Then, the Nothingness struggle reformed into Angel Flora, not in her normal defensive and protective stance, but in a position of offense, pushing Demon Flora back and driving her through the doorway.

Seizing his chance, Jan sprinted out of the room, across the hall, and through the door into the new storeroom. In the back of his awareness, his mind registered the door slamming shut behind him as he raced up the stairs. In the kitchen, he locked the basement door, then thrust his arms under the faucet.

As the cold water sucked the heat from his blistered arms, he gathered his thoughts despite the intense pain.

Locking the door was probably a useless gesture, since it wouldn't stop either version of the ghost, but having a physical barrier between himself and the terror in the basement gave him at least the illusion of security.

The cold water eased the searing pain somewhat, but a deeper, no less intense, ache that told of the damage done to the skin and muscles of his forearms settled in. Every movement, every flexing of his fingers sent shards of pain up his arms.

I need help. I need to tell Kathy.

He texted her.

```
I need your help.
Somewhere private.
```

Her response came as he was upstairs, changing his clothes.

Her address followed.

Every turn of the wheel sent jolts of agony through his blistered arms as he drove into Dundee, his GPS leading him to a house a block off Main Street. A set of wooden stairs climbed the outside wall.

"My God! You look like shit."

Kathy stepped back and waved him inside.

"What the hell happened?"

Jan just shook his head and gingerly peeled off his jacket. The blisters on his arms were white bulbous lesions stretching his skin.

"You need to go to the hospital."

He shook his head violently. "I can't."

"Why not?"

"Because I can't explain what happened."

Kathy frowned. "What do you mean? Did you wake up this way?"

He shook his head again.

"No." His annoyance was obvious. "If I tell them what happened, they'll lock me up. If I tell them a ghost with a split personality burned me because I was trying to read her journals, they'll put me in a padded cell."

Kathy's eyes went wide, and her hand flew to mouth. In a second, though, she recovered and took command.

"We need to treat these before they get infected. Come into the kitchen."

Jan followed her through the apartment's main room. His writer's eye scanned the small tidy space and was drawn to the open paperback lying upside down on the coffee table. He felt a twinge of disappointment and jealousy when he realized it wasn't one of his.

In the kitchen, Kathy waved him to one of the two chairs at the small kitchen table while she retrieved a first aid kit and a bottle of whiskey from a cupboard.

Jan eyed the bottle.

"Don't you have a bullet I can bite down on, too?"

She didn't crack a smile.

"I do. How about a .22 rim-fire? Maybe you'll bite down hard enough and blow your brains out."

"That would be hard to explain."

"And messy."

She yanked a dish towel from the oven door.

"Here. Shove this in your mouth so I can't hear your pussy screams."

"You also won't hear my story."

He raised an eyebrow when Kathy pulled on surgical gloves.

"Hey, I like you—I think," she said, "but that doesn't mean I want to catch whatever you may have."

He broke into a mocking grin. "She likes me."

Kathy snorted while she wiped a sewing needle with alcohol-soaked gauze, then did the same to the first of his blisters.

"Ow."

Kathy gave him a withering look, then said in her best Al Pacino voice, "I'm just gettin' warmed up."

Over the next forty minutes, Kathy cleaned, lanced, and bandaged twelve blisters on Jan's forearms while he related the events in the basement.

"Any sign of infection, get yourself to the hospital. Tell them you blew up a gas grill or something. Just don't tell them I did this."

She wagged her finger at her handiwork.

"My liability insurance won't cover you dying."

She looked at how he was cradling each arm in the opposite hand. "And keep your grubby hands off the bandages." She tossed him his jacket. "Long sleeves until they scab over."

Jan saluted. "Yes, ma'am."

His arms still hurt, but it was a much duller pain than when he had arrived. Pulling on his jacket, he said, "Seriously, they feel better. Where'd you learn to do that?"

Kathy shrugged. "Boy Scouts."

"You mean Girl Scouts."

She gave him a hard stare. "The little bitches teased me unmercifully, so I quit and joined my friends in the Boy Scouts."

"They let girls in the Boy Scouts? That must have been tough."

"According to the Supreme Court, they had to. Plus, after I beat up a little shit who tried to sneak into my tent, nobody else hassled me. And, like I said, that's where my friends were, so…" She shrugged.

"Well, thank you. I mean it."

Her voice softened. "Sure. We're both in this together, right?" Jan nodded and Kathy continued. "So, what's in the journals you almost became a Crispy Critter trying to see?"

He reached for his phone. "I haven't had a chance to look at them yet."

He started the video, but it was almost impossible to read the rough handwritten script on his phone.

"Hold on," Kathy said. "Email me the video. I'll get my laptop."

49

Angel Flora's Journal

I was Florence James, "Flora" to my family and close friends. My employers, the Smythe family, were old money and my family's employer, in one way or another, for at least three generations. In fact, my mother, Stephanie, was Mrs. Smythe's personal maid, as I was to the Smythe's oldest daughter, Jennifer.

As Jennifer was still unwed, she shared her parents' lavish mansion on Philadelphia's Main Line. This day, December 23, 1921, the Smythe parents, Jennifer, my mother, and I were leaving by train for a Christmas holiday. The younger Smythe children were left at home to celebrate Christmas with their dour, never-smiling nanny, Mrs. Forrest. Such was the Smythe family dynamic.

"Christmas can be whenever we wish to celebrate it," Mrs. Smythe said every year.

Her wish to enjoy an adult holiday, *sans enfants*, every year meant, of course, that my brothers, my sister and I celebrated each Christmas *sans mere*, as well. That year, since I attended Jennifer on their trip, our family was split neatly in two.

Mr. and Mrs. Smythe were habitually early risers, unlike Jennifer, whom, I was sure, would need to be rousted from her bed. The elder Smythes were at breakfast already, but that meant my mother was probably lingering about, ready to look over my shoulder and tut-tut over everything I did, as always.

To my relief, though, Mother was still packing Mrs. Smythe's bedclothes, hairbrushes, and the like when I slipped down the hallway into Jennifer's bedroom. To my surprise, she was already sitting up in bed.

"Ah, there you are! Isn't this exciting?"

"Exciting, Ma'am?"

Jennifer gestured to the newly fallen snow outside her window.

"Yes, look at the snow. It's the perfect setting to start our Christmas holiday."

I nodded, although my quarters in the mansion's basement had no windows, so I was not in the habit of gazing at the falling snow.

"And I don't have to spend another boring Christmas morning with that wretched Mrs. Forrest."

Jennifer had "come out" at the previous spring's Debutante Ball, and so was now considered an adult and eligible to entertain suitors—chaperoned, of course.

"Yes, Ma'am. That must be a relief."

"Flora," Jennifer's voice took on a mocking tone. "I've told you to call me 'Jenn.'"

"But your parents—"

"My parents aren't here, are they?" Her voice softened. "I so miss how we used to play together."

Since my family lived on the Smythe estate—my father oversaw their stables—Jennifer and I grew up, not together exactly, but sort of in parallel. I was not quite a year older than she, who was, in turn, four years older than the next Smythe child, her brother Andrew. Because of our relative ages and the isolation brought on by wealth, I was the perfect childhood companion for Jennifer. So, there were many occasions when we two girls had a chance to just be girls together.

But childhood gives way to adolescence, which itself yields to adulthood. With those changes come changing roles, as well. So it was that I naturally, almost without conscious thought or planning, transitioned from playmate to youthful confidante, and ultimately to servant.

"Sorry, Jenn. I just don't want to slip-up with either of our parents around."

"Don't worry, I'm sure you'll be careful. I just so much prefer to hear my name instead of 'Ma'am'. It makes me feel so old!"

She giggled like the child she still was, which made me break out into my own round of giggles. Our moment of camaraderie abruptly ended when knuckles rapped on the bedroom door preceding my mother's stern voice.

"Florence, get Miss Jennifer ready quickly or we will miss the train."

Jennifer suppressed her laughter with a hand over her mouth, but the admonition had the desired effect on me. I turned to Jennifer's travel wardrobe and continued selecting her clothes while she slid out of bed.

When I turned back, she stretched, arms above her head. Standing in front of the window, the low sun shone through her thin dressing gown, silhouetting her blossoming womanhood. I let out a small gasp when, in one motion, she reached over her shoulder and pulled her nightgown up and over her head. Letting it drop to the floor, she stretched again, standing naked before the window, visible to anyone who might be out front. The chilled air near the window raised gooseflesh on her breasts and her nipples stood proudly erect.

She turned her head to me, dropping her hands to her hips, but otherwise still exposed to whomever might catch a glimpse from below.

With a wicked smile, she said, "So, what are we covering this up with today?"

***

The Mackey Station looked like a Currier and Ives painting. Jennifer practically bounced with excitement as the train's whistle blew and the snow-shrouded station came into view. She and her parents waited in the salon car while Mother and I waited in the family compartment for porters to come and haul the wardrobes and trunks up the hill to the hotel.

The Smythes, being one of the older and wealthier families, were second of the six to be moved into their accommodations. The Mackey Hotel was a three-story affair, four stories if you count the kitchens and servants' quarters in the basement. It was built at the close of the Civil War and had been well-maintained and updated, first with gas fixtures—the supply piped in from the nearby town of Dundee at great expense—then most recently with electric lights in the parlors, dining rooms, and guest suites. Gas remained the only option throughout the service areas.

Above the center hall, with its extravagant staircase and second-floor gallery, a windowed clerestory rose, poking up above the hotel's roof. Its beveled windows and the crystal chandelier that hung from it were prisms, sprinkling spectral colors across the space below. The overall effect was of a fairyland populated by sprites dancing across the walls and marble floor as breezes in the high, open space twisted the chandelier's crystal drops.

The Smythes' suite had pride-of-place at the top of the curving grand staircase. Its two bedrooms, sitting room, and private bath overlooked the back garden, recently blanketed by a fresh fall of snow. The main door to the suite opened onto the galleried hallway at the top of the front staircase. A less-obvious staircase led up from that hall to the third floor where Mother and the other five families' maids were housed.

A second door opened from the suite's parlor onto a back hall, which was accessed by a second, back stairway that descended to the hotel's kitchens, service areas, and servants' quarters two floors below.

Because I was the Smythes' "Junior Maid," I was assigned as my quarters a spare closet-sized room at the front of the English basement under the hotel's entry portico. The narrow window set high in the room's outside wall let in little light, but an abundance of cold air. Although I would do little but sleep there, given the unpacking, repacking, and multiple changes of dress Jennifer needed throughout the day, I learned that first night that the time I had for sleeping would be wholly uncomfortable.

"Isn't this place beautiful?" Jennifer gushed the next morning as I brushed her long, thick, chestnut hair in preparation for the many pins and clips needed to hold it in the latest style. She didn't wait for me to answer, of course.

"Look how the snow clings to the trees." She gestured to the large window that let in the morning sun.

"The ballroom downstairs has the most amazing chandelier. There must be hundreds of crystal drops hanging from the gas jets."

I smiled at Jennifer's girlish excitement, but I was also glad I did not have to clean that chandelier or any of the dozen matching wall sconces.

"And did you see that Mr. Mulberry? Not the father. He's older than Daddy. No, their son Jonathan is home from college—Harvard, I think—for the holidays, and he came up here, too!"

I had noticed the young Mr. Mulberry when we arrived, as he helped his parents across the train station's snowy platform and up the walk to the hotel. He then stayed outside to direct the porters moving the Mulberry luggage. I also noticed how his eyes, if not his head, followed each woman as she passed. I thought Jennifer was going to swoon like a Victorian lady when he offered his hand to help her down from the train platform. But I also saw his wolfish grin as he watched her lift her skirts above the snow. When he turned and saw me watching him, his grin widened, and he gave me a devilish wink.

"I'd watch myself around that one," I said. But my warning went unacknowledged.

"He and I are the only young people here," she said in response.

I thought I could hear a mixture of excitement and fear in my mistress's voice.

Present company excluded, of course, I thought.

But I kept those thoughts to myself. Less than a year ago, back when we were still teenaged playmates and confidantes, I would have voiced those thoughts. But our relationship was forever changed by then. No longer were we viewed by the world, nor by ourselves, I suppose, as young girls who had grown up together despite being widely separated by money, status, and social class. Now we were mistress and maid, with our mothers as constant reminders of what the future held for the rest of our lives.

As often happened when Jennifer was prattling on, my thoughts drifted to my duties for the day. After this morning *toilette* and its attendant cleanup and straightening of the room, I would choose and lay out Jennifer's afternoon dress, coat, hat, and boots.

The family was taking a sleigh ride across the countryside. Mrs. Smythe had ordered a late lunch to be ready in the sitting room of the family's suite for when they returned. Mother was responsible for arranging that, so I would have an hour or so to eat and maybe read a little of the Jane Austen book I had sneaked into my bag. First, though, I needed to lay out Jennifer's gown, gloves, stockings, and all the accoutrements for the Christmas Eve gala that evening.

Mrs. Smythe still favored her heavy Edwardian dresses, but she had taken Jennifer shopping in Philadelphia, where they gawked at the Christmas displays and villages of the Big Six department stores. Their ultimate destination, though, was Wanamaker's, where they stood in the store's five-story main court with hundreds of other shoppers to hear the 18,000-pipe Grand Organ play Christmas carols. By the end of the day, Jennifer had a full wardrobe that represented the height of fashion.

Upon their return, much to my surprise and Mother's disapproval, Jennifer presented me with a set of new, low-waisted domestic servant frocks. Although she gave them to me as an early Christmas gift, to my mind, they cemented our relationship as mistress and maid. And I knew that, in her eyes, I needed to be as fashionable as any of her other accessories.

I put on a gracious, appreciative face, of course, but in that moment, I saw my whole life, a mirror of Mother's, spread out before me.

I came back to the present as I finished pinning Jennifer's hair into a faux bob—Mrs. Smythe might have given in to the new "potato sack fashion" as she called it, but she absolutely refused to allow her daughter's beautiful locks to be "hacked off to look like a boy."

"Hurry up, Flora! I don't want to miss Jonathan at brunch."

So, they're 'Jonathan and Jennifer' now. This could turn out to be a very interesting holiday, indeed.

Little did I know how true that premonition was.

***

Preparing Jennifer for the Christmas Eve Gala took the remainder of the afternoon once the Smythes returned from their sleigh ride. Hair, makeup, dress, shoes, and the *pièce de résistance*, Mrs. Smythe's diamond necklace, all needed to be perfect. I knew the Smythe parents had noted the attention Mr. Jonathan Mulberry had been paying their daughter. Adorning Jennifer's pretty neck with a fortune in jewels clearly signaled to the elder Mulberrys that they would be pleased with such a match.

For the servants' holiday, Mr. Mackey had, at least, provided a Christmas turkey, ham, and all the trimmings which, of course, the Hotel staff had to prepare themselves.

While the honored guests feasted upstairs, we had our own festive affair at the long table in the kitchen. I caught Mother sipping illegal gin punch for the first time. She gave me a half-smile and a shrug in response to my open-mouthed stare. She had only one cup, though, from which I sneaked a taste when she was not looking. The face I made nearly brought the other maids to tears with laughter.

But, too soon, the party broke up as the call bells summoned maids and valets to their masters' rooms. I departed with Mother to attend the Smythes, but when we arrived, only the parents were there. The upstairs partygoers must have had their own supply of illicit alcohol, since both Mr. and Mrs. Smythe were well into their cups. Jennifer, however, was nowhere to be found.

After exchanging "Merry Christmases" with Mother, then laying out Jennifer's night clothes, I descended the back stairs and made my way to my cold dark room.

But, to my surprise, when I arrived there, I found the door to my chamber locked. I was certain I had left it unlocked, as I simply had nothing of any value to steal. Searching the pockets of my dress and apron for the key, which I knew for certain was not there, I froze, motionless, when I heard a moan escape from the room. That moan was followed quickly by another, then a much deeper gasp accompanied by the rhythmic squeak of bedsprings.

Heat rose up my neck, setting my cheeks burning, while another type of heat brought tingles down below.

Stepping back from the door, I looked up and down the hallway in anger, wondering whom on the staff was so rudely using my chamber to make the increasingly passionate, yet somehow bestial, sounds. Revulsion briefly overtook my anger, however, when I distinctly heard Jennifer's voice call out Jonathan's name. But my anger returned when I realized that, as mine was the only bedchamber in this remote part of the house, anyone who heard the sounds of lovemaking coming from down here would assume I was the wonton female participant.

Reaching out to rattle the doorknob and bang on the door, if necessary, another thought stopped my hand. If I interrupted the scene playing out inside, I would have to keep not only Jennifer's secret, but Jonathan's as well— with their knowledge. That kind of unbalanced secret-keeping could lead only to resentment and ultimately dismissal, probably on some trumped-up lie designed to keep my mouth shut or discredit any truth I might disclose later.

All this flashed through my mind as I reached for, then withdrew my hand from the doorknob. If, instead, I simply slunk away to another of the empty rooms off the hallway, I could wait until they left and then return. The thought of sleeping in the bed after their escapade turned my stomach, however, so I decided it was better to just choose different quarters down there.

Fuming over being pulled into Jennifer's disgusting lie, I entered the room at the end of the hall furthest from the illicit liaison and lit the gas lamp. This room had not been made up, but I knew I could find fresh linens in the morning, so I curled up on the old mattress fully clothed, and promptly fell asleep.

My Christmas nap did not last long, however. Jennifer's muffled scream woke me with a start.

"Jonathan! Your cigarette! Wake up!"

Muffled curses floated through the walls.

"Put it out! No, the blanket! It's burning! The wall!"

Disoriented, it took me precious moments to realize where I was and what was happening. Lost in the dark, I lay in my makeshift bed a moment too long, frozen in confusion and a mounting unconscious, unthinking fear. It was Jonathan's voice that shocked me into motion.

"Leave it. Leave it! Run!"

A door banged open, echoing through the warren of basement rooms, and giving me a false clue in the dark, leading me directly into the wrong wall. Feeling along the wall, the plaster under my hands grew hotter and hotter. I reached a corner of the room just as a whoosh and a blast of heat from ruptured gas lines erupted through the wall and turned my trap into a roasting oven.

When they finished reading Flora's story, they were silent and shaken. Kathy poured them each a couple fingers of cheap bourbon.

"That's pretty nasty," Jan said, taking a sip.

"Which? The story or the bourbon?" Her attempt at humor fell flat. "Sorry. No wonder she's pissed off."

"That Jonathan guy married Jennifer Smythe. Last time I was here, back last Fall, Jeff and Naomi Tomlin were staying at Mackey House, too. He told Jennifer's side of that story. Of course, he left out the sex scene and the dropped cigarette. He basically blamed the fire on Flora."

Kathy shook her head in disbelief. "That little shit. I bet Sandy didn't like that."

"No, it was a pretty bad scene. I left the next day, and they…"

"They 'offed' themselves."

Jan nodded. "Yeah, about that. Why he would do that is beyond me."

"He?" Kathy finished her drink and poured another, waving the bottle at Jan, who shook his head.

"Tomlin."

Kathy seemed about to say something, then shook her head and took a sip.

Jan didn't notice her hesitation. "I've been thinking about them, and something clicked when we read Flora's journal. She wrote that Jonathan told Jennifer to 'Leave it.' I think he was talking about the diamond necklace."

Kathy's mouth formed an 'O.' "Yeah. That fits. You think Tomlin came here looking for the legendary Mackey Hoard?"

"I think he didn't think it was 'legendary.' I think he thought it was very real and hidden around the House somewhere."

Kathy downed the rest of her drink. "I'm gonna get drunk. Want to join me?"

Jan thought for a moment, then shook his head.

"I need to get ho—back to the House."

He hadn't told Kathy about the artist's renderings, but that could wait for another time.

"I'm exhausted," he gingerly touched his bandaged forearms, "and I need some Tylenol."

51

Why am I still here?

The question had disturbed him for days and it reared up again on the drive to the House.

What is the point? I should turn tail and run. I'm no detective. I'm no action hero. I'm a writer, for Christ's sake. And this last encounter was too close for comfort.

He felt the ache in his arms.

Literally. Is it Sandy? Yeah, there's Sandy. Sweet, vulnerable Sandy—until she turns into hot, seductive Sandy. The sex is great, no question about that, but is it worth getting maimed or killed over? And, frankly, it's only good until Angel Flora shows up. That's when it becomes great.

Jesus! You're infatuated with a fucking ghost. Literally a ghost who fucks. How sick is that? That's it. I'm packing my shit and leaving. Tonight.

Having decided, his mind stopped racing and his fatigue took over. His eyes first fluttered a few times, then closed. His chin fell to his chest, snapping him awake as his right front tire dove off the pavement onto the shoulder. He yanked the wheel to the left and jammed down on the brake pedal in a spastic overreaction, which sent the SUV into a sideways skid. It came to a stop across the two-lane road, with Jan shaking behind the wheel. The adrenaline coursing through his veins and the cold sweat that sprang from his pores cranked his senses to high alert.

Holy shit. That was too close.

He spun the wheel to point himself in the right direction again and sped off. The fight-or-flight chemicals that flooded his body flushed out of his bloodstream by the time he reached the House, leaving him shaking and even more tired than before. Slamming the SUV in Park, he let his muscles relax and his eyes close.

At some point, he must have adjusted his seat, because he awoke in the dead of night reclining almost flat in the driver's seat. The position and the premium seat were very comfortable, but the nighttime chill of late spring in the Pocono Mountains convinced him to head inside. That and his fifty-something bladder.

Climbing the sidewalk, he couldn't look away from the statue of Flora bathed in the pearly light of the full moon. As he came abreast of her, he stopped in his tracks, then walked across the lawn and stepped into the newly planted garden surrounding her. With a wry smile, he stood face to stone face with Flora. Then, in an act of pure spite, he unzipped his fly, took out his cock, and pissed on her feet.

Steam rose in the cold air from the stream, but it sizzled like oil in a hot pan when it hit the granite. When his bladder was empty, he tucked himself away, zipped his fly, and mumbled, "Fuck off, bitch."

It was the most satisfying piss he had ever taken.

52

Tuesday, Late Spring

"Hey, Jensen. What are you doing here during the day?" Spaz shouted across the squad room as he and Gheringer entered.

Gheringer elbowed him.

"Yeah, I thought bloodsuckers only came out at night. Although carpet cleaners do work during the day."

They both guffawed until the Sheriff appeared in the doorway of his office.

"Knock it off, you two. Deputy Jensen is showing some initiative, which is more than I can say about you mooks. She's investigating something, and if she needs any help, I expect you boys to be first in line to volunteer. Am I clear?"

Spaz and Gheringer glanced at each other, before nodding and saying almost in unison, "Ah, sure, Chief."

"Good. Jensen, get your butt in here."

He turned back into his office and Kathy fairly jumped out of her chair.

Gee, Chief. That was helpful. Like those two didn't hate me enough already.

She scurried into the office and closed the door behind her. Sheriff Peterson sat behind his desk, not even trying to hide his amusement.

"You didn't think I'd make this easy for you, did ya?"

He laughed out loud.

"But Spaz and Gheringer? Did it have to be them?" Kathy's voice reflected her annoyance.

Peterson just shrugged, then took a folder out of his desk.

"This is a list of databases you now have access to."

He took a sheet out of the folder and handed it across the desk.

"And this," he pulled out a sheaf of several pages stapled together, "is the list of things you don't have access to."

He dropped it on the desk.

"Basically, anything that needs a warrant or court order is off limits."

Kathy scanned the forbidden list with a growing sense of alarm.

Holy shit. Does the government really know this much about us?

"Chief, some of this personal stuff could be really useful."

He leaned back in his desk chair. Crossing his arms, he just stared at Kathy with a raised eyebrow.

OK, no help from that quarter.

"Anything else?" She could barely conceal her annoyance.

Peterson commented on her attitude by remaining silent, so Kathy stood up to leave. Then he spoke up.

"I'm not just being a prick, ya know. You're a woman of color in an overwhelmingly male profession out here in the boondocks. There's no Affirmative fucking

Action out here. You'll have to be tougher, try harder, and achieve more, just because you're … you."

Better to hear that now from him, I guess.

She nodded her understanding and left the office. Sitting at her desk, she pulled up the office directory and loudly read out two telephone numbers.

"Those are your cellphones, S&G? Or at least the ones your wives know about, right?"

They stared daggers at her, but said nothing.

"Good. Just wanted to make sure I can get ahold of you if I have something for you to do."

She logged off her workstation and headed for the door, smiling to herself.

53

Somehow, during the night, Jan's resolve to pack up and leave dissolved. The smell of fresh coffee and frying bacon woke him later than usual. Washing up as best he could with his bandaged arms, he got dressed in a long-sleeve flannel shirt and jeans and headed downstairs.

When he walked into the dining room, Sandy emerged from the kitchen with plates piled high with food, which she placed on the table.

She stepped up to where he held a chair for her, but instead of sitting, she faced him with her hands on his chest. Reflexively, he wrapped an arm around her waist and drew her in tight against his body. Taking her cue, she embraced his neck and the good morning peck she had intended became a deep, lingering kiss.

When their lips finally separated, she whispered teasingly, "Breakfast is getting cold," and sat in the offered chair.

Holding a piece of bacon, Sandy asked, "What are your plans for today?"

A clap of thunder sounded, and Jan nodded to the window. "Looks like I'll be writing today."

Sandy nodded. "It looks like it'll be a good day to stay home."

She offered him a smile that could have been an invitation.

"And curl up with a good book."

"Or laptop," he said, and they both chuckled.

The rest of breakfast passed with small talk and the occasional subtle sexual innuendo offered up by Sandy. But, despite the intimacy of their kiss, Jan didn't want to escalate things today. Not with his bandaged arms, which he would have to explain somehow, but also because Sandy's siren song was a gateway drug he feared would lead to an inescapable addiction. An addiction that he suspected would surely take his life, if not his very soul.

***

Memories of her pouting lips haunted him as he sat in his suite and looked through Santori's drawings. The studies of Flora's face matched the pictures taken by the quarrymen who hauled away the sculptor's failures. A progression from Innocent Flora to Sensual Flora was plain when he laid out the drawings in chronological order. Annotations added by Mackey made it clear who was behind the transformation.

"Too innocent looking!"

"She isn't a child."

"Too angelic."

"More sensuality."

The most telling note, however, appeared on the next-to-last sketch before Santori's final rendering:

"Make her look how she feels when she comes to you in the night."

Another set of drawings showed how little the back of the statue had changed while its front and face were being made more and more erotic. Only minor changes were made to lengthen her hair, make the folds of her gown more like angel's wings, and, in general, provide a counterpoint to the frontal transformation.

The newer of his photos showed what he had noticed before, a repair made to one rose on Flora's shoulder. Curiously, the photo he had taken on his previous visit didn't show the same blemish. Checking again, he confirmed that last fall, the rose in question was still pristine.

That's something to ask Sandy. How'd the damage happen, and who tried to repair it?

While he mulled this tidbit over, his phone buzzed with a text from Kathy.

Tavern?

He checked his watch. It was half-past noon and his stomach rumbled, so he texted back his agreement.

The rain had slowed to a drizzle when he left the House. Like a magnet, he was drawn again to the statue of Flora, but this time, he approached with a clinical purpose. Standing on tiptoe, he examined the repaired rose. Someone had sculpted a mixture of cement, tinted to match the grey granite, to mimic the delicate petals of the pristine roses flanking it. If not for a slight mismatch in texture, and the low-angled light of the morning sun, he never would have noticed the repair.

54

Jan picked up a potato chip from his plate and ate it half-heartedly. His club sandwich sat untouched. Kathy, on the other hand, was devouring her burger. She spoke around a mouthful of meat, cheese, tomato, and bun.

"They finally gave me access to some online databases. I'm still amazed by how much the government knows about us. Where we go, what we buy, who we talk to, you name it."

"Nobody in the government *knows* that about you until someone goes and looks. So, if you don't give them—or you—a reason to look, it's just data sitting in the cloud somewhere."

Kathy just looked skeptical, and he shrugged and continued.

"That's their justification for collecting it all, anyway. 'It's just data.'" He made air quotes. "Until somebody, or worse, some AI program, decides it's relevant. Then it becomes information, which gets aggregated into patterns, which are transformed into behavioral models that try to predict whether you're a terrorist, a drug dealer, or just some shmoe trying to get laid on Saturday night."

Kathy looked at him with wide eyes. "Seriously? How do you know this?"

Jan shut up, but Kathy's stare made him feel somehow important.

"If I told you, I'd have to kill you."

She scoffed, which bruised his ego a bit.

"Don't forget that I was a software engineer for thirty-plus years. I've worked on some hush-hush contracts for agencies that don't officially exist."

That last part was a bit of an exaggeration, although his security clearance was still valid the day they fired him. Anyway, Kathy wasn't buying it.

"Now you're just trying to impress me with bullshit."

He grinned. "Is it working?"

They both laughed, and Jan gave a mental sigh of relief.

Keep your conspiracy theories—although they aren't just theories, are they?—to yourself or you'll end up in a deep, dark hole.

"Anyway, what did your access to this vast data lake of personal information teach you?" he said, trying to move the conversation back to the present.

Kathy gave him one last, 'we're not finished with this conversation' look before pulling out her notes.

"Nothing. There's been no unusual activity on his credit cards or his bank account."

"No 'unusual' activity?"

"That's the thing. All of their accounts are in both their names. There have been plenty of purchases and ATM withdrawals, but they've all been in this area. Nothing over twenty miles from Dundee."

"But were the amounts or the frequency unusual?"

Kathy looked sheepish. "I didn't look for anything like that. There are hundreds of transactions to comb through." Then her face brightened. "You're a programmer. Can't you analyze the data?"

Jan scowled for a moment. "First of all, I'm not the one authorized to access the data. Second, you won't be able to download the raw data, only the report, and you can probably only print the report, not save it."

Kathy shrugged, but Jan nodded confidently.

"There are at least some safeguards to keep the information in official hands only." He thought for a moment. "What about online purchases?"

She shook her head. "Very little. A few books and women's clothes. That's about it."

"Can you access her browsing history? Or, better yet, Dan's?"

Kathy frowned. "What would that tell us?"

"Well, besides the obvious—searches for how to dispose of bodies—with a list of sites that Dan has visited in the past, we could try to find out if his accounts have been active lately."

She shook her head. "It would take a court order to get that data, and I don't have that much authority."

Jan didn't make eye contact, but said under his breath, "I know a guy…"

But Kathy interrupted him. "Look, this is my first case and I'm being watched like a hawk. I have to play this by the book. I'm not going to screw my chances of making detective by using some fucking hacker from the Black Web, understand?"

The Dark Web, he corrected her mentally, but just put his hands up in surrender.

"You're the boss, Detective."

He tried to keep any hint of sarcasm out of his voice. Apparently, it worked, because Kathy nodded and sat back in her booth.

"Good. I'm open to suggestions about what to do next, though. Legally, that is."

Jan just shrugged. "I got nothin'."

"We need a hypothesis."

"You mean like the scientific method? Propose a theory, then try to prove it."

She shook her head. "Nope, wrong approach. You propose a theory, then try to *disprove* it. Eliminate the theory, just like you eliminate suspects. If you try to prove your theory, you get emotionally attached to it and may ignore or discount contradictory evidence. But if you doubt your theory from the beginning, you can stay more objective. Then, 'once you've eliminated the impossible'—"

"'Whatever remains, however improbable, must be the truth.' I've read Sherlock Holmes, too. All of them, in fact. Not a bad role model for a detective. Aside from the opium, cocaine, indoor target practice, and general antisocial behavior, of course."

That got Kathy laughing, too.

He continued, "So, what're the possible theories?"

"Let's see," she flipped open her notebook and raised her index finger, "Sandy's telling the truth and Dan just up and left."

"Leaving everything behind."

"Right. Not very likely, but not eliminated yet, either."

Jan nodded reluctantly, and Kathy raised another finger.

"He could have been kidnapped." Jan made a face. "Again, not likely, but not eliminated, either."

"Wait a sec. I think it's eliminated simply because there has been no ransom note."

"None that we know of. Maybe Sandy didn't tell anyone."

"But it's been over six months."

"True." She made a note in her notebook. "Not eliminated, but way down on the list."

A third finger went up. "Now we get to the one I least want to be true."

She paused as if she didn't want to say it, but Jan held his silence. He knew what was coming, but he also knew that she had to embrace it as her own theory. If he said it, she wouldn't internalize it like she needed to.

"Or, he could be dead, either accidentally or … murdered."

Jan slowly nodded, but remained quiet.

"But how do I disprove that theory without flat out finding him, which is the whole point?" She took a deep breath. "I keep going around in circles."

Jan finally spoke. "The truck."

"What about the truck?"

"A person can stay hidden, either being off the grid by choice, or because they're locked away, or … because they're dead. But a truck can't just vanish. It needs to be registered. It needs to be insured. If it goes through any toll booths, either its transponder pays the toll or its license plate gets recorded." Kathy was nodding vigorously. "Plus, it's a new, high-end model, right?"

"Yeah, with all the bells and whistles. Including a nav system." She thought for a moment. "I can get at least some of those records. I don't know about any GPS tracking, though."

Jan shook his head. "That's a common misconception that Hollywood loves to use as a plot device. You can't track something just because it uses GPS. GPS satellites only broadcast, they don't receive—at least for civilian use. You can only track someone or something if they are actively using a navigation program which is reporting their speed and direction to service in the cloud so it can detect traffic jams and stuff."

"You're talking about Waze or Maps."

"Right, but not just when you're using those apps. Any time you have location services turned on—which we probably both do right now—some server in the cloud is recording your location. To get that data, though, you have to go after his subscriber account from either Google or Apple. That'll take a court order and they'll still fight you. Apple for political reasons, and Google because that's how they make money. His truck's nav system data might be easier to get, though."

"Shit. Where's the Deep State when you need them?"

Jan raised an eyebrow and stared at Kathy until she said, "What?"

"You still want to stay strictly 'by the book'?"

"What are you saying?" Kathy asked.

"Like I said before, I know a guy."

"I wouldn't be able to use any off-the-books info officially."

Jan shrugged. "So, if my guy finds Dan's been moving around, case closed. He lit out like Sandy said he did. But, if he doesn't find him, well, that pretty much eliminates that theory."

He held up a hand to stop Kathy's protest. "Yes, I know he could be totally off the grid living in a cabin in the woods, which is why you keep looking for his truck, bank transactions, or anything else you can think of. But, you have to admit that theory moves way down the list."

He pointed at her notebook for emphasis.

"That leaves the worst possible scenario. That he's dead. Fuck."

Jan nodded in sympathy. "Just like you can't wish a theory to be true, you can't wish one to be false, either. You need to find the truck."

Kathy picked up a cold French fry. "What have you been doin'?"

Jan blinked at the sudden change in subject. He had completely forgotten his research into the statue.

"When I was in the basement, before I got these," he held up his forearms, "I got a look at Santori the sculptor's working drawings."

He pulled out his laptop and spun it around so Kathy could see a composite image on the screen.

"I overlaid Santori's final drawing with a picture I took last fall and one I took this past Saturday. What do you see?"

"Is this one of those 'Find the Differences' puzzles in the Sunday paper?"

Jan just nodded his head toward the screen.

"OK," she muttered in response, then her eyebrows went up. "One of the roses on her shoulder is different."

"Yeah. It was broken and delicately repaired. It must have happened over the winter, because the picture I took in the fall," he clicked a few icons and brought that image to the forefront, "doesn't show the damage."

"You think it was the winter weather?"

Jan shook his head.

"Then what broke it? It's granite, for God's sake."

"I think somebody was chipping at it." He zoomed the picture in to the maximum. "See the scratches on the flowers around the broken one?"

"Definitely tool marks. Somebody was chiseling at it. Who do you think?"

"Well, I took this one when I got here in late September and it was fine—"

"Holy shit! I just remembered." Kathy slapped her forehead. "I'm such an idiot!"

"What the hell are you talking about?"

"September, you said?" Jan nodded. "I was on patrol, and I cruised past the House when I saw a flashlight shining across the lawn. By the time I got the cruiser pulled over and fired up my spotlight, whoever it was disappeared. I assumed it was Dan, although now that I think about it, he would have either gone around the back or waited for me."

Jan looked at Kathy with a quizzical expression. "Did you shine your spotlight on the statue?"

"Yeah, of course."

Jan nodded excitedly. "That happened while I was here. I saw you from the upper porch. I saw something else, too."

His voice faded away on the last sentence, but Kathy pressed the issue.

"What did you see?"

Jan maintained his silence for a few seconds, trying to think of a way to explain.

"Your spotlight drew my attention, and I walked to the porch railing."

"Did you see who was attacking the statue?" Her voice carried more enthusiasm than Jan would have expected.

"No. I guess I got there too late."

He stopped talking, and Kathy's enthusiasm evaporated.

"So? What did you see?"

"A week ago, I would have believed I had just imagined it, but not now. When your spotlight was on the statue, it cast a long shadow across the lawn, and the full moon cast a different, fainter one. After you turned off the spotlight, I swear I saw the moonlight shadow *detach* itself from the statue and slither into the house."

Kathy looked thoughtful, then started nodding.

"Two shadows from one statue. Two ghosts from one dead girl. She's a dual *murti*," she whispered.

"A *murti*? What's that?"

Kathy came back from wherever her mind had gone.

"It's a Hindu thing that my mom told me about before she gave up on raising me that way. A *murti* is a statue, usually carved from stone, that embodies a deity or traps a demon. A deity, either a major one like Shiva or Ganesha, or one of the many minor gods or demons, resides within the *murti* as long as the carving is perfectly flawless. The slightest blemish in the carving releases the deity—or the demon. For centuries, Islamic invaders knocked the noses off thousands upon thousands of *murti* to defile them and expel the deity inside."

"And Tomlin damaged Flora's *murti*."

"That must have been what released her, but not enough to send her into the Brahman."

"Maybe because the damage wasn't done to her directly, but to one of her roses."

"But that means Santori carved her specifically to entrap the ghost, which would explain the duality of the carving. Benign versus savage—*Sattva* versus *Tamas*, *dharma* versus *adharma*."

Kathy looked satisfied that they solved the mystery of the statue's origin, at least, and maybe they had learned something significant about Flora's internal conflict, too.

"So you think Tomlin did it?" she asked.

"Who else? The timing fits. They were the only other guests here besides me at the time. Did you ask Dan or Sandy about it?"

"Naw, like I said, I thought it was Dan, so I didn't even write it up. I forgot about it until just now."

Jan thought for a moment. "Tomlin gets caught chipping at the statue, then the next morning he spouts off about his grandmother losing her jewels and practically accuses Sandy's family of stealing them." He looked confused. "So why would he kill his sleeping wife and then himself?"

Kathy was shaking her head before he finished.

"No, no, that's not what happened."

"What do you mean?"

"I was first on the scene in the morning. And let me tell you, that's something I can't unsee."

She took a big gulp of her beer before continuing. "It was the Tomlin *woman* who did the killing. She still had the weapon stuck in her eye." Kathy shuddered. "They were naked. She was on top. She hacked his throat, then jammed the thing through her eye into her brain."

Jan felt his gorge rise and covered his mouth while he swallowed it back down. Kathy was looking pale herself.

"How big was the knife?"

She shook her head again. "Wasn't a knife. It was a nail file."

"What?"

"Yep. Stuck it straight into her right eye."

"She ripped his throat out with a nail file?" Jan was incredulous.

Kathy slowly shook her head. "Officially she did. But the coroner, Doc Smith, figured she did it with her teeth. Even found bits of him in her mouth. Sheriff Peterson wouldn't let him put that in his report, though."

Jan had to swallow again, and his eyes darted to the men's room door. His glance wasn't lost on Kathy.

"If you head for the shitter to hurl, I'll crawl over your back to get there first."

"Oh. My. God. You must have been traumatized."

Kathy shrugged, then nodded. "They gave me a week off after. But I still see them in my nightmares." She shuddered again.

"I'm sorry," Jan said.

"What do you have to be sorry about?"

"Sorry I made you relive that."

She shrugged and said in a monotone, "Just going over the facts of the case. You think it relates?"

Jan nodded. "Oh, yeah, I think it does. Jeff Tomlin chipping away at Flora one night, then the next his wife turns into a crazed maniac while fucking him? Oh yeah, it relates."

Jan heard the voices in the kitchen as soon as he opened the front door. One was clearly Sandy's, but the other was a snarling distortion that Jan instantly recognized as Demon Flora. His blood ran cold, and he froze in place. But, unlike when he heard mumblings from the basement, this *tête-à-tête* was crystal clear.

Sandy was whining, "I've been trying. I don't know what else you want me to do."

The other was raspy and harsh.

"*Try harder. He's just a man.*"

"But he's a nice guy. I—I like him."

"*Don't be stupid, you simpering child. He is a man, and he is after the same thing they all want. You need only distract him for long enough and let me do the rest.*"

Suddenly, a third voice spoke. Angel Flora's was calm and melodic, though no less powerful than the snarl.

"Leave him alone. He simply wants to tell our story."

"*You know what that will lead to. I will not let that happen.*"

"He is a writer, not a treasure seeker. Telling our story will free us. You know this."

"I do not want to be free! I want to keep what is mine."

"But it is not yours and never was."

"It is mine by right. I died because of it and I will keep it for eternity."

"*We* died because of it, that is true, but I want no part of it. It is tainted and foul."

"Just like me, eh? Say it. You despise me."

"How can I despise you? You are me and I am you. You and I—we—cannot spend eternity guarding trinkets."

The voice of Angel Flora, which had been calm and soothing, rose in stridency. Jan looked at the staircase.

Two minutes. That's all I need. Two minutes to throw my stuff in a suitcase and get the hell out of here.

Realizing these two halves of the same ghost were arguing his fate, he froze with his hand on the banister. Could he pack his things and get out before Demon Flora won the argument? He then glanced at the front door, still standing open. Unconsciously, he reached back to his satchel to reassure himself that his laptop was still there. Accusations and recriminations flew between the Floras, growing ever louder over an undercurrent of Sandy's frightened mewling.

Finally, a growling shout of *"He's mine!"* convinced him to forget about his clothes and all the replaceable things in his room and bolt for his car.

Then Sandy screamed.

"Get out of my head! Both of you. Go back to whatever Hell you came from!"

In two strides, Jan ran down the hall and burst into the kitchen. Sandy stood in the center of the room, jerking from side to side as if she was a rag doll being shaken by a tantrum-throwing child. Her eyes were empty, and her mouth was a yawning portal to nothingness. Less than empty, she appeared to be hollowed out of this universe entirely.

"Get out!" Jan yelled, his cracking voice a poor imitation of Flora's guttural growl.

The shaking of Sandy stopped, and her eyes took on a little of their natural blue color.

"Get out!" Sandy screamed, and the non-presence that was Flora slowly drew out and away from her as her face contorted with the strain.

Hovering half-in and half-out of her, the two Floras flickered between the snarling, hissing Demon, and the worried, protective Angel.

Sandy let loose another scream, this time a wordless expression of mental and physical anguish, which drove the formless form fully out of her body. The terrible, hideous, and rapid transformation between Flora's bestial face, clawing hands, and pendulous breasts, and her equally protective flowing locks and angelic wings, continued as Sandy's will forced them away from her.

When all links to Sandy were severed, Demon Flora turned her face with its fang-filled mouth to Jan. Drawing her lips back even further, slather hung from jaws which protruded out from her face like the snout of a rabid dog.

Terrified, but unable to abandon Sandy, Jan knew his fate was sealed until the growling snarl became a yip of pain and Flora folded in on herself again, revealing her Angel persona.

"Run!" it said. "Run away and leave this place. You cannot help her, for she is ours."

Then she opened her arms as if embracing her alter ego and drove them both across the floor and through the open basement door. It slammed shut in their wake.

Jan darted for Sandy and caught her as she collapsed. He lifted her into his arms and her eyes fluttered closed. With shaking legs, he carried her into the parlor and gently lay her down on the couch. Relieved of their burden, his own legs gave out and he sat down hard on the floor.

56

"She's shaken up, but physically she's alright."

Kathy walked into the parlor after putting Sandy to bed. Jan slumped in one of the club chairs. A drink sat ignored on the end table.

"Did she say anything?"

Kathy shook her head.

"She can't remember anything. Or at least that's what she says." She flopped down onto the couch. "You need to tell me exactly what happened."

"I wish I could." He shook his head. "I've never been so scared in all my life."

He picked up his drink, but his hand shook so badly it sloshed onto his sleeve.

"They were arguing. The two Floras were speaking through Sandy, and they were really going at it."

He took a deep breath, and by concentrating on his hand, he managed to sip his bourbon without spilling it.

"Then Sandy screamed and—expelled them, I guess. When Demon Flora came for me, Angel Flora did something that hurt her somehow. She took control and drove both of them into the basement."

His glass rattled again when he set it down.

Kathy looked him over appraisingly. "Are you sure you're alright? You look, I don't know—"

"Like I've seen a ghost? How about two of them? You know, I was ready to run out the door and back to Philly when Sandy screamed."

"You saved her," she said matter-of-factly. "If not her life, at least her fuckin' sanity."

Jan felt like a betrayer, not a hero. He knew if she hadn't screamed when she did, he'd be on his way to Philadelphia right now. But what would be left of Sandy?

I won't run again. I won't be a fucking coward. I've got to see this through to whatever the end is.

"It's probably good she can't remember. But I'm not sure about her sanity," Jan said. Kathy looked surprised. "I've heard her talking to herself on multiple occasions."

"Hell, I do that."

"In different voices?"

"Oh. Well, no."

Jan gave her an I-told-ya-so smile, then got serious. "We've got to get her out of here."

"How do you propose we do that? This is her house, and she doesn't remember being…"

"Possessed. There's no sense hiding that. This house is haunted, and Sandy is possessed by both a killer demon and a horny angel."

"When you put it that way …" Kathy stood up and started pacing around the room. "Then there's the case of her missing husband. It's all circumstantial at this point, but there's no sign of Dan anywhere. Assuming he bit it, was Sandy involved? If we can prove that, I'll get her out of this place."

It took Jan a moment to process her statement.

"You mean you'll arrest her."

He said it matter-of-factly, but he didn't like the idea one bit.

"So, is she responsible for what Flora does?"

His tone of voice made it clear he didn't think so.

"Well, somebody is. If she killed Dan, whether or not she was possessed when she did it, she has to face the consequences."

He'd held Sandy in his arms and shared her bed. His conflict showed on his face.

"I think that's bullshit."

57

It was late when Kathy left, but she was far from sleepy. The change of shift, coming off midnights, staying up all day investigating Dan's disappearance, and Jan's panicked calls for help had her sense of time totally screwed up. Add to that the argument that raged all evening over Sandy's culpability, and she felt mentally, emotionally, and physically drained.

I ought to be asleep. I'm exhausted. Yet here I am driving around in the middle of the night, too wired to sleep.

She didn't have a destination in mind. She just let her instincts guide her along roads she had driven thousands of times.

What happens if I find the truck in the woods out here somewhere? That'll look really bad for Sandy. Maybe I could warn her off before reporting it. Or just not report it at all.

I'm the only one lookin' for Dan. If I don't make a stink, everything can stay the way it is. Well, not everything. I'll know, and eventually, she'll know that I know. Once she knows that I know, will the Floras know, too? Probably, and I don't want to cross those bitches.

What would Dad say?

She pictured her father's craggy features, then the image changed into her memory of him standing in his State Police dress blues when he received a commendation from the Governor.

I know what he would say. He'd say, "Good job." And I know what he'd say if I didn't turn her in, except he wouldn't say it to me, because he'd never speak to me again.

Shit! If I find the truck, I have to turn her in, maybe even arrest her myself. If I don't, I'll never know. And if someone else finds it abandoned somewhere, it'll look like I covered up a murder.

Agitated, Kathy pulled to the side of the road. Looking around, she realized her subconscious had brought her to one of her favorite spots in the entire county.

Getting out of her car, she walked around it and stood on a ridge overlooking a hollow with one of the many long, thin, and deep lakes the region was known for. This area was riddled with off-road trails running around the lake and all through the woods. Kathy had been four-wheeling here many times growing up, and even with Dan and Sandy a few times.

The vista from this spot was stunning, and it tickled a memory from another early morning ride in the fog. She could see across the valley to the state highway on the other side, as a bright, full moon lit the scene with an eerie, yet beautiful, pale glow.

In fact, the light was doubled, as the moon was reflected in the perfectly still waters of the lake. Kathy stood enraptured by the sight of the two moons, one hovering above like a protective angel, the other seemingly climbing from the depths of the underworld.

I'm obsessed. Now I'm comparing the moon to Flora. But hold on, what's that?

Something that wasn't quite right about the scene below caught her attention. Barely visible in the moonlight, the faintest rainbow sheen flickered on the water's surface, close to the opposite shore. The patch of oil floated just below a cliff at the end of the access road from the state highway.

With a series of mental clicks, the puzzle pieces fell into place—the state road leading to Dundee, the dirt access road running downhill to a high drop-off into the deepest part of the lake, and a network of off-road trails.

Envisioning what must have transpired, Kathy jumped in her car and sent mud flying as she sped back onto the road.

58

Jan sat at the dining room table well into the night, his fingers flying across the keyboard in a mad rush to chronicle the events of the last few days and capture his thoughts on them. A dreaded sense of finality had settled over him when Kathy left, hours before. The writer in him wanted—needed—to tell this tale, though he knew it would be called the worst sort of pulp horror. Nobody wrote ghost stories anymore.

The backspace key had gotten as much work as any other during this session, simply because he had no expectation that there would be any opportunity to rewrite or even edit any of his hurried prose. He had made a decision, sitting in his room, unable to sleep.

I've felt more alive in the past week than I have felt in years—maybe my entire life. This house and this town feel more like home to me than my stupid little shithole apartment. Besides, Sandy needs me.

No woman had ever needed him before, other than needing his mortgage payments and his credit cards.

She's no damsel in distress, though. She kicked those bitches out of her head. If she did it once, she can do it again, and permanently this time.

It also occurred to him that the sexual pull he felt toward Angel Flora was the beginnings of an addiction, one that already held Sandy in its thrall.

She needs my help and support to keep her strong.

He looked up from his laptop in surprise when the kitchen door creaked open. Sandy stood in the doorway, squinting and pushing her wild hair from her eyes.

"What are you doing up?" she said around a yawn.

"Ah, just doing some writing." He stood and walked over to her.

"Down here?"

"Yeah, well I wanted to be close by in case you needed anything."

From her blank look, he got the distinct impression that she truly had no recollection of the previous evening's events.

"You really don't remember?"

She looked confused. "Remember what? Kathy asked me that, too, I think. What am I supposed to remember?"

Jan paused, his mouth open, ready to speak.

How do I tell her she's possessed by a ghost with multiple personalities?

"You … had an *episode* earlier." Sandy's face darkened. "You were talking to yourself, ah, with different—"

"Oh, my God! That wasn't a dream?"

Her face contorted into a look of pure terror when Jan shook his head. Her eyes darted back and forth, then her head turned from side to side. She crouched as if ready to run for her life.

Jan stepped up close and tried to calm her with hands on her shoulders.

"It's OK. They're gone."

Or at least they're not here now.

Sandy relaxed a little, but her panic was still present enough to see through his lie.

"But they aren't actually gone, are they?" He shook his head. "Then those other times weren't dreams, either? All those times when I fell asleep writing in my journal? And when we…?"

Jan ignored her last question. "Didn't you go back and read what you had written?"

He could feel her shoulders trembling. Oh, how he wanted to hold her in his arms and make her fears go away. But he knew her moment of self-realization was a catharsis that he shouldn't cut short.

"I tried once, but it was too painful and angry. And I didn't remember writing the worst parts of what was there. It was like I wrote them while dreaming."

Tears flowed down her cheeks.

"But I wasn't dreaming, was I?" A sob escaped her lips. "What am I? Am I a monster?"

"No, God, no. You're not a monster."

But there are monsters among us.

"You just need a break. Some time away from here."

Her body went rigid. "I … I can't leave here," she whined. "This is my home. My life. I need to keep this place going."

Jan's tone was soothing. "Just a break. A vacation. We can take a trip, together."

"Together?" Her voice sounded hopeful. "You'll stay with me?"

He understood the real meaning behind her question, and without thinking, he nodded. The change in Sandy was immediate. She leaned into him, wrapping her arms around his waist and burying her face in his chest. He embraced her in turn.

"We can make our plans in the morning," she murmured without looking up, relief obvious in her voice. "Come to bed, now."

He jerked back, reason returning, and pushed her to arm's length. She gazed up at him with a look of pure innocence.

"Just to sleep. Nothing else, I promise."

Believing the honesty he heard in her voice, and also because he dearly wanted to believe her, he nodded and smiled, knowing full well that his life had just fundamentally changed. Whether for the short term or long, whether for good or ill, he couldn't say, and didn't care as he pulled her back into his embrace.

59

Wednesday, Late Spring

His phone's insistent buzzing woke Jan. The sun was already high in the sky, and he was amazed to see that it was past noon. He was alone in Sandy's bed. Thinking back, he realized that she had been true to her word. They had done nothing but sleep, wrapped in each other's arms. His phone beeped this time, indicating a new voice mail.

Kathy's annoyed voice came through the tinny speaker. "Check your texts. I sent you a map link to the place I want you to meet me. Come now."

Sandy was nowhere around when Jan got dressed, though he found a note taped to the bathroom mirror.

Gone to Scranton. CU later.

***

The ten-mile trip on the winding mountain road took a good twenty minutes to arrive at the GPS coordinates. A Sheriff's squad car blocked the turnoff to a one-lane dirt road. A deputy approached, making a shooing motion when Jan pulled the car onto the shoulder.

"Nothing to see her, Buddy. Move along."

Before Jan could protest, the deputy's radio squawked, "Spaz, let him through."

Deputy Spatz eyed him suspiciously. "You ain't a reporter, are you?"

"No, definitely not," Jan said as he tried to think of a good reason for getting through the barricade.

Before Spaz could question him further, though, Kathy's voice spat out of his radio, "Spaz!"

The deputy muttered, "I don't know what's up Jensen's ass, but the Chief said to let her run this shitshow, so…"

He turned and walked to his car. When he had backed it up just enough, Jan slowly drove past and down the unpaved lane toward a small lake.

Several squad cars and SUVs were parked in the weeds to the side of the lane, where it turned to follow the shoreline, so Jan followed suit. A flatbed truck carrying another vehicle sat idling just past the turn. Kathy stood talking to two men in scuba gear, and when he hesitatingly walked up, she thanked them and turned to him.

"It's about damn time you got here." Her voice carried a tone of authority he hadn't heard her use before. A little too loudly for the private conversation he was expecting, she said, "I asked you here, Mr. Sorrensen, to see if you could identify this vehicle."

She pointed to the flatbed, which Jan realized carried a blue pickup truck that had been winched out of the muddy bottom of the lake. He instantly recognized it as Dan's truck.

Before he could say anything, though, Kathy stepped in front of him and said in her best detective voice,

"You don't know whose truck this is, do you, Mr. Sorrensen?"

He caught the clues of her tone and formally phrased question and didn't need the tiny shake of her head to confirm how he should respond.

"Sorry, I don't recognize it, Deputy—" he leaned forward as if reading her nametag, "Jensen."

Her scowl practically shouted, "don't overdo it." Instead, she grabbed him roughly by the arm and started marching him back to his car.

Keeping his voice low, Jan said, "Was he in it?"

Kathy shook her head, but under her breath she said, "Once we run the VIN and I have a positive ID, we'll get a warrant."

She pulled him to a stop and tugged him around to face her.

"You know what that means, right? This will become a murder investigation, and I'll be shut out by the real detectives."

She raised her voice so it would carry. "Do you understand, Mr. Sorrensen?"

He nodded quickly, genuinely a little frightened by this version of Kathy.

"Of course, Detective," he said just as loudly. Then he whispered, "You can't be sure since he's not in it."

Kathy gave him a withering look, then shook her head and let go of his arm.

"Not a word of this to *anyone*. Do you understand, Mr. Sorrensen?"

Jan could only nod, and with a flick of her wrist, she dismissed him.

But as she turned away, she whispered, "I know what you're thinkin', but I have to tell you if she's not there when we bring the warrant, I'll be hunting *both* of you."

She didn't wait for a reply, just turned back to where the divers had re-emerged from the lake.

"What else have you got there, guys?"

They held up a metal ramp. As she strode toward the salvage operation, Jan heard one of the other deputies say, "Jesus, Jensen. You really tore him a new one."

"Fucking tourists," she replied, and everyone else laughed.

60

"The VIN came back to Daniel Adams."

Kathy had just laid out the evidence she had gathered around Dan's disappearance to Sheriff Peterson and the other two detectives, Lewis and Stevens. Detective Lewis had sat with his arms folded throughout her recitation until she wrapped up.

"And the ramp they found with the truck confirms my theory about how Mrs. Adams disposed of the truck."

Lewis spoke up. "So, where's his body? All you've got now is a littering charge."

"Illegal dumping," Stevens said. Lewis snickered.

"Dan's body could be buried somewhere on the property," Kathy said sharply.

Lewis raised his eyebrows. "'Dan' is it? Sounds to me like you're a little too close to this family. Maybe even a little jealous—"

"That's way outta line."

"OK, knock it off both of you." Sheriff Peterson gave all three of his detectives a scowl. "Give me the proposed timeline again."

Kathy took a deep breath to compose her thoughts. She looked down at the written report in her hand.

"Some time after Mr. Adams was last seen on January twenty-ninth, Mrs. Adams, *or some other perpetrator*," she cast a sidelong glance at Lewis, "caused the death, or sufficient bodily injury, of Mr. Adams to warrant the disposal of his distinctive vehicle. The perpetrator loaded an off-road vehicle—a dirt bike or four-wheeler—into said vehicle and drove them to the Bennett Lake drop off. The perp then unloaded the off-road vehicle using the ramp that was recovered at the scene, rolled the truck and ramp into the lake, then returned to Mackey House using the various trails through the mountains."

To her surprise, she saw both the Sheriff and Detective Stevens nod when she finished. Lewis at least kept his silence.

Sheriff Peterson turned to Stevens. "Ed, talk to Judge Collins. Get a search warrant for the Mackey House property. We need to look for evidence of a violent crime against Mr. Adams."

Detective Stevens held out his hand to Kathy, but before handing over her report, she turned to the Sheriff.

"You're giving this case to Ed? This is my work, my case."

Peterson's expression softened. "Kathy, this is a murder investigation now. We have to do everything strictly by the book from now on. Ed needs to take the lead from here. You'll be in on the search, and if there's an arrest to be made, you can have the collar."

He looked over at Ed, who shrugged and nodded.

"Good. So, while Ed gets the warrant, I want you to keep an eye on the place. It'll take an hour or more to get the paperwork filed, and the writ issued. By then half the town will know what's going on." All three detectives nodded their understanding. "I don't want any evidence to walk between now and then."

All three stood, and Detective Stevens held out his hand to Kathy. She had already handed over her report, so at first she didn't understand why. But then realization dawned, and she shook his offered hand.

Stevens held up the report. "This is good work, Detective."

Kathy felt a rush of pride, but then the reality of the situation set in.

"I just wish it wasn't about my best friends."

One of whom I may be sending to Death Row.

61

The drive back to Mackey House was like awakening from a dream. He felt as if he had been sleepwalking for several days, being led by the nose and thinking with his heart and his cock, not his head. Finding Dan's truck and the missing ramp in the lake brought the horrible picture into clear focus.

Sandy must have loaded the ATV, along with the ramp, into the pickup; then driven the ten miles to Bennett Lake, where she unloaded the four-wheeler and pushed the truck and ramp over the cliff that formed the deepest part of the lake. The lake was ten miles along the winding country roads, but probably only two or three miles as the crow flies. And, given all the trails running through the countryside around there, she could have ridden the ATV almost all the way home without being seen.

It was a simple, yet clever plan, but there was still one key piece of the puzzle missing.

Where is Dan's body?

Jan pulled up to a stop sign where the county road met the lakeside Route 590. A turn to the right would take him back to Mackey House, where a vengeful ghost and her slutty alter-ego routinely possessed his lover—who was probably a murderer.

The road to the left, however, would lead him southward, back to his normal life; a life of writing on the balcony of his studio apartment when the weather was good; a life of takeout food from the local pubs where all the bartenders knew his name; a life of never-ending sameness and safety. Making that left turn would end this madness, or at least his involvement in it.

To the right, a life on the run from the law awaited, if he could convince Sandy to leave. To the left, a life as a mid-list author struggling to pay the rent.

To the right lay an unfinished story waiting to be told. To the left lay a depressing normality.

He turned right.

Sandy was still absent when he got home. He glanced at the main staircase which led to his room, where his suitcase still waited to be packed. With a slight shake of his head, he strode past the stairs and into the kitchen. Kathy's spare keys were in his hand.

This is crazy. Not just crazy, this is stupid.

He unlocked the basement door and held his hand next to the knob before grabbing it. The brass doorknob was warm to the touch, though not hot enough to burn. But the warning was clear. Dreading what he would find on the other side, he grabbed a dishtowel from its hook and used it to protect his fingers as he gingerly turned the knob.

As he feared, Angel Flora blocked the stairway. She seemed in control of her shadow-shape, although it did flicker menacingly around the edges. Jan stared into the negative space where her face should have been.

"I need to go down there," he said with as much authority as he could muster. Angel Flora didn't move or answer, although the flickering became more pronounced.

"I need answers, dammit. I need to know the full story. Besides, if I don't find whatever evidence is down there before the police do, Sandy will be hauled off to prison, and you'll be stuck here alone again."

If a shadow of a shadow can appear indecisive, Flora did. Jan pressed his advantage.

"Besides, if I'm to tell your story to the world, I need to know it all. Which means I need to go through that door. Beyond that blocked-up wall at the end of the hall. That's where you were, right? That's where you … died."

Flora wavered. Her non-form seemed to contract, allowing the reality of the physical world to gain a purchase.

When she finally spoke, her voice was that of a woman-child, high-pitched and plaintive.

"I can hold Other-Me back as long as we are alone, but Sandy makes her stronger."

She contracted to a disembodied head, a hole in the universe inside which black nothingness seethed and twisted. Though no light could penetrate or escape, Jan knew, through some other long disused and atrophied primordial sense, that an intense struggle for domination was happening in whatever higher-dimensional world the two Floras inhabited.

Seizing his opportunity, he edged past the hole in our world whose spasming edges reached out and grazed his shoulder as he passed. A new blister erupted beneath the hole burned through his flannel shirt. Wincing, the pain sped his feet as he stumbled down the basement stairs and through the storage room door into the main hallway.

He felt Flora follow him, and a quick glance over his shoulder revealed her to be a writhing ball of darkness floating at head height. Sweat sprang from his pores as waves of heat testified to the two manifestations of Flora's conflicted will, fighting to own her space, her existence.

With a rush of hot dry wind, she soared over his head, singeing his hair and reddening his upturned face. She stopped in the middle of the passage, just past the door to the storage room that held the racks of archives. Her message became clear when the storeroom door creaked open.

Jan shook his head vehemently.

"I need to go through *there*."

He pointed at the nearly completed cement block wall, behind which, he was sure, there would be another passageway beneath the lawn, ending in a tiny, dark room.

"You said you would tell our story," Angel Flora said, though the timbre of her voice wavered toward Demon Flora's snarl.

"I will tell your story. All of it, I promise. But I need to find Dan first. He's behind that wall, isn't he?"

"I can't—I can't hold her back if you go in there."

Jan wiped sweat from his eyes. "But I need to find him … before …"

He thought, *before Sandy gets home*, but he said, "before the police get here."

"*Let him pass*." Demon Flora's raspy voice emanated from the void, along with a blast of heat. "*We need Sandy here*."

He never expected that Demon Flora would become his advocate, but her argument seemed to win over her other-self. The ball of blackness calmed its writhing and drew back to the threshold of the open storeroom, allowing Jan to sidle past, pressed against the opposite wall.

The smell of newly laid mortar was strong at the end of the hallway. This explained the dragging and tapping sounds that Jan heard Sandy making down there. She was sealing off the space beyond to hide evidence, he was certain.

The top course of block was incomplete. Pieces of cement, broken off to make partial blocks to fit the opening, lay about the floor, along with a short hammer, a mason's trowel, and a bucket of quickset mortar.

Jan reached up and tugged at the end block in the topmost row. It didn't come free, though he felt the slightest give, like a stuck lid on a jelly jar. Grabbing with both hands, he anchored himself with a foot against the wall and pulled with all his might. The combined force of his weight and his leverage broke the block free. Unbalanced with no support, Jan fell over backwards and landed on shards of broken cement blocks. Adding insult to injury, the one he pulled free landed squarely on his chest.

Pushing the heavy block off, he heard—or maybe only imagined—Flora snickering.

The hell with this.

He looked around the hallway for something to make the demolition job easier, but all that was there were tools to build the wall, not tear it down.

Wait, the sledgehammer.

He remembered the abandoned tools that Dan had probably used to knock a hole in the old wall that closed off the front of the Hotel. He found it lying on the floor in the storeroom with the wheelbarrow and shovel.

Swinging wildly, he attacked the obstacle with all his might. As course after course came crashing down, he felt the temperature of the air in the confined space climb. Within minutes, he was bathed in sweat. The slickness of the wooden handle made his hands slip as it twisted and turned in his grip. Blister after blister rose on his fingers and palms, then ripped open, adding their weeping pus to the already well-lubricated, sweaty wood.

When he was half-way through his task, he realized that heat was radiating, not just from the ghostly non-form blocking the hallway behind him and waiting with surprising patience, but also from the door he was struggling to expose. Caught in this oven, the hot dry air sucked the sweat from his skin and threatened to add more blistering burns to join those on his arms, whose bloody leakage soaked through their bandages.

And still, he swung.

This is probably going to kill me.

Swing, thunk.

Is it worth it? Do I really want to know what's behind that door?

Swing, crash.

I can't go back. She won't let me.

Swing, smash.

But every swing seems to make her stronger, hotter.

Yet still he swung.

Ten minutes later, though the hammer had done its job, Jan was exhausted. His furious blows had turned the freshly built wall into a field of debris that littered the floor. Cement dust speckled his hair and irritated his eyes and nose. He had inhaled so much of the stuff that his throat burned and complained with jolts of pain every time he swallowed.

Swinging the hammer with every ounce of force he could muster left his arms limp and his breathing ragged. The sledgehammer slipped from his grasp and clattered to the floor. Before him stood a heavy metal door set into a rough opening in the foundation wall, a strong padlock keeping it closed. With aching hands, he pulled the ring of keys from his pocket and slowly flipped through them, searching in the dim light for the correct key.

With trembling hands, he tried three times to insert it in the lock before the heavy ring slipped from his bloody fingers. His clumsiness was met with an angry increase in the heat emanating from the black void behind him.

Fishing around in the pile of cement shards on the floor, he found the key ring, but the dust that coated his hands as a result stung terribly as it infiltrated the open sores of what were once blisters.

But it did dry them enough to give him a better grip on the small key. With the padlock opened and off its hasp, he wrapped the doorknob with the tail of his shirt and turned.

Freed of all restrictions, the door flew open and a cry of vicious joy came from Demon Flora, who stood, impossibly darker and immensely more powerful. The smell that was also trapped in the space beyond the door rushed out and assaulted Jan. He turned his face away from the onslaught, but the musty odor of disturbed earth combined with that of burned, rotting flesh, made him gag and vomit against the side wall.

Straightening and wiping his mouth on the back of his sleeve, he saw a gaping hole whose entrance the basement lights barely penetrated. With his cellphone lit and recording, he peered into the darkness. Before him lay a low-ceilinged tunnel through the dirt that filled in the unused portion of the Hotel's basement. Six-by-six posts and overhead beams shored it up.

The heat behind him ratcheted up as Flora, now dominated by her Demon persona, stepped toward him, driving him deeper into the tunnel.

Flora's cackling, demonic laughter echoing in the tight confines of the passage drowned out the sounds of Sandy's arrival through the outside door in the storage room. She surprised both Jan and Flora when she appeared in the hallway, carrying a cement block in each of her hands.

"What did you do?" she yelled.

Jan and Flora jerked around in a strange synchrony, both frozen for a heartbeat. Then, with a whoop of triumph, Demon Flora started toward Sandy, who dropped the blocks and raised both hands to ward her off.

Flora oscillated between her Angel and Demon selves, a four-dimensional wrestling match for control of her presence in our world. She let out an inhuman scream, and the flickering stopped, with Demon Flora in control.

All traces of Angel Flora disappeared for a moment, but then the oscillating began again. This time, though, it was not a struggle for dominance, but rather a show of solidarity, of common purpose.

Sandy's eyes bore into Jan's. "You fucking idiot," she said when Flora's Nothingness advanced toward her.

She looked directly into Flora's snarl, and her own face became serene. With a final glance at Jan, she opened her arms, accepting possession by the now doubly powerful spirit. Flora engulfed her, and Sandy's scream of agony turned into a stream of terrible laughter.

That scream jolted Jan out of his frozen terror. He stumbled backwards. Flora's scorching heat drove him down the length of the tunnel, despite the increasingly fetid air. Backing away from Sandy-Flora, he tripped over the threshold of a battered opening in another concrete wall.

In the semi-darkness of the tunnel, Jan could see shimmering tendrils of absolute black floating in the air. Strings of Nothingness connected Sandy-Flora to the ceiling above his head.

His phone light revealed him to be in an eight by ten foot room. There, huddled in the far corner, lay the source of the stench—a body. Despite its severely burned and rotting state, the distinctive shock of Dan's jet-black hair and his ever-present work boots identified the victim.

A wave of blast-furnace heat washed over Jan as Sandy-Flora stood silhouetted in the doorway. As she slowly, deliberately, walked toward him, he backed as far into the tiny room as he could until he pressed himself into a back corner, precisely as Dan must have done. With no way to escape, he lowered his hand and let the phone drop to the floor, its light casting ghastly shadows about the room.

62

Kathy stewed in her patrol car parked out of sight up the street from the Mackey House. She could see the logic of Sheriff Peterson's decision to sideline her, but it still rankled. That frustration, combined with the feeling of betrayal toward Sandy that she couldn't shake, had her on edge. Should she warn her? She had already given a heads-up to Jan, which would probably cost her job if anyone found out.

His car's still here, the idiot. Is he so pussy-whipped that he can't see what's going down?

But Sandy's car was missing.

Maybe they lit out together in her car. But that doesn't make sense. We'll have BOLOs out for it in no time.

As she tried to convince herself that things were out of her hands now, the sound of an approaching vehicle snapped her back to the present. She watched with a mixture of sadness, guilt, and vindication as Sandy pulled her car into the driveway.

They're both idiots. Maybe they deserve what they get.

But there was no conviction behind that thought, just a deepening sense of doubt.

I'm sending my best friend to prison. Maybe to Death Row.

She watched as Sandy opened the car's trunk and lifted two building blocks from it.

What is she doing with them? she thought as Sandy opened the side door into the basement and carried them inside.

Sandy's shout a few seconds later was muffled, but raised the hair on the back of Kathy's neck. She was already reaching for the door handle when she heard the scream.

Sandy-Flora stood on the threshold of what was once a tiny bedroom. Jan was pressed against the back wall, but with a final resolve, he stepped forward. Standing defiantly before her, his voice wavered a bit before he got control.

"This is where you died, isn't it?"

His calm, hard-fought as it was, seemed to have the same effect on Flora.

"I read your journal," he said, addressing Angel Flora. "What happened to you was terrible. I understand your need for revenge."

Sandy, her eyes black, her mouth an empty abyss, shook her head, and Angel Flora spoke, "I do not want revenge. She does."

A low, throaty growl followed that statement.

"I simply want to be free of your flat, three-dimensional world. Can you help me be free?"

Her voice broke into a sob, and Sandy's face contorted into a snarl.

She said with Demon Flora's voice, "*Enough of this bullshit. She says she wants to be 'free' and then she fucks anything that comes through the front door. We both want the same thing. We want this.*"

Sandy/Flora slowly walked toward Jan, her chin cupped in her hand.

"*And we want these.*"

She wrapped her hands around her breasts as Jan did during his unnatural encounter with her other body, the statue on the front lawn.

She stopped within reach of Jan, who struggled to suck in hot breaths, though his gaze never left the twin holes that had once been Sandy's pale blue eyes.

"*And most of all, we want this.*"

Sandy undid the fly of her jeans and slid them down her hips, then reached between her legs. As her hand moved front to back and back to front, slowly at first, then with increasing urgency, Jan, to his horror, felt his cock hardening. As the force and speed of her ministrations increased, Sandy's lips parted. She tilted her chin up and arched her back into the perfect imitation—more a recreation—of Flora's pose.

The shadow tendrils that he had seen floating in the hallway swirled around Sandy-Flora with increasing speed, matching the rhythm of her hand. When she gasped in ecstasy, they became a column of the deepest black, extending straight up through the ceiling. He realized that could signify only one thing, that they stood directly below the statue, the source of Flora's power. With a deep, stentorious moan, Sandy closed her eyes and shuddered.

The clatter of running footsteps shattered the tableau as Kathy appeared in the basement hallway, her service weapon drawn. Sandy-Flora's response was immediate.

She spun her head almost all the way around and screamed, "*He's mine, bitch!*"

A blast of scalding heat stopped Kathy in her tracks and the steel door, glowing a dull red, slammed shut. Several gunshots thundered down the tunnel, but Sandy-Flora held the door firmly closed from twenty feet away with an outstretched hand. She laughed when they heard Kathy's gun clatter to the floor.

Jan found his voice. "Kathy, it's over. Get out of here!" he croaked through his parched throat.

When silence reigned, he hoped that his last words had done some good.

Slowly, Sandy-Flora turned toward him with a leering look of pure lust as she licked spittle from her lips. Jan raised his hands and tried to back away from her heat, but in an instant, she closed the gap between them, and six hands pulled him to the ground.

As two fiery, pure black hands pinned his own to the floor, a resounding clang echoing in through Flora's *sanctum sanctorum* accompanied his scream.

Then another loud bang of the sledgehammer slamming into the door sounded. Another pair of the otherworldly hands branded their fingers into the flesh of his ankles. Jan's screams grew weaker as Sandy's searing heat scorched his throat and lungs.

After another few ineffective bangs, the pounding on the door stopped, and he knew Kathy's efforts with the sledgehammer were in vain. Sandy-Flora tilted her head, waiting for the assault on the door to resume, but when it didn't, she turned back to Jan, and with a hideous smile, she undid his belt and yanked down his jeans.

With no hope of rescue and every struggle against Flora's grip searing his flesh more deeply, Jan resigned himself to whatever tortuous death Flora had in store for him.

64

Sattva versus *Tamas*, *dharma* versus *adharma*. *Sattva* versus *Tamas*, *dharma* versus *adharma*.

The phrase echoed in Kathy's head in time with each swing of the sledgehammer against the red-hot door. Again and again, she chanted, but as Jan's screams grew weaker, so did her body and her will. Seeing how little damage she was inflicting, and with aching arms, she stood panting.

Sattva versus *Tamas*, *dharma* versus *adharma*. The chanting in her mind assumed her mother's voice.

"Kaveetha, '*Sattva* versus *Tamas*, *dharma* versus *adharma*?' The *murti*, you Silly Child. Remember your lessons."

Realization came at last, and she knew what to do, although Jan's screams were reduced to agonized moans, and she feared she was too late. Still, her will and her strength renewed, she tightened her grip on the sledgehammer and rushed up the outside stairs.

65

What should have followed, as Sandy-Flora positioned herself above him, was a pleasure he had grown to love. But instead, as she descended and engulfed his inexplicably hard cock, he was plunged into the deepest fires of Hell. Each time Sandy-Flora rose, he felt the slightest bit of relief, but then she pushed back down, and he was thrust again into the purest burning pain. His vision narrowed, replaced at the edges by blissful unconsciousness, as her rhythm increased.

Looking through the tunnel of his fading awareness, he felt her stop her bestial thrusting and saw her jerk sideways as if struck in the head. Before she could recover, another jolt slammed her in the opposite direction. Jan saw a flash of blue in her eye sockets where there had been only blackness moments before. Then a third invisible blow snapped her head backwards, and the room echoed with a terrible keening scream.

A swirling vortex of nothingness erupted out of Sandy, releasing her. Unconscious, she slumped down onto Jan. Freed from Flora's sexual and demonic grip, he nevertheless wrapped his badly burned arms around Sandy in a protective embrace, shielding her from the ongoing battle in the tiny room.

By the faint light of his cellphone, Jan watched the hideous shadow fly back and forth about the room in synchrony with the sounds of hammer on stone coming from above the chamber. Finally, he heard a resounding crack from above and, in a roaring rush, the Nothingness flew up through the ceiling.

As the demonic blackness ascended, and the blackness of unconsciousness descended on him, Jan saw reflections of his cellphone light twinkling from the ceiling in its wake.

The Hoard?

66

Early Summer

The scar tissue forming beneath his bandages itched. The medically induced coma the hospital staff placed him under when he arrived gave his body a chance to begin healing, but his road to recovery was going to be long and tortuous.

When the nurses visited every half-hour, they reminded him not to scratch, but his bandaged hands could provide little relief, anyway. Just one day after the University Burn Center staff brought him out of his coma, he still hadn't adjusted to the fact that two weeks of his life were gone. Anxious and fearful to know how extensive his injuries were and what he had missed in those lost days, the nurses simply shook their heads and told him it was best he didn't know for now.

All the young doctor who attended would tell him was that the spinal block which kept him from feeling anything below the waist was a godsend—trust him on that one—and that he would have a long road to recovery.

"Some things might not work as well as they used to," he nodded to Jan's crotch, "but hopefully you'll get at least some function back."

Getting *that* function back was the furthest thing from his mind, though. Any thoughts along those lines quickly turned to visions of Sandy-Flora leering at him through those abyssal eyes.

Despite his internal turmoil, he pretended to be mentally stable when the nurses came to fuss over him, but left alone, his mind returned to memories of the terror he felt when he faced certain immolation. He repeatedly asked what had happened, since he couldn't admit that he remembered it all too vividly, but they again shook their heads and told him to rest, then left him to drift back in his mind to Flora's tomb.

So it was that his eyes were unfocused and his face blank when Kathy pushed open his door.

"Jesus. You look like shit."

He blinked twice before returning to the present and offering a rueful smile.

"Back at ya, and you don't have to call me 'Jesus.'"

He got the same smile in return. Neither spoke for a few seconds, then Kathy pulled out a mini-recorder and held it up to show him she was turning it on, before setting it down on the hospital table.

"Mr. Sorrensen, I am Detective Jensen with the Dundee County Sheriff's Department. I'm here to take your official statement."

Jan waved a dismissive hand at the recorder, and Kathy hit Pause.

"Detective?" He smiled, realizing he was genuinely happy for her. "Congratulations."

Kathy beamed, but said, "Provisional. I'm scheduled to go back to the Academy when the next class starts in the fall."

He looked at the recorder. "You want an *official* statement?"

"Well, you are a well-known author of fiction, are you not?" Her smile took the sting out of her words.

"I am, but I always do my research first. So, maybe you should tell me what the hell actually happened. The last I remember, I was being raped by a blowtorch."

Kathy made a sympathetic face. "You sure you want to hear it?"

"God yes. Nobody around here will tell me anything."

"That's because I told them not to say anything until I collected this." She pointed at the recorder, still on pause.

"Well, you better tell me what to say, because I sure as hell am not recording what really happened."

Kathy sat on the side of the bed.

"Well, officially, I heard screams coming from the basement while staking out the House waiting for a search warrant."

Jan nodded. So far, so good. Clearly, Kathy knew the best way to lie is to stay as close to the truth as possible. She switched to an official-sounding voice.

"When I descended into the basement, I found the victim, Mr. Sorrensen, disabled on the floor and Ms. Adams in the process of setting Mr. Sorrensen on fire. After subduing Ms. Adams, I retrieved a fire extinguisher from the kitchen upstairs and extinguished Mr. Sorrensen."

"So, how did I get 'disabled' with my pants around my ankles? And what about the busted-up wall?"

He stopped and his eyes got wide.

"And just exactly how did you 'subdue' her? Thanks for that, by the way."

Kathy nodded modestly. "When I couldn't break down the door, I took the sledgehammer outside and started wailing on the statue. The head was a bitch to knock off, but once it broke free, Flora shot up out of the neck like she was on a rocket."

"What made you think of attacking the statue?"

She sat silently for a moment, then when she spoke, her voice was quiet.

"Remember I told you my mom used to teach me about Indian culture and Hinduism?" Jan nodded. "Not much of it stuck—too many gods and deities and other kinds of spirits. But one thing she said stuck with me. She would show me pictures of these incredibly intricate carvings of deities in temples. She told me the spirits of these minor gods lived within the statues, but only if the carvings were perfect. Even a little chip would weaken their hold over the spirits, and any major damage would cast the spirit out."

Kathy stopped. Her eyes glistened, and she wet her lips before continuing.

"*Maan* passed a year ago, but I swear while I was wailing away at the door, I heard her say, 'The murti, Silly Child.'"

The tears broke free of her eyes and left streaks on her cheeks, which she quickly wiped away with the back of her hand. Jan laid a bandaged hand on her arm.

"Well, thank you for saving my life. And thank your *Maan* for me, too."

There was no joking or teasing in his tone, and Kathy cradled his damaged hand.

"I will."

He winced when she gave the tiniest squeeze with her fingers.

"Sorry," she said as she let go. "Anyway, when I got back down in the basement, both of you were unconscious." Kathy looked over her shoulder at the closed door. "I had to stage the scene so I could come up with a reasonable explanation."

Jan nodded throughout her explanation. "So, what does Sandy have to say for herself?"

His tone was unintentionally callous. Kathy's response was uncharacteristically subdued.

"Right, I guess you haven't heard. She's not saying or doing anything. She's totally catatonic: doesn't speak, doesn't move, doesn't respond to pain, doesn't hardly blink."

Jan lay in his bed in stunned silence. Finally, he mumbled, "They took her with them."

Kathy shuddered. "I hadn't thought of it that way. Thanks for that image."

Her sarcasm fell flat.

"So, what happens now?"

Kathy shook her head. "Nothing until she comes out of it. They've got her in the psych ward over at the State Hospital."

She lifted the mini-recorder off the table and waved it in front of Jan's face.

"OK, Mr. Best-Selling Author, give me something I can put in my report." She locked eyes with Jan. "Ready?"

He nodded, and she hit the Record button.

Late Summer

"What's this I hear about you leaving 'Against Medical Advice'? Oh—" Kathy said as she barged into Jan's hospital room.

He stood there naked except for the bandages that still wrapped his groin. The dead fish color of his scar tissue started at his collarbones and covered his torso, thighs, ankles and wrists in a tracery of lines, ropes, and large patches of white, puckered flesh. When seen full-on, a pattern of the scarring emerged, radiating outward from a central point hidden beneath his bandages.

"Oh, my God," she whispered behind the hand covering her mouth.

Jan stood unashamed. The daily inspections and wound care administered by the nurses, along with the ministrations of the physical, occupational, and emotional therapists, had inured him to any such inspection.

"Oh, my God," Kathy repeated. "I'm so sorry."

"What are you sorry about? If it wasn't for you, I wouldn't even be standing here. I'd be buried under that fucking statue like Dan was."

He took the bag of clothes he had asked her to bring and dumped them on the bed. She watched, silently horrified, as he sat on the bed, then fought to slide his boxers up his legs. After taking a deep breath, he groaned as he stood and reached for his shirt. Gingerly, he slid his arms into it before pulling it up his back. Fumbling for the buttons with his swollen, inflexible fingers, he cursed under his breath.

Kathy, freeing herself from her momentary paralysis, stepped forward and took the front of his shirt in her hands.

"Why don't you wear a pull-over?" she said as she worked her way down the row of buttons.

"Can't," he said and lifted his arms to just below shoulder height. "This is as high as they go."

Kathy dipped her head to look for the last button, so he wouldn't see the tears brimming in her eyes. Then she pivoted to the bed and grabbed his jeans. She gently pushed him to a sitting position on the edge of the bed and knelt down.

"Kaveetha, you don't have to do this."

His use of her real name, which normally would have drawn a sarcastic response at the very least, instead made her smile.

"Shut up and put your foot in here," she said as she guided his leg into the pants.

When he was fully dressed, she again confronted him with her initial question.

"The docs say you aren't ready to go home yet. So why are you leaving?"

"I've been stuck here for almost three months. I want—no, I need—to get out of here. I haven't written a thing since I've been in here, and it's driving me nuts."

"I can bring you your laptop—"

"No! My mind's made up. I want to go…"

"Where?" Kathy asked quietly. "You can't drive yet. Where you gonna go?"

Jan sat on the bed, wincing in pain. "I don't know." His voice cracked. "My whole world has collapsed. Everything I believed in—or didn't believe in, actually—has been overturned. I can't drive. I can't type. I can't even button my fucking shirt."

A sob escaped his throat, but he quickly swallowed the growing hysteria.

"I don't know what I'm going to do, or where I'm going to go. I just need to get *out of here*."

Kathy stared at her feet and scratched the back of her neck.

"You could move in with me."

He looked at her sideways, but she didn't make eye contact.

"You have a one-bedroom *walk-up* apartment."

She shook her head, then looked at him. Her voice returned to its normal imperative tone.

"Actually, I have plenty of room. I have four bedrooms and five suites just sitting empty."

It took him a moment to understand, then his eyes went wide.

"You moved in? *There?* How? *Why*, for God's sake?"

She raised her hands to calm his reaction. "It turns out that I'm Sandy's closest relative, so they appointed me her guardian. Her finances were a mess. She hadn't paid the mortgage in three months and the bank was ready to foreclose."

"But she told me she owned the place free-and-clear, and she was OK financially."

"Well, she lied. She inherited the house, but she and Dan took out a mortgage to renovate it, which they paid off. But she borrowed against their line of credit the day after Dan—you know. She never made a payment on that one. So, to avoid losing the whole thing over ten grand, I paid it off and moved in. Besides, the front lawn needs work before anybody else can have it."

Jan just shook his head. "I can't believe you want me to move back in there. After all this."

He swept his hands down his scarred body.

"Look. I'm in the apartment in the back. You can have the first-floor suite and the run of the parlor, dining room, and kitchen. You won't have to go upstairs, or downstairs for that matter."

"Especially not downstairs."

Jan thought for a moment, considering the fact that he had no other options.

"Well, maybe temporarily. Just until I can take care of myself."

Kathy nodded. "Sure. You can get your therapy at home, and I can drive you to your other appointments and stuff."

"What about your job, Ms. Detective?"

She laughed. "It turns out detectives have a lot less to do in this county than beat cops do."

Jan chuckled, but he was thinking of something else.

"You haven't dug up and filled in Flora's tomb yet, have you?"

Kathy shook her head. "No, that's the 'lawn work' that needs to be done. Why?"

"I think you'll want to be careful digging it up, especially the ceiling."

THE END

Author's Note

Writing this story was one hell of a ride. I hope you, Smart Reader, enjoyed reading it as much as I enjoyed writing it. The story was inspired by an actual statue standing in front of an actual bed-and-breakfast where my wife, Ona, and I stayed. One look at Flora, standing there in front of the old Mission-style house, and the skeleton of the plot blossomed in my head.

The real joy of writing it, though, came from watching our characters emerge, especially Kathy. A minor character to start, she pushed herself to the forefront and claimed her place as Jan's full-fledged partner. You gotta love headstrong women.

<u>The Ghost of Mackey House</u> is a standalone novel, but I'd love to see what's next in store for Jan and Kathy as they reset their lives, so stay tuned, perhaps, for their next adventure in the wilds of Eastern Pennsylvania.

As always, Smart Reader, thanks for spending your precious time with us. I hope it was worth it.

R.A. (Rob) Johnson
April 2021

Acknowledgements

For the most part, drafting a novel is a solitary effort. For me, those solitary hours lost in the act of creating a story are thrilling. They can be incredibly frustrating at times, but in the end, when the characters have come to life on the page, it is so satisfying.

The draft is just the beginning, though. The hard work comes when it's time to restructure, revise, edit, and repeat. For that, a community is really needed. I'd like to thank the members of my community.

First, I need to thank Cathy, whose wonderful statue inspired this book, and which occupied my thoughts for most of a year.

First impressions are most important, and people *do* judge books by their covers. So, thanks, as always, to my excellent cover artist, Lance Buckley (lancebuckley.com), for capturing the essence of Flora.

Next, thanks to Prashant Gupta for his impromptu lessons on Hindu theology and for teaching me what a *murti* is while visiting the temples of Southern India.

Thanks to my developmental editor, James Osborne (https://reedsy.com/#/freelancers/james-o), for showing me what was strong and what needed work, especially the importance of Jan and Kathy's relationship.

And a special thanks to my beta readers, Sarah Inforzato, Carly Johnson, Robert Piatt, and Ichabod Ebenezer (www.theichabodebenezer.com).

Finally, thanks to Judy Maxfield, whose copy editing made the text infinitely more readable. Any typos

or grammatical miscues were most assuredly inserted by
me after her review.

Other Titles by R.A. Johnson

Fiction

The Enclave Series

#1 The Templar Lance

#2 Lady 355: Mother of Freedom

Non-Fiction

Mental Crudites – Appetizers for the Creative Mind Series

#1 Helping Science Fiction Writers Get Their Stories Off
the Ground

To connect with Rob, check out his website www.RobJohnsonWriting.net. There you will find his blog, which contains dozens of flash fiction pieces, and you can join his email list to get monthly newsletters and special offers.

Rob is also active in the Fiction Writers Group on Facebook.

You can contact him directly at rob@robjohnsonwriting.net.